# TRACI HALL

# BLOOD OF RA

## GUARDIANS OF THE UNDERGROUND

KENDELLE PRESS

# TRACI HALL

"…writes with gripping emotion and engaging twists, whether it's for teens or adults - Ms. Hall pens a fabulous tale!"

- Cherry Adair, New York Times Bestselling Author

"As always, Ms. Hall manages to beautifully convey real characters--and the human emotion that rules us through all time. I love her work!"

- Heather Graham, New York Times Bestselling Author

"This fast, fun read is about a teen girl who is easy to love and hate."
- Lauren Becker, Romantic Times (4 Star Review)

"…I recommend this exciting book, and I think it will especially appeal to readers who like stories about ghosts, the paranormal, and trying to fit into high school life. It's got all that good stuff, along with a spicy touch of romance."

- K. Osborn Sullivan, Courtesy of Teens Read Too (4 Star Review)

"Traci Hall is a magical storyteller!"

- Rhonda Pollero, USA Today Best Selling Author

# More TRACI HALL

"A new talent to watch!"

- Amy J. Fetzer, Award Winning Author

"Traci Hall brings ALL the issues of being a teenager to life through Rhee, her friends, and her magical family. The balance of Wiccan beliefs and psychic powers kept me reading into the early morning hours, reminding me of my trials as young woman, studying Wicca and managing the ability to see spirits. A great read for young and old alike!!"

- Ginger Quinlan, Author & Certified Psychic Medium

"Well developed characters, an accurate portrayal of psychic abilities, an intriguing plot combined with teen angst will keep you reading this book into the night. Traci Hall has created a wonderful protagonist in Rhiannon Godfrey and wonderful secondary characters. Now I have to read the rest of the series!

- Melissa Alvarez, Author and Intuitive Clairvoyant

"No one does teenage angst like Traci Hall... It's a paranormal feast at warp speed!"

- Michael Meeske, Author of FRANKENSTEIN'S DAEMON

# More Reads by TRACI HALL

## Young Adult:

### The Rhiannon Godfrey Series

Her Wiccan, Wiccan Ways
Something Wiccan This Way Comes
Wiccan Cool
Wiccan Wishes – a short story
Wiccan Chalice

### Mile Post 42

### Zombyre, My Love

### Diary of a Bad Boy

## Historical Romance– Traci E. Hall

### Boadicea Series

Love's Magic
Beauty's Curse
Boadicea's Legacy

### The Queen's Guard Series

Violet

©Kendelle Press: 1095 Military Trail, #121, Jupiter, FL 33458

Published by Kendelle Press: August 2012/trade edition

For information about special discounts for bulk purchases, please contact Kendelle Press Special Sales at1095 Military Trail, #121, Jupiter, FL 33458

Book Cover Designed and Illustrated by: ©More Than Publicity

Interior Pages Illustrated by: ©More Than Publicity

MoreThanPublicity.com

Edited by: T. Hayes 2012

ISBN-10: 0985993413
ISBN-13: 978-0-9859934-1-2

Published & Printed in the United States of America
10   9   8   7   6   5   4   3   2   1

# DEDICATION

For Greg, Brighton and Destini, Mom, Sheryl and Trena – when I imagine my reading audience, you all are always front row.

# BLOOD OF RA

# CHAPTER ONE

All alone, I had nobody's butt to kick and too much time to think.

"Lorelei? Are those lamb kebobs I smell?"

I whispered the question into my lapel mic, ignoring the growling of my empty stomach as the aroma of spiced meat wafted up the staircase from the party below. The clink of champagne glasses as toasts lifted in honor of Mrs. Marcos's birthday offset the low, rhythmic *thrum* of Egyptian drums. My foot tapped against the marble floor, as close to dancing as I dared while on the clock.

My mentor didn't answer me, but an angry buzz of static echoed in my ear. For the millionth time in my life, I wished I could mind link like the other guards.

I adjusted my position so I was in regulation Bazmeht Bodyguard form – sketch five, page three. As taught, I envisioned each pore of my skin opening and absorbing everything around me through the filter of my hypersensitive flesh. Memories. Ancient knowledge. *Secrets*.

It's hard to concentrate with a rumbling belly.

"At least save me a piece of the Gullash..." The back of my throat tightened at the thought of the flaky, phyllo pastry filled with cinnamon, walnuts, and honey.

"Shani, focus on something besides food – like your *job*," Lorelei commanded.

My 'job' is to guard Joshua Sherif Johnson, the Ambassador's nephew – or at the moment, his empty bedroom.

This is my first assignment, and I couldn't be safer if I was standing in the middle of the Bazmeht Control Center. Joshua is a wanna be archeologist majoring in Egyptian Studies, which is practically cheating since he lives in Miami with his pure-blood Egyptian mother. To be fair, Zelda Marcos Johnson Pierre Callahan Cortez hasn't stepped foot in Egypt since her first runaway marriage. Like her brother, she's a fixture in the Daily Star; unfortunately for the ambassador, Zelda can be found in the 'scandal' section.

"This is *boring*. At least you get to be at the party."

"I'm blending with the curtains."

"The ones by the kitchen?" *I might starve to death before the night is over.*

"Do you want me to write you up?"

"No." My ears twitched as I thought of the disappointment on Bastet's face if I came home with a demerit. But it was the imagined fury on Sekhmet's that held my tongue.

Being a guard is an honor. Not all Felidia shifters are accepted into training. My inner GPS system, combined with acute hearing and out of this world reflexes, balance my inability to mind link. Some guards whisper I only got in because of my mother.

Gritting my teeth against bad memories, I swept my gaze along the upper floor of the mansion.

*Do not think about food. Think about duty.*

"What's Joshua doing?"

"Playing the drums. He's not bad."

I heard reluctant admiration in Lorelei's tone. My brow lifted. "Abhar let an American touch his *doumbeck*?"

Lorelei gave an indelicate sniff. "Joshua Sherif is half Egyptian."

"Not that you can tell." Blond as a Swede. Blue eyes. Cute mouth. Great laugh. Before I started a fan club, I reminded myself he was completely off limits as anything but eye candy.

I'd found a picture of a pretty brunette, most likely his girlfriend, on the nightstand by his bed. Only other thing of interest was the locked leather case at the bottom of his backpack. Inside were folded letters on lined notebook paper.

Joshua's terrible handwriting made deciphering the first sentence difficult. I wasn't snooping, really. It's my job to know what my client is doing. In this instance, writing bad poetry.

"Shani…" Lorelei warned.

Easy assignment. Boring assignment. It wasn't like the Marcos family had received a threat from the hated Uraeli faction. No, we were here because the Bazmeht *always* provided guards when the family hosted an event in Zamalek. It was our honored duty to protect Egyptians who carried the Blood of Ra. Lorelei said that a true Egyptian has sand in his veins.

"Don't forget, Lorelei, you said you'd show me the sarcophagi before we left." I couldn't wait to see the ancient collection housed in the Marcos vaults.

"If we have time. If the ambassador agrees. And *if* you shut up."

I laughed, determined to get through the night with a perfect report. I looked around the hall. Patted my suit jacket pocket where I'd hidden my blinged out, orange iPhone. Glanced at the video camera hidden behind a blue tile mosaic.

*Just one game of BeJeweled?*

No.

Having a cell phone on duty is forbidden. I'd tried telling Dahlia at the control desk that I hadn't been separated from texting since the age of ten, that I needed my phone to breathe. She'd shown me rule number forty-six – no personal cell phones on duty.

By nature, I am not a rule breaker. I consider myself an enforcer of justice. Other people have teddy bears, or amulets. I have my phone, my life line, which is worth the risk of a demerit. Just knowing it's near calms my nerves. Nerves drawn tight by hunger, boredom, and too much time to think. Why had I skipped dinner in favor of Pilates and toned abs?

I double-checked my posture. My polished shoes shine, my hair pulled back into a bun so vicious it's cutting off circulation to my brain. I can run as fast as a panther, disable an alarm, speak seven languages, or kill someone with a pencil.

My talents are totally wasted guarding an empty room. "Lorelei?"

"What now?" I didn't blame her for sounding pissed.

"If I'm supposed to be guarding Joshua, then maybe I should come downstairs." *With the sparkling cider and crab dip.* "We can trade."

"Forget it. Did you check inside? You're guarding that room until he goes to bed."

That could be *hours* from now. "Of course." In addition to rifling through his things, I'd used my heightened senses to make sure the bedroom and adjoining half bath were danger free. "No poison in the sheets, no black adder hiding in the roll of toilet paper."

"Shani," Lorelei *tsked.* "Being a guard isn't all glamour and glory. It's work. Why do you think the training is so selective?" She lowered her voice. "What about the drawers? Last week, I killed a brown horned viper inside the pyramid."

"Lorelei!" *Ew.* A bone deep shiver of revulsion rippled from my belly at the thought of touching a snake. I rubbed the ticklish spot behind my ear, which is always the first to change, and sighed with disappointment. "It's just that I'm doing this, and Joshua's not even a *real* member of the sacred family."

"Don't say that," Lorelei scolded. "Listen. Try reciting the myth. Maybe after a millennia, you'll be the one to crack the riddle."

She snorted, and this time, *I* turned down the mic. Some people thought they were soooo funny.

Minutes passed. It felt like hours. The weight of the regulation Glock, tucked into the holster at my waist, tempted me. What would happen if I practiced my soon to be signature release and spin move? Who would know?

All I needed to add fuel to my mother's fire was to get kicked out for breaking a major Bazmeht Bodyguard rule. It had taken me, *me*, a full week to memorize them all, and playing with your weapon sits right at the top of the 'Do Not Or You're Out' list. No warning, no write up, no demerit. Just banishment. Total humiliation. I'd have to go rogue, and live in a colony for other rejects on the edge of the desert.

I tugged at the hem of my black suit jacket. Five seconds ticked by. My nose itched. I smoothed back a non-existent loose hair. My stomach rumbled again as an interesting scent tickled my nose – something between cantaloupe and cucumber. What could it be? *Not food.* My body tensed, fully alert.

The soft hush of a rope unfurling reached my ears seconds before I was hit in the face with a lightning fast kick, followed by another to my shoulder, crushing my lapel mic and cutting off communication with Lorelei.

I hissed in a surprised, pain-filled breath before dropping into a defensive stance, quickly assessing the enemy and the danger, just as I'd been taught.

Glancing up, I saw where a plaster square had been cut away, leaving an opening just big enough for the tiniest Ninja I'd ever seen to slip out.

*How had I not heard that?*

The ninja wore a black belted robe over loose black pants, and a satin ski mask over his face. He carried no visible weapon.

I reached for my gun, my fingers flexed to unholster it and release the safety in under a second, but the ninja was faster, and I dropped my elbow to block a swift kick at my kidney. I swallowed the pain, using it to clear my head.

I sent a prayer of thanks to the Mother Goddess that Joshua was downstairs with the drummers and Lorelei. I jerked back, my ears ringing from a blow to the temple. Biting my lip, I demanded focus. *My name is Shani Nebit. I am a Level One Bazmeht Bodyguard. I am highly trained to kick ass.*

Lame, so far as mantras went, but it worked.

Holding my hands up, I blocked my face against a wicked punch before returning the favor. I heard him grunt and felt a swell of pride.

He stepped back, as if reassessing the situation. That tiny reprieve was enough for me to jiggle the broken mic. Blood dripped into my eye. "Lorelei? A little help here?"

The ninja pulled back then rushed forward in a speedy attack.

I ducked then managed a solid right clip to the masked ninja's jaw. "Who are you?"

Ninja came at me with a roundhouse kick that hurt like Hades as it connected to my left side. I heard a rib crack as the air *whooshed* from my lungs. Goddess knows I can take a lot of pain but this was insane. "What do you want?" I jabbed forward, pleased when the ninja sucked in a hurt breath.

"You."

*Me?* The whispered answer sent chills up the nape of my neck.

Caught off guard, I didn't move away fast enough from another pop to the brow. Dizzy, I felt my left eye swell, and knew I was running out of time.

Bazmeht rule number whatever – *never interrupt the client. Never cause a scene.*

I'd always compensated for my inability to mind link, but now I understood my mother's fears. That I might be a detriment to the guard. Shaking off the cloak of failure, I decided that protecting the sacred bloodline mattered more than the rules of how to do it. Scene or no scene. Taking a deep gulp of air, I readied a shout so loud it would drown out the damned drums. Instead, I choked as the ninja's foot caught me in the throat.

Black spots danced before my eyes, and the sensitive skin behind my ears tingled with the urge to change into true warrior form.

*No, no shifting in front of a human.* Desperate, I concentrated all of my energy, sending a mental shout out to the other guards in the house. I didn't have a lot of faith that it would work.

Ona and Ferimi guarded the ambassador's twin sons on the third floor of the other wing. One of the boys carried the rare mediated Y chromosome, the Blood of Ra, necessary for Felidia breeding.

Lorelei was downstairs. A few guards marched the outer perimeter. This party was supposed to have been a cakewalk – excellent training for a new guard.

*My gun.* I drew in a breath of courage and pretended I was in the training field shooting blanks at a fellow trainee instead of shooting a real live human being.

Who was trying to kill me.

I'd aced my psych evaluation, testing as driven and morally flexible. But this was my first time, and I felt like a timid virgin. I didn't let that stop me from aiming at the ninja's chest.

The drums played on like mood music at a movie.

The ninja seemed to have anticipated my move, and with a slash of leg, kicked the gun from my hand, sending it across the marble tile until it teetered at the edge of the staircase.

To add insult to injury, the ninja followed that kick with a lunge, catching me off balance.

What in the hell? I breathed in, searching for a clue as to the identity of my enemy. I got nothing, not even the smell of falafel the ninja might have had for dinner.

The enemy was scentless...and the only thing a cat can't smell is a snake.

*By the Goddess!*

With all of the disgust that an Egyptian cat-shifter bodyguard has for the deceiving snake faction, I violently shoved the ninja off me and jumped to my feet. Soundless, scentless, and sneaky, I should have put it together sooner.

I'd been too busy defending myself. I'd never fought a Uraeli before.

*No excuse.*

The Bazmeht handbook spelled out the danger that all snakes pose to the Felidia, and they gave carte blanche orders to kill.

*Now what?* The panic I'd been fighting down sprang to life in a smattering of tawny fur across my knuckles. *No.* I reached inside my torn open suit jacket and grabbed my non-regulation, write-up worthy, bright orange cell phone.

The ninja sprang up and spoke in a feminine English accented voice. "You aren't supposed to have that."

I paused, wondering how the ninja knew what the rules for a Bazmeht guard were then I called Control with a single push of a button.

After the slightest hesitation, Ninja pulled a deadly looking knife from thin air, or at least that's what it seemed like to me, and threw it with lethal accuracy toward my rapidly beating heart.

Dahlia at Control answered and snapped, "You'd better have a good reason for using your personal cell phone while on duty!"

I saw it coming. Life or death. I chose the lives of the ambassador's family over my own. My knees shook.

I stepped back, pushed by the force of the blade piercing through my regulation blouse.

The tip was cold, followed by icy pain. "The mansion's been compromised!" Blood welled up my throat, spilling from my lips. It tasted like death. "Send someone," I added in a garbled whisper, my life energy fading.

I couldn't escape the hard thrust as Ninja's foot jacked at the knife handle like a hammer to a nail. It hurt so badly, worse than the time when I'd almost died as a little girl. When I'd left the compound to chase after the red ball.

I'd broken the rules then too, and now look. Dying. My first time out as a guard and I'd gotten myself killed.

The promise of nine lives was given to the Bazmeht but only if they were worthy. My knees crumpled and time slowed as I folded to the cool, marble tile. It occurred to me in abstract that the ninja warrior was a female. She bent over me, and I found the strength to rip off her mask.

I stared at her, the warrior with the white skin, black spiky hair, and reptilian cold, gray eyes.

"I hate you," she informed me with a devious smile. Fangs grew from her mouth, and I squirmed, as weak as a newborn kitten.

"I'm not worthy," I mumbled, thinking of my next life.

"That's right," the ninja said before sinking her fangs into my throat. "You're not worthy. Which is why you will die."

The sting of poison rushed through me. My body immediately tried morphing into my semi-feline self. My jaw cracked, my carnassial teeth elongated, and fur itched behind my ears. I fought against the change.

Eyes drawn to the arc of poison from her fangs as she was ripped from my body, I didn't trust my sensitive ears when a male voice asked if I was all right.

I turned my head, in slow, slow motion, my heart giving a series of death thumps. Disappointment surged. Joshua Sherif Johnson, the young man I'd sworn to protect, kneeled at my side.

"Go," I whispered, wanting him safe.

Blue eyes filled with concern, he studied my face and I wondered what he saw. Fur, whiskers? He shook my shoulder and I groaned, even though I tried to hold the sound inside.

"I'm sorry," I said, breathing in short, desperate sips of air.

"Sorry?" He cupped his palm to my cheek, confusion in his tone. "I don't understand."

"Please leave." I coughed, tasting blood.

"I won't leave you." He stroked my arm with compassion, something I hadn't suspected. Perhaps he'd been worthy after all. *Go. Before Ninja returns.*

Then Lorelei came into focus. Brown hair, brown eyes. Her pretty face tightened with emotion as she rubbed her knuckles along my forehead, smoothing the fur over my ears. "I heard you," she said, tugging Joshua to the side, where another guard held his shoulders.

"Ninja?"

"Hush now. Control is on the way. You did it, Shani, you did it. Natalie's got this one tied for questioning. Ona and Ferimi found another intruder in the attic, but the boys are safe. Now hold on. Goddess willing, we will meet again."

I felt my life ebb, but a smile tugged at my lips.

*I'd done my duty.*

# CHAPTER TWO

## REBIRTH
## UNDERGROUND TEMPLE OF BUBASTIS

Death is a real bitch. Seriously. She has scorpion tails in her hair and six breasts. I wanted to head toward a ray of light, and she stopped me with a long staff that had a knife tied to the tip. Taunted me about being a true Bazmeht.

I told her I'd never wanted to be anything *but* Bazmeht.

*Then where are you going?* She questioned me with a wide grin, her eyeteeth yellowed and curved, like a tiger's teeth. Stay, she ordered me.

Stay?

Staying is hard work. My body ached. My muscles contracted and it felt like one giant leg cramp. I swear on the Goddess' crypt that I heard my own blood as it moved sluggishly through my veins.

I think I cried. I might even have called for my mother, for all the good that would do. She's off in the Mayan Jungle, trying to figure out how to stop the end of the world.

My mind bounced around like my favorite red ball. What happened to that thing? The sandy desert outside the old temple flashes once but then it's gone. My memories shy away as if there's a magnetic force protecting the truth inside my fragile psyche.

The pain is constant. My soul cries for peace, but I am a warrior who has chosen to fight, just as Ancient Mother Mafdet fought the rebellious serpents for the first Pharaoh, dropping the severed heads at his royal feet.

Serpent Slayer.

Warrior of Justice.

Guardian of the Underground.

*I like it.*

Time passed, and the melodic *tinkle* of water dripping into a fountain brings me back, giving me my bearings. I am in the Sacred Rebirthing Chamber. In my mind's eye, I can see the ebony lioness-headed statue of the Warrior Goddess Sekhmet on one side of the underground limestone chamber. On the other side, in perfect balance, is the golden cat-faced statue of Bastet, Goddess of Hearth and Home.

The universe is constantly in chaos. The demi-goddesses do what they can to maintain balance in Egypt, as Mafdet ordered them to do over a millennia ago. Together, they govern the Bazmeht – bodyguards dedicated to protecting the sacred bloodline of the ancient pharaohs.

I was born to a Bazmeht warrior, the great Sharifa, and chosen to be a handmaiden at the secret underground temple near Bubastis. Above ground is a wasteland of pink granite ruins and broken monuments where hundreds of thousands of cat mummies once rested. I grew up reading ancient hieroglyphics, learning the legend of Mafdet, soaking in the history as blood soaks into a dirt floor.

This is my world, it always has been, and it always will be. Egypt is my legacy. This chamber houses my rejuvenating body as my soul travels the cosmos, waiting for my second birth. The *ka* cannot return if the body isn't ready.

I can't see, I can't smell, I can't taste, but I can hear. Damn me, I can feel. Agony is my fingernails growing. The birth of each individual eyelash is like a needle piercing flesh.

My new skin itches, but I can't scratch. I am mummified as I wait to be brought back to life.

Time skips and suddenly, I hear, "Stop wiggling!" Bastet's soft voice is soothing and instantly the itching recedes. "You will scar, young Shani, and you don't want to go through a millennia with scars."

"Bastet, only you would think of that." Sekhmet spoke in a no-nonsense way that made my pulse skip. The demi-goddess was tough, but she had the interests of the Bazmeht – of all the Felidia – at heart. "Scars are badges of pride."

"If won in battle, yes," Bastet agreed with a charming laugh. "If gotten because one couldn't control their wiggling, I think rather it would be a mark of shame."

Sekhmet sniffed. "You have a point."

I stayed totally still. I felt their separate energy as Bastet stood at my feet and Sekhmet at my head. It would take their joined magic to bring me back.

I'd been handmaiden to the demi-goddesses, and I knew the

ceremonial preparations to a rebirthing. This was special. *Sacred.*

Eighty-one layers of linen strips protected me from the chill of the granite table I rested on. Centered in the chamber, the table balanced on four carved granite pillars. Between each pillar would be a canopic jar that theoretically held my liver, intestines, stomach, and lungs. Since I actually needed the organs, they'd stayed inside my body instead of being ceremonially removed.

Once the ceremony was over, I'd return the jars to my personal cat sarcophagus.

I felt the light weight of Bastet's fingers on my wrapped feet at the same time as Sekhmet placed her heavier, ringed hands on either side of my head.

I heard the crackle of hemp wicks as oil lamps burned in the four corners of the underground chamber.

It wasn't that long ago that I'd folded linen strips and filled the woven baskets stacked with oils and herbs, doing a handmaiden's chores with a grateful heart. Never dreaming that I'd need this table when I was so-

"Young." Sekhmet finished my thought in a guttural bark.

"Now Sekhmet, you were young..." Bastet chided.

"It was war! My sword arm was stiff with the blood of the enemy."

My heart hammered in my chest. If it wasn't for the tight wraps, it might have burst free. What if Sekhmet didn't want me to come back for a second life?

"Hush." Bastet slowly massaged the arch of my feet and the heat brought a tingling sensation, reminding me of the time I'd stepped into an anthill. "Shani died protecting the ambassador and his family. Like you, she did her duty."

I wanted to speak in my defense, to tell my story. But what was my story? I couldn't remember.

Sekhmet applied more pressure to my temples. "You guard your thoughts with the usual thick walls, Shani. We were unable to get a complete read on what happened. We saw enough to know that you were taken by surprise." Her thumb moved in circular motions down my cheekbones, and I could have purred as the hurt in my head disappeared. "You took a beating, but you didn't leave your post."

"Hetmet would be proud. She trained you well." Bastet's

healing hands moved up my calves. Rosemary oil, so pungent it got past the wrappings covering my nose, soaked life into my skin and burned like fire onto my sensitive flesh. "Stay still!"

I heard Bastet's warning, but it was hard to follow direction when it felt like flames engulfed my body.

"A warrior doesn't acknowledge pain." Sekhmet's pronouncement hit me like cold water, and I stopped moving.

"We know you must have many questions, as do we, Shani. Now that you are conscious, we will be able to see your thoughts. Stay focused and form clear images in your head for answers," Bastet said.

I've never understood why the demi-goddesses were the only ones able to read me, at least, most of the time.

"We can discuss your guardedness later." I heard the underlying bite in Bastet's tone and wondered if I'd made her angry.

"No," she answered. "But council convenes in the morning hours and if you are not up and well..."

*What?*

Sekhmet grunted, her strong hands digging into the lax muscles at my shoulders. The linen wrappings were looser now, as was my body. "Lorelei spoke without thinking and told a few people that you were bitten by that Uraeli we captured."

"Your mentor was angry on your behalf! Lorelei wanted revenge." Bastet's words were unusually harsh and defensive.

"Nobody expected you to live. And there were quite a few who objected to your rebirth. The law says that any Felidia bitten by a Uraeli should be put out of their misery immediately. No sense in prolonging the suffering before death." Sekhmet grunted and prodded another sore muscle.

*What? I was bitten?* I was bitten. Snake venom is lethal to the Felidia. The memories came rushing back like a flood, carrying me in the torrent. Since Sekhmet, Bastet, and I were linked, they came too.

*Ambassador Marcos, his wife's birthday, my first assignment. Joshua Sherif Johnson, a wanna be Egyptologist with surfer hair. Natalie, Lorelei, the ninja warrior with gray eyes and venom dripping from her fangs. She defeated me. She knifed me then bit me, and it hurt, by the Goddess' spear, it hurt, and I tried to call – with my mic, with my mind, and with my cell phone. Ninja hated me, she said so.*

*Told me I wasn't worthy. The red ball bounced along the floor, but that's wrong and my memories are mixed up, and I want to live and fight the Uraeli who are slithering scum with fangs.*

"You are a true warrior, Shani," Sekhmet said proudly. "Bazmeht. That is why we took the chance. You should have died from the snake bite. You'd taken a lethal knife wound. Perhaps it is because you were already dying when she bit you that you didn't succumb to the venom. We don't know."

Bastet jumped into the conversation, her mothering voice much more soothing to me than my own mother's voice. "Forty days have passed, to the hour. Your ka has returned to its body. It is time to wake up. We must see if..."

I hadn't heard another heart beat in the chamber. *Who else is here?*

"We are alone." Sekhmet gave no explanation, and my insides chilled with foreboding. The unwrapping must be quick, the skin of the newly reborn Bazmeht saturated with magical lotions and oils. My muscles massaged before they stiffened. There was usually a handmaiden to the demi-goddesses to assist.

I'd performed the ritual twice.

"Patience."

"Shani hasn't ever shown patience, why do you expect her to start now?" Sekhmet argued as I shivered with apprehension.

I thought of my forbidden cell phone. *I'm sorry.*

"I'm talking about your mad rush to graduate, your break-neck speed through training, and having your first death before you are even eighteen."

Chuckling, Bastet snipped through a layer of linen at my feet. "Shani is mature for her age, and she's shown us dedication, loyalty, and strength. Nobody is more focused."

"She can't mind link."

Surprise and alarm added to my nervous state, especially since Sekhmet previously sided with me, against my mother's warning. Remembering how worthless I'd felt, being unable to connect with anyone during the attack, forced me to acknowledge they could be right.

"Nonsense." I heard the drop of linen on the floor as Bastet unwound another layer. "Her *ka* is protecting something."

*What?*

"That worries me," Sekhmet announced.

"We've raised Shani to be a Bazmeht Warrior – a great one. She needs time and experience to fulfill her destiny. She knows the inner secrets of this chamber, because we trust her. Are you saying that now she *can't* be trusted?" Bastet's voice rose as she defended me, as if I couldn't hear them as they spoke over me.

Sighing, Sekhmet peeled linens from my head and shoulders. "She survived a snake bite. It's never happened before. I've heard the others grumbling."

Her worry transferred to me. Would I be brought back to life, only to have the council banish me to death?

"See what you've done, Sekhmet? Stop. Shani's not supposed to stress right now. Think soothing thoughts, Shani, and ignore the Voice of Gloom. I've read the stars and you are meant to be Bazmeht. Tied to the ancient bloodline and trained to protect it. The rest…" I heard the ivory bangles on her wrist *jangle* together and it was easy for me to imagine her making the 'so be it' gesture with her delicate hand.

"Hmph," Sekhmet mumbled. "We need to turn you over."

My body was one big nerve ending, but I bit the inside of my cheek. I would prove myself, over and over again if I had to. *At least Joshua is safe.*

"Yes. He's…safe." Bastet hedged.

*What aren't you telling me?*

Hesitating, she launched into a complaint. "A rebirth is supposed to be coming into the world again with new eyes. Into pure light and calm – not this discord."

Sekhmet, Queen of Chaos in addition to being the Voice of Gloom, made a rude sound in her throat. "The Uraeli want one of the Marcos family members. We know that Ramy Marcos carries the mediated Y chromosome. We were surprised to discover Joshua has it too."

*No! He has American blood – he's mixed – not pure! Impossible.*

"Not pure." Sekhmet sounded furious. "Zelda should have been under lock and key from the time she was fourteen years old. Running away to marry an American?"

"Water under the bridge," Bastet said softly. "If the Uraeli discover Joshua's secret, he will be in danger, so we've kept him under guard. He doesn't like it."

"He's like his mother – defying convention! Tradition."

*The angry poet is a rebel with the sacred Blood of Ra?* I couldn't get past it.

"We've asked him to stay," Bastet said. "I tried to tell him how important he is to us, within reason. He doesn't understand and demands to return to America for fall classes at Miami University."

Sekhmet growled low in her throat. "An Egyptologist should study where the real history is. *Egypt.*"

Egypt. My home...a shadow cast itself over my active mind.

"We did a mind sweep, so he doesn't remember you. He thinks he was downstairs at the party during the attack on Ramy. He's not convinced he's in danger. Also..." Bastet began.

Sekhmet finished her sentence. "Both of the Uraeli escaped. We think we've been betrayed. From the inside."

"Anything you can recall about the night of the attack would help us." Bastet's perfume, gardenia and lilac and rose water, was like a caress. Sekhmet smelled of subtle sandalwood. These women were my mentors, the demi-goddesses I served out of love. Mothers.

I remembered wondering how the ninja had known the Bazmeht rules...but who among us would jeopardize the Bazmeht? In some form or another, we'd been guarding the ancient bloodline for over four thousand years.

*Betrayal.*

"Your heart is racing, Shani." Bastet worked her way through to the last layer of linens between my new skin and me, then helped me to sit.

I wanted the linens off. I wanted a chance to prove I could be the Bazmeht Bastet thought I could be. But Sekhmet's doubt worried me.

Bastet slowly lifted the last cloth. Tense, I wondered what I would see. Fur I could handle.

Scales? A death sentence.

# CHAPTER THREE

## COUNCIL OF NINE

"I didn't think I'd rest, not after sleeping for forty days." I reached over to smooth a pleat on Bastet's sheer white sheath.

"Rebirth isn't easy, Shani. Your body and soul have to heal together. We worried, Sekhmet and I, that you would get lost in the darkness."

"I don't get lost, remember?" I tapped my temple and smiled, careful not to tear the thin skin at the corners of my mouth. I'd coated my lips in olive oil just as a precaution. I'd already torn the sides twice, and it stung worse than a paper cut.

Bastet hummed her agreement. I'd dusted her skin in gold, shimmering paint before applying thick kohl around her eyes. Red ochre flushed her cheeks and lips, and her black ceremonial wig curled to perfection.

"You look smokin'," I said with a self-satisfied nod.

"Smokin'?" She laughed. "You watch too much American television." Studying herself in the long, oval mirror, Bastet agreed that I hadn't lost my touch. "No handmaiden since has your way with folding my skirts. Dendera might be close, but then she burns my wigs."

Our eyes met in the mirror. I felt her love and concern wrap around me. "Perhaps being a handmaiden to the Goddess is a kinder fate than what is in store for you."

Fear froze my vocal chords.

Bastet's eyes went dark, black as the kohl lining them, and for a second, I thought I saw death. She was the golden flame of justice in an Egyptian wig.

I stood behind her, a few inches taller, my eyes as brown as the water of the Nile. My black wig was not as bright, my white sheath not as sheer.

Had I thought her maternal? I bowed my head before her power. "You are a Goddess."

Her painted mouth lifted in a brief smile. "And you are Bazmeht. You are my sword arm, despite your talent for pleats." Bastet sighed, gesturing me toward the bench seat beneath the window. "I asked you to help me this morning, even though you've outgrown your duties here."

"Never!" It was my honor to serve her.

"Not just for nostalgic purposes. I have a warning."

She sat, tugging my hand until I sat next to her. I couldn't breathe in anticipation of the bad news. It had to be bad, and I'd been stupid not to see it coming. I wasn't a child anymore.

"Sekhmet knows what I'm about to say, but she doesn't agree with me. To keep balance between us, she will accept my decision."

*I was being banished, and I hadn't stepped foot before the council.*

"Pah! You are not being banished."

I breathed.

My mistake.

"Not exactly."

"What then?" My pulse *thudded* through my body.

"It's about your mother."

*My mother?* "Is she all right?" I cleared my throat, embarrassed that after all this time I cared. "I meant, will she be here for the council meeting? She almost blocked my votes before." Cold seeped into my heart as I considered all the ways she'd shown me her hate, while I foolishly waited for love.

"Sharifa always lands on her feet," Bastet noted dryly. "We tried to locate her in the jungle, but couldn't get word to her about your death or the circumstances around it. Sekhmet even sent Natalie to find her, but-" Bastet shrugged.

"I see." I blinked, my eyes scratchy with disappointment. When would I stop hoping? It had to be *now.* If gifted a second life, I'd keep the power I gave my mother to hurt me. I lifted my chin, my voice cold. "Then what?"

"You know she's on a mission to the Mayan ruins."

"Yes, but I don't know why, exactly."

"You don't need to know. Suffice it to say, we're worried. Sekhmet thinks you should go to the jungle and find Sharifa. Be with your mother. Learn from her."

I shook my head, my mouth too dry to speak.

"I don't." Bastet held my gaze.

Relieved, I jumped to my feet, accidentally smearing a gold

patch on Bastet's hand. I marched to the cosmetics on the table and grabbed a small paintbrush and the jar of gold. Professional. Duty. *Exhale.* "I'm not talented enough to track my mother in the jungle."

I dropped to my knees before Bastet. My heart shriveled to the size of a date, and I concentrated on covering each whirl of skin.

"I disagree, but more importantly, I feel that your mother is fine."

I briefly closed my eyes in thanks.

Bastet tapped my shoulder. "It isn't a sin to love your mother."

"It is when she can't stand me."

"Shani, I wish I could heal this hurt inside of you."

"I'm fine." I capped the jar and stood. "I'm happy. Thanks be to the Goddess that I acted as Bazmeht, despite my mother's doubts. What did she call my inability to mind link? A defect?" I swallowed the dull pain.

Bastet's mysterious eyes remained troubled. "We will be re-evaluating our stance on the cell phone. Lorelei heard you from the mic and tried to reach you, fighting the waiting assailants at the stairs. Ona mentally received your warning, but Ferimi didn't. Control only knew there was trouble because you called."

The acknowledgment warmed me.

"Sekhmet is right, and this had to have been an inside job. Shani, I need to trust you and burden you with more than I should. You've proven how strong you are. You've showed your loyalty. Go get me my Utchat and the Sistrum too."

"*Tamam,*" I said, my mouth dry. "Okay." When Bastet held the sacred eye and her ceremonial rattle, she became Goddess. I knew I was about to be judged, here in the privacy of her chamber rather than in front of the council.

Bastet had to be worried in order to break the rules like this.

"Sometimes," she winked at me and my head filled with the image of my orange iPhone, "the rules must be broken." She took the Utchat and Sistrum and told me to kneel before her, with my heart clear.

Closing my eyes, I sent prayers to the oldest of Gods and Goddesses that my fate be filled with honor and courage, that I meet my destiny with a worthy soul.

Dendera interrupted our impromptu ceremony by bursting into the chamber.

I looked up from my prayers, noting the surprise on her young face. Had I ever been so innocent? Her clear, amber eyes widened, showing without words that she'd heard the rumors. I'd been bitten by a snake and survived. That I was evil.

She couldn't help searching my skin, my body, my face for anything out of the ordinary. Like scales or a Cobra's hood.

"Boo," I said with a smile.

Dendera flushed with guilt, and Bastet cleared her throat, her tones deep. "Is there a reason you've barged into my ceremonial room without knocking? Without remembering you are a mere servant in the presence of the Goddess?"

"I am sorry, Goddess Bastet!" Dendera dropped to her knees, her forehead to the floor as she cried. "I apologize for-"

"Stop that," Bastet ordered in a stern voice I remembered very well. "And tell me what possessed you to behave so badly?"

Dendera leaned back on her heels and hiccupped, her gaze over Bastet's shoulder. "The council is ready, Goddess. Some of the members are already pounding the floor with their staffs, demanding their turn to speak. Before you, and the Goddess Sekhmet are even seated! What will we do?" The young handmaiden risked a half lidded glance toward me.

Bastet, in either demi goddess or full Goddess form, was not one to mess with. She gestured at me. "Go get Sekhmet. I refuse to step foot before the council one grain of sand early. Sekhmet will let them taste her wrath, by the Ancient Mother, I can promise that."

She lifted the golden Sistrum and rattled it, awakening the slumbering gods. My early judgment was not to be.

I returned with Sekhmet, who stood in glorious anger as she heard the pounding coming from the small auditorium. "In the old days, we'd claw the heads off the rebels and drink their blood."

Dendera moaned, while Sekhmet's personal handmaiden, her narrow shoulders stiff, looked ready to go to battle on behalf of her Goddess.

I liked her. "You're Keket, right?"

Her dark eyes were oval, her irises shaped like a sand cat's. "Yes. Isn't your mother the greatest warrior of all time?"

*Ouch.* I guess my popularity with the younger set hadn't

improved. I thought of Natalie, who always had a following of young girls. I'd never taken time to braid palm frond crowns. Training took precedence.

We walked through the limestone tunnel, the floor smoothed by thousands of years of bare feet. We entered the auditorium from the side. Dendera removed the lids from the baskets of dried ice, creating a mysterious screen of smoke. Side by side, Bastet and Sekhmet passed through the cloud of fog and onto the stage.

Keket guided the Goddesses to the dais where they sat before the mix of Bazmeht women, young and old, retired and trainees. The council leaders of nine, four to the left of the dais, and five to the right, also faced the audience, though the chairs turned toward the pair of goddesses.

The council was a democracy – the judges ancient.

The pounding of the staffs stopped as Sekhmet stood, spreading her arms toward the people. "Welcome! You are called together to welcome a sister, a warrior, back from the dead. To judge her worthiness and reward her with the next level of life among the Bazmeht. Shani Nebit, step forward!"

My insides trembled like rice pudding, but my outsides were as solid as Lorelei's nut cake. I strode out before the council, my judges, my jury – with my chin lifted and my back a straight line of steel.

Less than a year ago I'd walked this stage, scared I'd faint. New, uncertain. It hadn't helped knowing my mother argued against my acceptance of the Bazmeht birthright.

I'd buried that particular nightmare, but the bright lights and dry ice fog brought it back. Humiliation tastes like defeat, and I don't like it much.

My mother is beautiful. Tall, with auburn hair and golden eyes. She has a thin muscular build made for running like the wind, eyesight so sharp she doesn't need binoculars, and she blends into her surroundings as if one with nature. She's a superhero in a world that can't know she exists.

I, by contrast, have muddy brown eyes, hair that can't make up its mind what color it is, and I'm only five foot four.

She holds all of the records in Bazmeht history.

I barely made the team.

But I want it – I want so badly to succeed and prove that I'm good enough to be her daughter – even though she doesn't want me.

Stepping further onto the stage to face my enemies and allies, I glanced to the right of the dais.

I tripped, catching myself before I fell.

My mother, the great Sharia, sat in her council chair.

How had Natalie found her and gotten her back on time? I squinted into the shadows, fine-tuning my sight to include the tiny bit of jungle dirt at her scalp, and I saw her frown. I can feel her disapproval even though we are fifty feet apart. Her lips didn't move, but I heard her whisper my name.

"Shani." Then, "Don't do this."

I turned my back on her, and I know that the jury watched me do it. *Me, the terrible daughter of the Bazmeht's greatest warrior.* I lifted my gaze to Bastet, but she is pure Goddess now, her eyes onyx in her golden cat's face. No mask, but real whiskers, real fur, real ears.

The crowd behind me gasped, and I saw that Sekhmet completed her transformation - a lioness head on a stunning, ebony, female body. She and Bastet stood, side by side, Sekhmet holding the Utchat and Bastet holding the Sistrum. They will listen, and at the end, offer their judgment.

I prayed for courage.

My mother started first, cutting off anyone else who would speak with a slash of her hand through the air. She pounded her staff to the floor once. "My name is Sharifa Nebit. My daughter is Shani Nebit. I protest her acceptance as a Level Two Bazmeht."

My stomach did more than twist into a knot; it took the other intestines with it. *How can she be so cruel?*

Lorelei banged her staff against the stage floor. "Shani has earned her right to be a bodyguard. Her death came at the hands of the enemy."

"Don't you mean fangs?" Tefnut, another council member who had previously been on my mother's side, yelled into the crowd.

Shem-tet, the oracle, stepped forward, cracking her staff against her chair. "Out of order, Tefnut!"

Everybody had something to say and all exploded into opinion as I stood with my head bowed before them.

I was the cause of the chaos. It hit me that I split the council when the goal of all Bazmeht was a United Egypt under true-blooded rule.

Natalie, Goddess smite her, wore a large smile from her seat in the front row.

The council leaders forgot protocol. Sekhmet released a deafening roar, bringing us all to our knees.

Nobody dared to look up, not even me. Time crawled. Urgent whispers wafted from the dais. The council leaders went forward, one at a time, to speak softly with the Goddesses of Judgment.

I waited in vain to speak, or explain. To defend my life. Training held me still though my instincts bade me jump up and yell my innocence.

The Sistrum rattled, signaling the end of the conferences. "Sit," Goddess Bastet said in her deceptively sweet voice. "Be ready to hear our decision."

I shook. Trembled. Nerves, apprehension. Fear. Emotion raced through my body, not allowing me to be still any longer.

My mother's energy called to me, but I didn't look at her, I couldn't. I refused to let her hurt me again. My hearing is acute, better than most guard-shifters. I've often wondered if instead of the ability to mind link, the Mother Goddess gave me this instead.

I'd overheard the whispers, and I knew that the numbers were five to four, in favor of banishing me.

The Sistrum's loud *rat a tat tat* commanded my attention. The auditorium remained as quiet as night.

"We heard fear in your voices instead of fairness. We are shamed for the council." Goddess Sekhmet's loud voice boomed around the auditorium.

Salty tears gathered at the back of my throat. I swallowed them down, refusing to show weakness in front of my enemies.

Goddess Bastet shook the rattle of justice. "Shamed," she echoed sadly.

This was not the time for the council to speak, and I could feel their frustration. Mews of distress came from the watching crowd.

Goddess Sekhmet raised her arm and shouted angrily, "We should rejoice!" Her eyes pierced each person her gaze landed on. "Shani Nebit is a miracle. No Felidia, no Bazmeht in all of our five thousand years of known history has survived a bite from a Uraeli agent." Lowering the Utchat as well as her voice, she continued, "I would think, Tefnut, council leader of poisons, that you would want to find out why."

I blamed the gathering tears in my eyes on being newly reborn. The Goddesses made their bid for me, but they'd lost. Been out voted.

Death loomed. Or banishment from the underground temple to live with the rogue Felidia, which seemed a fate worse than death.

"We've thought it over, together, and searched our hearts and souls for the right thing to do." Goddess Bastet grasped Goddess Sekhmet's hand. "We are *not* banishing a brave member of our pride because some of you fear what she might become."

I looked up, blinking away any trace of moisture.

Goddess Sekhmet wouldn't meet my eyes as she boomed my fate. "Shani Nebit is on probation for a period of forty days."

Probation? My shoulders eased. I could do that. Catch up on my reading, renew my iPod list...but my sentence wasn't over.

"She will be sent to America." Goddess Bastet's dark gaze didn't meet mine. She'd had a warning for me. About this? The demi goddesses wanted me out of Egypt? I'd never left my home soil, *I needed it.* I patted my phone, securely tucked into my chemise strap.

My heart ached with denial, but I could breathe.

I hadn't done anything wrong. I had no scales, no fangs. And what was in America? Fast food, loud music.

My head whipped up, and at last Bastet met my eyes.

*Joshua Johnson.*

# CHAPTER FOUR

## WINDS OF CHANGE

I quickly bowed my head before I said something really stupid. Like, uh, no.

"Shani," Goddess Bastet said softly, "you will leave immediately. Wait for us in our chambers."

With that, the lights from the wall sconces dimmed and the council meeting was over. I hadn't been given a death sentence, but I hadn't been welcomed back into the fold, either. Thanks to my mother, the great Sharifa, I'd been put on probation.

*America.*

Girls Gone Wild videos, MTV, Kim Kardashian and Tyra Banks – that's what I knew of America.

Nobody dared speak to me as I followed the Goddesses and their handmaidens out the side door of the auditorium. Lorelei sent me an unreadable look. The ultimate failure, my inability to mind link.

Keket skipped the sarcasm portion of her good-bye as she left us to prepare the Goddesses special baths, and Dendera eyed me as if I might start speaking with a forked tongue.

*Hissssss.*

Goddess Bastet gave Dendera the Utchat and the Sistrum and told her to lock them safely away. The young girl left, and in that instant, Bastet and Sekhmet became demi-goddesses again.

They were approachable, and I could argue without getting my head chopped off.

"I don't want to go to America!"

"You speak English better than anybody else, well, besides Tabitha, but she came from the outside world." Bastet sat on a stool and gestured for me to start helping with her wig.

Sekhmet paced the room like a caged lion. "Did you hear them? They've been riled, against Shani, but I fear it goes deeper than that. Who has that power?"

"My mother." I pulled a pin from Bastet's hair.

"She's been gone, deep in the jungle where she can't get into trouble or cause harm," Sekhmet said. "And first thing tomorrow, back to the jungle she'll go. She had to be notified for the meeting, Shani, you do understand that, don't you?"

I nodded, wishing I didn't understand. The goddesses were all about fair play.

"Sharifa is a born warrior. And a strategist! She's onto something, a clue in the Jaguar. Hmm. Anyway," Sekhmet made another turn around the room, "the bottom line is that you are in danger if you stay here. I can't tell from who, so you have to go. I wanted you to help your mother, but Bastet and the oracle both say America is where your destiny lies."

Bastet reached to pat my hand. "Joshua refuses to stay here. He wants to go to college in Miami, and he will need a guard. One that's college-aged, who can understand him. You are the best suited for many reasons."

"Natalie likes him!"

"Natalie speaks German. That doesn't help." Bastet rotated her head from side to side as soon as I lifted the heavy wig. "That feels so much better." She scratched her scalp.

"I'm glad someone feels better," I mumbled as I put the wig on the shelf.

"It won't be horrible," Sekhmet said. "We're sending Lorelei too. If I remember correctly," she paused to let us all silently acknowledge that she never forgets a thing, "Zelda Marcos, whatever her latest name is, has some Egyptian Artifacts that every other year she lends to a local museum. Lorelei will be there to guard Zelda's collection. She will be there to assist, only if you need it."

"You don't trust me." This was a terrible assignment and they didn't think I could do it alone. *Great.*

"You have proven that you have what it takes to be an honorable guard."

I brushed a piece of blue thread from my white sheath, anxious to remove my own wig and scrub the five layers of make-up from my sensitive face. "Sekhmet, I've proven I know how to die. And Miami is a long plane ride away."

Bastet laughed as if my fears were harmless. "If you use up all your lives in the first year, you won't last a century – be careful, dearest Shani. Just pack enough for a few days, and we will do the rest. Send Lorelei to us, please? We'll meet for a light supper before you go."

I'd been dismissed.

My head reeled, keeping me off balance. What would happen if I had a screaming, tearing out my hair tantrum? I shook off the need to scream, knowing that warriors, especially warriors on probation, were not allowed crying jags.

Walking down the corridor toward my room, I slipped my cell phone from the specially made strap I'd designed for all my undergarments and checked for messages. One from Martina, asking me to come dancing in Cairo.

Temptation. A way to release the primal energy building within me. The lights, the unrestricted movement of dancing in the dark was as close as I dared come to acknowledge my rage. I preferred to dance alone.

I'd explained my sudden disappearance over the past forty days on an unexpected death in the family. Martina didn't need to know it was mine.

Too tired to come up with another lie that would excuse my next forty days in purgatory, I texted my few friends – all Felidia or humans outside of the Bazmeht - a generic good bye. I doubted they'd actually miss me.

Lorelei waited outside my chamber. Her eyes blazed in her pale face.

"I was just going to call you," I said, waving my phone. "Bastet wants to see you."

She nodded with a tough jerk of her chin. "Good. I'm going with you, they can't send you to America by yourself! It's crazy over there. Don't they watch the news? You'll need your own bodyguard! I'll refuse to work with anyone else."

My heart filled at her show of loyalty. "Bastet told me you're going. Act surprised when she tells you. I'm to pack for a few days and they are sending the rest of what I'll need. Forty days. That's not long. Right?"

Dark shadows of foreboding clouded my thoughts.

As I'd recently learned, forty days could be an eternity.

Lorelei grinned, traces of white make-up still visible in the creases around her mouth. "Thank the Goddess. If I stay here with Tefnut, the temptation to kick that crone's bony tail might prove too much. That old woman doesn't just study poison, she *is* poison."

"I didn't realize how many of the Bazmeht don't trust me." Chills dotted my skin as I opened the door to my room and stepped inside. Neither one of us brought up my mother by name.

"They don't understand, that's all. Not much of a decorator, are you?" Lorelei joked as she followed me.

I looked around, seeing nothing wrong with the plain, plastered walls. My hammock had two pillows piled at the head, with my serviceable teak trunk tucked beneath it, against the wall. My wooden desk was uncluttered, holding my closed laptop and my iPod dock with speakers.

"I haven't been here for a while," I said defensively.

"Who are you kidding? It always looks like this. You're in the Bazmeht, not prison, you know. You make plenty of money to buy nice things."

"I'm fine." The truth was that I didn't really care about 'stuff'. I stored my cash in the bank for retirement – or emergencies. A girl can't expect to live for three hundred years and not put a little something away.

Muu, my silver Persian with green eyes, woke from her nap on top of the wardrobe and blinked at me, as if the forty days I'd been gone were nothing. "Hi pretty kitty."

She yawned, showing a pointed pink tongue.

"Do you know where in America we're going?" Lorelei pulled out the chair from my desk and sat.

"Miami. They seem to think that Joshua Johnson is in danger, from the Uraeli."

"Explain, please?"

I paused, wondering if I should share what the demi-goddesses told me. But this was Lorelei – my mentor and only Bazmeht friend. "Joshua has the Blood of Ra."

Her mouth dropped open, and she shot to her feet, accidentally knocking my computer to the floor.

Muu, startled by the crash, jumped from her place on the wardrobe, landing at my feet. I reached down to scratch behind her ears when she suddenly hunched her back and spat at me. Eyes wild and slitted, she looked furious and terrified at the same time. "Muu? What's wrong?"

She reared back on her haunches and swiped at me with her claws extended.

"What in the world is the matter with you?"

Apprehension spread through my veins at the look in Muu's eyes. "She hates me."

"She doesn't hate you." Lorelei quickly opened the door and shooed Muu out to the hall, where she took off running with all the speed an aging, overweight cat could get.

"Really?" I watched the tail disappear around the corner.

"Don't be sarcastic. She probably smelled the rebirthing herbs."

Somehow, I didn't think so. "Well...I guess she won't miss me while I'm gone. Who was feeding her while I was, uh, asleep?" It's hard to say that I'd been dead. Truth or not, some things just don't slide off the tongue easily.

"Dendera."

Great. The two could bond over their mutual dislike of me. I had a feeling it had more to do with surviving a snake bite than being reborn. "Will you ask her if she will keep Muu for me? I mean, I would, but she doesn't really..."

"I'll ask. When do we leave?"

"Immediately." Just the thought of not being in Egypt made me ill. "Goddess's mercy, I don't even own a suitcase."

I heard the panic in my voice and coughed to cover it. I picked up my laptop, checking it for damages. "The lid was closed, so I'm sure it's fine." Set it on the desk, centering it. Wiped a fingerprint smudge from the corner. Exhaled.

"Relax." Lorelei put her hand on my shoulder. "I have an extra carry on."

"I don't know what to wear." I detested sounding like a girl but this was serious.

"It's Miami. All you need are a few bikinis."

"Huh?" I whirled around, my hand over my toned, yet very pale, stomach.

"Bring what you have, but you can buy more when you get there. Miami has raised the bikini to an art form."

My face flushed as Lorelei rummaged through the drawers of my wardrobe. "You fold your underwear?" She went to the next dresser. "Bless me, your jewelry is even labeled. What's this?" She held up a picture I kept beneath my pajama pants.

"Me and Mom." I resisted the urge to snatch it from my friend's hand. I'm about five in the photo, and my mom actually smiles at me like she loves me, which is the reason I keep it hidden. And probably why hope won't actually die. "Just leave it."

Lorelei nodded, then dragged out my lone swimming suit with distaste written all over her face. "A one piece?"

"I hate the water." I shuddered.

"You'll have to get over that." Lorelei stood, dropping the suit back into the drawer. "Forget it. I'll take you shopping. You don't have to swim anyway. You just have to look good. Blend in. You can do that."

"Where do we put our guns?" My specially made bra had a spot for my ultra slim phone but there wasn't any room for a Glock.

Laughing, Lorelei flung open the wardrobe doors. "No guns. You'll have to be on your toes. Use your senses, but no shifting. Ever."

"What about at night when-"

"Never. You're on probation, remember?" Lorelei sorted through one black jacket and pants suit after another. "Where are your other clothes? Girl, you need a -ooh, this has possibilities." She'd found my peacock blue, silk dress that I wore to my secret life at the clubs.

"I don't want to go." I crossed my arms over my chest as if I could physically block the change Fate demanded. "Help me tell Bastet that I need to be here. I'll be careful – nobody would actually *hurt* me! This is my home."

Lorelei's scream cut me off mid whine. She fell back from the wardrobe, my silk dress in one hand and a black snake clutched in the other.

Snake!

The surge of adrenalin made newborn fur sprout behind my ear. I ran the five steps to where Lorelei sprawled on the floor, my mouth dry with fear.

Her thick, dark braid tumbled over her shoulder, her lips pinched, her face a mask of fury as she ignored my outstretched hand. "Jerks." She vaulted limberly to her feet, the snake dangling from her clutched fist.

I couldn't breathe under the onslaught of memories. Being bitten. *Dying.*

"Rubber." She tossed the toy snake to the floor then kicked it across the room. "Somebody's idea of a joke."

*Not real.* It took a minute to realize that there wasn't any danger.

Lorelei put her hands on her hips, her chin angled for a fight. "The demi-goddesses are right. You can't stay here."

Somebody had broken the bounds of privacy.

And scared me half to death.

# CHAPTER FIVE

"Call me Josh." His Miami drawl dripped with disdain.

Pouting behind my bland expression, I tightened the buckle over my lap, then looked to see if he was strapped in too. *Check.* I dipped my head, resenting his resentment. "This is a business arrangement, Mr. Johnson. It's better if we keep things on a professional level."

"And what am I supposed to call you? Ms. Nebit?" He sent me a grin that in no way reached his angry eyes. The next forty days were going to be pure Hell. Joshua had not taken the news of his guardianship well, and once he'd met me, he'd burst out laughing.

Until I'd given him a sleeper hold that brought him to his knees.

He hadn't gotten over my display of capability, obviously.

"We don't have to talk." I'd planned on cat napping during the flight to the states on the Bazmeht's private plane. First class was leather seats and warm blankets. Hot cocoa. Candied almonds. Pure luxury.

"Ever?"

"Don't get your hopes up," I said dryly.

"I don't need a bodyguard. It's insulting that Uncle Marcos thinks I can't take care of myself. I never should have asked to visit, now he thinks he owns me! No wonder Mom took off."

Would he complain the entire way, and ruin my first flight experience? "Do you need a valium?" I popped one eye open, daring to hope.

He frowned, his dark blond brows drawn together. "I don't do drugs. Not even the prescription kind."

Too late, I remembered Bastet saying something about Zelda in rehab. "Sorry." I knew all about mother issues, and it was one area I would give him a pass. "Aren't you tired?"

"No. I'm not. I'm pissed off and I want answers, which nobody is giving me."

"They talked to you. You were too busy arguing to listen." I rolled my shoulders, settling in.

His jaw clenched. Perhaps I hadn't taken the right approach. Trained to fight, I struggled to play nice.

Sighing, I sat up all the way and listened to the droning of the airplane's engines. Diplomacy was harder to ace than target shooting. "Bastet and Sekhmet told you about your family carrying a special gene, one purely maintained throughout history."

"Impossible."

I bit my lip before trying again. "Our organization has protected that blood line, and...co-mingled." We hadn't told Joshua about our ability to shape shift. Or the Council of Nine. Or that if the Uraeli enemy found out about his genetic abnormality, they'd want him for experimentation, or just plain dead. Bastet said that a guy could only take so much.

"You're like some female Knights Templar? Protecting the Holy Grail?"

It was exactly like that, so I just smiled.

His answering smirk told me that he wasn't buying it. "I've studied Egypt, and nowhere does it say anything about the real Bastet and Sekhmet – ancient *feline* goddesses, by the way – being human and having ancestors survive to today."

I tried not to roll my eyes. But I'm seventeen, and it's hard. I could tell him more about goddesses than his mind could take.

"And there isn't even a rumor about a pure Egyptian bloodline, which might be believable if you said, say, five hundred years back. But pre-dynastic?" He shook his head and I worried that I might have to put him in another sleeper hold. Just because he won't even try to believe. You have to have a little faith.

"Mom's collection stays under lock and key, and I'm all for a private security guard for when it's at the museum." He jerked his head back to the rear of the plane, where Lorelei was already sleeping. "But me?" His blue eyes grew stormy, pulling me in. "I can take care of myself, and the last thing I need is some chick following me around campus. You," he leered, "will totally cramp my style."

My temper simmered. Nothing in my training prepared me for guarding a moron. "And Lorelei called you charming..."

"When? I've never met her, so how could she know what I'm like?"

ᵞ𐤉𐤎ᛟᛝᛝ𐤇𐤊𐤒ᛚᚣ 𐤉ᛗ ᛦᛤᛝ 𐤀ᛗᚣᛝᛟᛦᛣᛝᛠᛝᛝ

Great. Half an hour into the assignment and I'd almost blown cover. Totally forgotten about the mind sweep they'd done on him.

"She heard it from Mrs. Marcos, your aunt." I glanced at him, and he nodded but still wouldn't relax. Maybe some small talk would bore him to sleep. "Did you enjoy your visit?"

He looked at me as if I was crazy. "Let's review," he droned. "I wanted to see the pyramids and study the Egyptian drums. Instead, the family went into lock-down because some weirdo tried to kidnap my cousin Ramy. I've spent the last month imprisoned-"

"The Cairo Hilton is hardly prison." I tapped my fingers over my knee.

"Every time I left the room, I had a shadow!" His glare intensified, and as much as I wanted to argue with him, I kept my mouth shut.

He was seriously mad about the whole thing.

Having been born into the Bazmeht world, I know how rare a male with the mediated Y chromosome is, just as I understand, on a pheromonal level, how important Joshua is to our species. A Felidia female can only produce a cat shifter by mating with a male with the special gene.

The Bazmeht take the very rare instances of shifters born outside the compound and train them to be guards, as is their destiny. Like Tabitha. Most Bazmeht are planned pregnancies, kept within the pride. There's not a lot of us.

But Joshua was raised outside of the compound, outside of Egypt, outside of tradition. His brain can't even comprehend what we really are. If Zelda had stayed in Egypt, Joshua would be comfortable in his role as Prince among the Bazmeht.

Fate.

Destiny.

You can't outrun it.

Was that what Zelda had been trying to do?

"You have no idea what it's like to have every move you make monitored just because you supposedly have some stupid family gene. What does that do for me anyway? Why does it put me in danger? It's not as if someone is going to want to kill me for an organ transplant – that kind of stuff doesn't really happen. Your organization is warped, totally twisted." Joshua dared me to argue.

Indignant, I narrowed my eyes and prepared to set him straight, but Lorelei cleared her throat from her seat a few rows back.

"It seems surreal," she acknowledged with kindness dripping from every syllable. He turned, and Lorelei held his gaze until his shoulders slowly relaxed. Hypnotism. Calming him down without ever leaving her seat.

Someday I should be so talented.

Joshua turned around, the fight leaving his body like air from a balloon. "I'm beat."

Just like that, he started snoring. I heard Lorelei chuckle as I made myself as comfortable as possible for the rest of the flight.

Clearly, I had a lot left to learn.

I slept but awoke when the plane hit turbulence. Excitement warred with nervous tension as the private plane descended toward Miami International Airport.

Joshua stretched then stared out the window, completely at ease as we bounced through the sky.

"Are you sure our pilot knows what he's doing?" I clutched the armrests as we bounced through the clouds.

He looked at me, realization dawning in the beginning of a smug smile. "You've never flown before?"

"I've never left *Egypt* before." My cheeks burned beneath his gaze.

Joshua exhaled, one side of his blond hair sticking up from where he'd slept on it. "Sorry. I assumed that in addition to your mad bodyguard skills you'd be a world traveler. I mean, you're almost eighteen, right?"

This time, his smile was genuine, and I quickly looked away before I smiled back.

We weren't supposed to be friends.

I didn't know how to be friends.

"Are you afraid of heights?"

I thought of the rooftops I'd leaped and shook my head with disdain. "No."

"So it's just flying you're scared of."

"I'm not scared. I've just never done it before." The plane skipped. I choked down a squeal.

Josh lifted his can of root beer. "Uh huh."

I sent him a glare. "I'm not afraid!" My belly lodged in my

throat as we skidded across a cloud.

"You're fearless, then?" He saluted me then drained the can. I was surprised he didn't crush it in his hand to prove his superiority.

"She's been trained, Joshua, to be fearless," Lorelei said, making her way toward the front of the plane. "That is what will keep you safe."

He snorted and pointed at my white knuckles. "Good thing I can take care of myself."

I forced my fingers to release the armrests, which retained finger indents in the vinyl.

"Let's solidify our plan before we land." Lorelei sat in the seat ahead of me then turned so she faced us both.

"Shani is your Egyptian cousin come to live with you and possibly go to college. Thank the Goddess, er, goodness, that you two don't have any *spark*."

No spark? For some unfathomable reason, this revelation annoyed me. Was I not fun enough? Attractive enough? I stole a peek at his scruffy cheeks and chin. He wasn't *that* cute...

"As family, it will give a believable reason for the both of you to be around each other all the time. Living in the same house. You are showing her Miami and the college. She might be interested in taking a semester or two." Lorelei held out her hand, palm up. "What do you think, Joshua?"

"My name is *Josh*. I have a girlfriend, okay? So don't think I'm spending all of my time with you." Scowling, Josh crossed his arms over his chest. "Bastet and Sekhmet are like two meddling aunts from a bad romance. How long do we have to pretend that I'm in danger?"

"Fort-"

"For as long as it takes," Lorelei smoothly over-rode my truthful answer with a lie.

I smiled tightly. "We just want you safe."

"I'm not in any trouble." Joshua's jaw tightened with testosterone.

"Oh look, we've landed!" Lorelei announced brightly.

I'd been so irritated that I hadn't noticed the plane was finally on the ground.

A black limousine idled as we stepped outside into the hot, humid air. I immediately broke into a sweat. Egypt is hot, yes, but not damp. This was like stepping into a misting machine, without the refreshing coolness of a river's breeze.

Lorelei delicately dabbed at her brow. "Just as I remember it."

"You've been here before? Why didn't you say so?" I fanned my face with my hand.

She winked. "It was a very, very long time ago."

In cat years, code for possibly centuries. "Hmm."

"My mom's been here for twenty-five years," Joshua said. "She says Egypt slumbers in her blood." As if he realized what he'd just admitted, he stomped to the back of the limo.

"I don't see how he's ever going to be a successful Egyptologist if he hates Egypt." A concept I would never understand.

The broad shouldered limo driver took our luggage from the plane and stored it in the trunk. "*Bon jour!* Will this be all?" He seemed surprised that we only had three carry-ons. His accent was French, his hands groomed. I noticed the snug fit of his jacket. No bulge of a gun.

"We travel light," I assured him. "You were sent by the control center?" He nodded and didn't seem to mind as I did a routine car check before crawling into the air-conditioned interior with a relieved shiver. Chilled sparkling cider and crystal glasses waited for us. I sighed with pleasure as we each took a seat. "This is the way to go." Luxury wasn't something I had in my daily life, but I could get used to it - as part of my job, of course. "How long before we get to your house, Mr. Johnson?"

I mentally listed everything that I'd need to do first, starting with the home security system. Then the windows. A backup list waited on my Notes app. "Do you have a basement?"

Joshua – Josh - stretched his legs out in the center of the limo. "This is Florida. We don't do basements. We're about a half an hour from the house, but do you want the beach tour? I can ask the driver to take us down to the ocean road. It's touristy."

Lorelei didn't give me a chance to say no. "Yes! How fun. We can see the beach, Shani."

Forcing a smile, I nodded. I wanted to say that we weren't here for fun; we were here to work. To make sure that the Uraeli stayed blissfully unaware of Joshua's genetics. But Lorelei looked happy, so I kept quiet. As long as he was in my line of sight, I supposed it was all right.

Still...

Joshua knocked on the partition, and the glass between the driver and us slowly slid open.

"*Oui?*"

"Take us by Ocean Drive, would you?"

"Of course. Tell me again your home address?"

Joshua gave the driver his address and the partition slid shut. His voice held an edge as he stated, "So. We're family."

Lorelei poured us all a fizzy glass of chilled cider before sitting back and crossing her legs at the ankle. "It's perfect."

"I wouldn't say perfect," I said, sipping, then sneezing as bubbles went up my nose. Joshua refused to laugh, even at my expense.

"Cousins," I forged on. "But I can't change my name," I said. "My luck, I'll forget it."

"Right." He lifted his glass in a sarcastic salute. "Here's to my cuz, Shani Nebit..."

*Level one Bazmeht Bodyguard. Highly trained to kick ass.* Once I was back from probation, I would be a Level Two. I smiled into my crystal flute.

"May her visit be short and uneventful." Joshua drained the cider in one long drink, eyeing me as if I was a bug in his salad. "I was blackmailed by my uncle into having you come with me to Miami. But what's your gig? You don't seem to like your job that much."

I tilted my head, wishing I had Lorelei's gift of hypnotism to put him down with a mere look. I'd promised to keep my hands to myself. "I am seventeen, practically eighteen. Trained to protect, as I proved to you earlier with the sleeper hold." I pinched my fingers together like lobster claws. "What's not to like?"

"You got lucky." His eyes glittered, blue shards of ice in his tanned face.

I heard the resentment, and yes, embarrassment, in his voice. "Taking you down was nothing personal, Mr. Johnson." I kept my chin firm. "I did it to prove a point. I can take care of you. It's what I've been taught since the day I knew my vocation."

His brow quirked, and again, I realized too late how that must sound.

Rather than make it worse, I turned my gaze out the window. I didn't need a friend, so why let his irritation bother me?

Egypt was home. In order to get back I had to spend my probation *not* growing fangs while keeping Joshua safe from the Uraeli. Easy enough, since the few Bazmeht who knew about Joshua - Bastet and Sekhmet, two scientists in our testing department, Lorelei, and me, were sworn to secrecy.

My duty now was to *make sure* that nobody else knew about his genetics, and if possible, tempt him into returning to Egypt where we could introduce him to the Bazmeht way of life. Without telling him too much. I'm used to obeying orders. Doing what is good for the pride. For Egypt.

What was this like from Joshua's point of view? He had a girlfriend, college classes, a real life. All he'd been doing was visiting his uncle in Egypt while his mom was on her honeymoon. His family had been attacked, and his privacy torn to shreds as he'd been saddled with an unwanted bodyguard.

Across from me, Joshua fumed. Perhaps the sleeper hold had been a bad idea.

Swallowing my pride, I choked out the words, "I'm sorry."

# CHAPTER SIX

## TROUBLE AHEAD

Lorelei smiled at me as if to say, 'That wasn't too hard, was it?'

Well, as a matter of fact, it sucked.

Joshua, the ingrate, simply shrugged, neither accepting nor rejecting my apology.

"I won't do it again." *No matter how much you deserve it.* Draining my glass, I reached into the pocket of my suit jacket and pulled out my phone. Palms damp with stress, my breath caught when I saw the black screen of my iPhone.

Until I remembered I'd turned it off for the flight.

My pulse slowed to normal as I turned it back on.

"Three messages," I said into to the tense silence of the limo. Scanning them, I added, "Nothing from Bastet or Control. Keket asked if I'd enjoyed my going away present, which I assume means she's the one that put the snake in my wardrobe."

"I'll speak to Sekhmet," Lorelei pronounced. "That is unacceptable behavior. She should be written up, at least."

"Please don't. Sekhmet's handmaiden isn't my biggest fan."

Joshua looked at me over his glass. "Not good at making friends, Shani?"

I ignored him.

The weather report said Miami was a sunny eighty-nine degrees and my daily horoscope said to watch out for unexpected trouble.

I rolled my shoulders and cracked my neck before checking the road for anything unusual. I'd know it when I saw it.

"This is ridiculous," Joshua said in a dangerously quiet tone. "You guys act like you're in a James Bond movie. Black suits, Control, ancient bloodlines. I used to think my mom was crazy, and now here you are, talking about ancestral duty."

"Your mother spoke to you about your legacy before?" I exchanged a look with Lorelei. Maybe he wouldn't be so hard to reach after all.

"Not really. Not when she was sober anyway."

I bit my lower lip. What could I say to that?

"You know, there probably isn't any danger, but you have to let us check. For your own good." Lorelei put her hand on Joshua's knee but he jerked it away. "There are people who might want to hurt you."

"I don't *have* to do anything. I'm going to school, for my degree. I want to understand my history – the real thing, not your trumped up bullsh-."

I was discovering that I didn't have Lorelei's patience with idiots, and my good intentions flew out the window to be with the passing palm trees.

"We are offering you a chance to learn Ancient Egyptian history, and yet, you turn your American nose up in the air at it." I stared back at him from the opposite end of the limo. "You have no idea what you're leaving behind."

"You're not being honest with me." His blue gaze swirled with accusation.

"You refuse to believe anything we say!"

"Because you're lying."

"I don't lie." My grip tightened on my phone as I fought for control.

"Hey, didn't you tell the driver to tour the ocean?" Lorelei leaned over and knocked on the partition between the driver and us. "Excuse me? Sir?"

While I realized we'd left the freeway some time ago, I didn't understand that we shouldn't be cruising through a residential area. From Joshua's, "What in the hell?" I assumed something was wrong.

My unsettled instincts flared, and I wished I had my Glock. Since I was on probation, I couldn't have it. I was not, however, without options. Not only did I have my phone, but with a twist of my shoulder, a slim switchblade slid down my arm and into my left palm, where I hid it from view. I watched Lorelei do the same.

She knocked on the partition again, all traces of the privileged, sophisticated lady gone. "Lower this window!"

"He's picking up speed," I said, wondering who found out about Joshua arriving in Miami so fast. Bastet's fear of betrayal within the council had to be true. Calm descended over me as I went over each step of the procedure manual.

*Keep the client safe at all costs.*

𓂀𓏤𓈖𓅱𓏏𓆓𓏏𓏏 𓈖 𓏏𓆓 𓂋𓈖𓃭𓂋𓅱𓏏𓈖𓏏

Joshua pounded on the glass then tried to open the locked doors. "Let us out! Pull over."

I dialed Control with my right hand. "I should have asked to see some identification."

Lorelei gave a clipped nod. "I didn't think of it. He said he was from control."

Shame burned in my belly. "No. I asked him if control sent him. I gave him the information."

Joshua's cute smile flattened in a line of fury. "What's happening?"

I'm not one to gloat when I'm right, but the fact that we were being kidnapped by a limousine driver pretty much assured Joshua that his life was in danger. He needed me.

I didn't have to rub it in as I saved his life.

Dahlia answered in her usual friendly tone. "Didn't you leave the country?"

Not taking the bait, I stayed cool. "Yes. Could you please check to see if Bastet arranged the limo pick-up at the airport? We're being kidnapped by the driver."

"What? Goddess have mercy, child. Hold on. I'll call from here. Can't believe the demis let you out of their sight."

Lorelei tore the back of the limo apart, looking for anything to use as a weapon, in addition to her blade. I picked up the crystal flute and smashed it against the edge of the ice bucket. The stem made a great handle, and the jagged pieces would make a bloody mess when poked into someone's bare flesh.

"Did they teach you that in summer camp?" Joshua took the broken glass as if it had germs.

I lifted my hand to mime how to use it. "Plunge it, like a dagger, anyplace that isn't covered, all right?"

I heard Joshua grind his teeth in frustration, but then he accepted the makeshift weapon. "Try not to cut yourself," I warned with a teasing smile.

"You're enjoying this?" He looked incredulous, but I had no doubt that between Lorelei and I, we could keep Joshua safe from the giant Frenchman. And what was wrong with a little adrenalin?

Dahlia got back on the line. "The driver service said they sent their best driver – Cadee McGarrity. Female. You know the demi-goddesses prefer to hire women."

I sighed. "This is a guy. French. So now what?"

"Get off the phone and call the police. Twit! And Bastet said to protect the client - with your life, if necessary." Dahlia's voice softened, just a bit. "You can do it."

The click in my ear signaled the end of the call.

Lorelei arched a dark brow, the ice bucket in one hand, her knife in the other. "Well?"

"This isn't the driver the service sent. Surprise, surprise."

"I've been kidnapped before." Joshua rubbed the bridge of his nose.

"What?" My attention spiked. "When?"

"Did you tell Bastet and Sekhmet that?" Lorelei balanced on her knees, staring out the rear window.

"Uh, no. I was a little angry at the time they were grilling me about my background."

"What happened?" I wanted to throttle him myself. "How old were you? Were you hurt?" *Were they snake shifters? Uraeli?*

He shrugged. "It was my mom's second husband. He was using me as a hostage to get her back. He sent a ransom note; she sent him my Xbox so that 'we boys' could bond while she went to the Caribbean with future husband number three."

"No." My anger melted in sympathy despite my best intentions not to care.

"Yeah. No biggie. He still sends me a birthday card every year."

And here I'd thought I had the world's worst mother.

"Some women just don't have that maternal gene," Lorelei said quietly.

"Are we back to genetics again?" Joshua lowered his broken champagne flute.

I had 9-1-1 on my phone, and my thumb on the dial button.

"What are you waiting for? I don't think he plans on pulling over." Joshua reached for his own phone, but I shook my head as ideas and plans tumbled like numbered balls in a bingo machine.

"Wait. Just...see what happens. What if this is a message? From the Uraeli?" My instincts cautioned against being hasty.

Lorelei frowned. "I hate to alert the police to our presence in Miami if we don't have to. Police and private security don't usually mix."

I lifted one shoulder, playing both sides of the argument. "We haven't done anything wrong, and we aren't carrying anything we shouldn't be. It might be better to play it safe."

"Hellloooo? We're talking about my life here? I vote for calling the police right now." Joshua shook his phone for emphasis.

The limo came to an abrupt stop, and I fell forward so fast I almost sliced off the tip of my nose on Joshua's glass. He dropped it and checked my face to see if I was all right.

His eyes, up close, had green flecks in them. His arms were strong and he smelled like...early morning sunshine.

I pushed off him, not liking the way butterflies fluttered inside my belly. "You should be more careful..."

"That wasn't my fault," he said defensively.

The side door opened and I jumped out, taking the driver unaware. Before he knew it, I had him pinned to the ground, my knee on his throat, the blade of my knife pointed beneath his eye.

"Get off," he said, unable to move me.

I deliberately dilated my eyes at him, and he stopped struggling, too scared to move.

But not too scared to speak. "What in the hell was that? Freak!"

I dug my knee into his neck a little harder.

"My turn to ask questions. Who are you? And what's up with the little detour? And the bad French accent. I can't believe I didn't catch that." I shook my head in self-disgust.

"Don't kill him," Lorelei advised.

"Kill him?" Joshua's voice cracked.

"What's your plan? Murder? Ransom?" I lifted the driver's lips, looking for fangs. Nothing.

"I *did* my job."

"We're still alive," Lorelei pointed out.

"My job," he coughed so I lifted my knee a fraction of an inch. "Was to bring you here. I did. Now we wait."

"For what?" I pressed the tip of my knife to his flesh. I heard Lorelei walk in a square, searching for danger.

"Yeah. For what?" Joshua knelt beside me.

The limo driver barely glanced at Joshua, which was odd, considering Joshua was the target. *Or was he?*

The driver tried to buck me off him again. "You're strong, but you sure don't look dangerous to me," he said. "Freaky eyes, but I bet its contacts."

"*Who* is coming?" Cold sweat broke out along my shoulders,

and I leaned forward until the driver's eyes bugged open due to lack of oxygen. I released the pressure, and he gasped for air.

"She said to tell you – an old friend."

*An old friend?*

Suddenly, Lorelei shouted, "Goddess' spear, grab his keys, Shani! Joshua, get in the limo. Shani, should we bring him? Never mind, just leave him there! Two cars are speeding this way. Without guns, we can't hold that many off."

*What to do?* We had to keep Joshua safe, which meant leaving the area immediately. "Tell that old friend that next time, I want a formal invitation before meeting for lunch." I pinched the nerve at the base of the driver's neck, knocking him out cold. Quickly patting him down, I took his wallet, with a thousand dollars cash, and keys.

"Cool," Joshua said from my side. "Can you show me how to do that?"

"Get in the car!" Springing up, I pushed Joshua in front of me, shoving what the driver had said to the back of my mind for later processing. "I've got to drive."

Crap. I wasn't exactly an expert. Camel riding. Running. I could even do horse back. But a car?

"I'll do it," Joshua said, sprinting for the driver's side.

"No!" I pulled his shirt to keep him back.

He snatched the keys from my hand so fast I didn't even realize they were gone until he dangled them in front of my face. *How had he done that? What other surprise skills was Joshua hiding?*

"I know which side of the road to drive on," he said with a shrug. "You don't."

Excellent point. "Lead the way." We piled onto the front bench seat, not made for three, but we made it work.

"We're at a dead end." Lorelei, squished against the passenger door, pressed a few buttons on the dash. "I figured out the GPS. Our driver didn't know how to turn it on and wrote Joshua's address on the back of a business card." She held up the paper as if it offended her.

I took the card and shoved it in my jacket pocket. Power surged beneath my skin. "What should we do?"

"Stay calm, you're doing great. Are you ready to call the police? This is your assignment." Lorelei's steady gaze lent encouragement.

"No," I said, glad for her show of trust. "I'll explain later. How are we going to get out of here? Mr. Johnson, does this area look at all familiar to you?"

"After what we've just gone through, dude, you've got to call me Josh." He grinned as he gunned the engine.

"Dude?"

"American term of affection. Friendship, not dating, so don't get any ideas."

Lorelei snickered and looked out the window.

He turned the limo around. "We're gonna drive right through them." He gunned the engine.

"You are insane." I noted with wonder, realizing he wasn't scared, but having fun.

"Hurry!" Lorelei pounded the dashboard.

"We're supposed to keep him safe-"

"You did that already." Josh stepped on the gas. "Now it's my turn!"

# CHAPTER SEVEN

### HOME SWEET HOME

"It doesn't say anywhere in the handbook that the client is supposed to help in his own rescue." I leaned forward, watching in awe as Josh bravely faced the two dark sedans heading toward us.

"Seat belt?" Lorelei buckled up.

I leaned over Josh, grabbing the metal clasp and tightening it until it clicked over his lap.

"Oof," he said. "How'm I s'posed to drive if I can't breathe?"

"Sorry. Safety first." There wasn't a seat belt for me but it didn't matter. If anything happened to Josh, and it was amazing how easy his familiar name came to mind, I didn't want to face the demi-goddesses alive.

Lorelei noticed and giggled. "Such courage, Shani."

"Did you..." I tapped my head. Would this second life finally make me the same as the other shifters?

"It's written all over your face."

*Great.*

Josh pressed down on the gas and it felt like we were air born. The two cars came closer, we raced toward certain death, and I prayed that Josh would eventually come to his senses and slam on the brakes. Or that the two cars would get out of the way, possibly creating a space for us in the middle. Rational Thought never showed, and the Goddess wasn't answering prayers.

Instead, Josh showed off his incredible dexterity by swerving at the last possible second – belly in my throat, I gripped the dashboard so hard the plastic cracked – taking us between two parked cars and an abandoned bicycle to get to the sidewalk.

Our tires took out a strip of lawn, and the front bumper killed a dolphin mailbox before Josh got us past the sedans and onto the road again.

"Amazing," Lorelei breathed out.

I still couldn't talk past my stomach in my esophagus.

"NASCAR," he said in an exaggerated southern accent. Left, right, down alleys and through parking lots - he took a series of turns, and the next thing I knew, we were flying on the interstate, our 'friends' in the black cars nowhere in sight. "We lost 'em," Josh started laughing first, but within seconds, Lorelei and I joined in. Nervous laughter, that we'd survived, together.

Then his hands started shaking, and he had to pull over before he puked. Josh's face turned as white as the salt in the desert. "Breathe," I instructed. "In through your nose, that's right, and out – a good long exhale."

I gave his back a solid pat as he hunched over the steering wheel.

Lorelei climbed back through the partition and grabbed a chilled water bottle, uncapped it, and handed it forward. "Drink this. You're just crashing off a pretty big adrenalin rush. See?" She held her hand out and shook her fingers a little, "it gets to me too."

*Liar*, I thought. But it was a nice lie, and I liked her for it.

Josh drained the bottle. "Thanks." His cheeks flushed pink. "I can get us home now."

"Are you sure? Once you point me toward your house, I can drive, or Lorelei." I just wanted to get to a private space and search the wallet I'd taken. I had to fill Lorelei and the demi goddesses in on what the driver said. Joshua hadn't been the target. Not this time. *It had been me.*

I'd checked my texts and there were five new ones from Bastet. My inside jacket pocket vibrated. Six. Six texts. Probably all from Bastet.

Josh's grip on the wheel relaxed as he eased into traffic. "Are we going to talk about what happened? I mean, you're not going to keep me out of the loop, are you? I want in. Whatever this is about, I want to know."

I swallowed, preparing to give him a watered down version of the truth, but Lorelei beat me to the punch. She widened her eyes and lightly swatted his shoulder. "Of course, we'll talk. And you *must* be in the loop. We are a team!"

Josh smiled – wobbly, but a smile – and switched lanes. I wanted to mind link, so I could ask Lorelei why she'd just lied to our client. But surely, he'd need to know what was going on

– right?

One of the rules in Chapter Three, Client Safety, was all about keeping the client on a need-to-know basis. Lorelei whispered for me to relax as she touched my arm. I coated my *lips* with gloss, which I chewed off in seconds. Relax. *Not feeling it.*

"Who are the Uraeli?" Josh asked, now driving the limo as if born with a steering wheel in his hands. Fast reflexes. Very fast.

"Bad guys." I coughed, pretending to have a scratchy throat. I turned around. "Lorelei, can I have one of those waters?" My phone vibrated like crazy, and I knew Dahlia had to be worried. I mouthed the problem to my mentor, but Lorelei gave me a slight shake of her head. *Wait.* I accepted the water and faced forward, sliding over to the passenger side, since Lorelei stayed in the back. "Joshua, Josh," I had to stop thinking of him as anything but that. "Please tell me we are going straight to your house?"

"Yeah. We'll save the ocean tour for another day." Josh's body heat, heightened due to adrenalin and danger, warmed me. Made me aware of his hands as he gripped the steering wheel. I wondered what it would feel like to hold his hand.

I unrolled the window, but the fresh air was like steam from a sauna and I rolled it right back up. "I desperately want a change of clothes. Do you ever get used to the humidity?"

"Yes. What kind of bad guys? Terrorists?"

How to answer? Unlike my mentor, I didn't have the gift of fabrication. The silence lingered too long.

"If you don't want to answer me about the Uraeli right now, just say so." Josh's jaw tightened, and his foot pressed a little harder on the gas pedal.

"Fine. I don't want to talk about it right now."

"But-"

"No." I held up one hand to stop his argument. "You said I could just tell you that I didn't want to talk about it now and I did. You have to accept that." Unable to take the buzz of my cell anymore, I one-handedly texted a message to Control that I'd be in touch soon. "And don't speed. The last thing we need is a ticket. I've seen COPS." The demis would flip completely if we ended up arrested on television.

Josh glared at me. I kept my expression bland. "You're too bossy," he accused. "Nobody is going to believe you're only seventeen."

"You need to make up your mind," I countered, stung. "I'm either too young or too old."

He kept his eyes on the road ahead as he muttered, "I didn't say too old. I said too bossy."

*Why did he irritate me?* Normally calm and unflappable, Josh grated on my nerves. Some members of the pride consider me cold, but there are benefits to being all about the job. Focus and concentration are my trademarks on the training field. Nobody ever referred to me as 'bossy'.

I stared out the window, praying for a miracle. It's bad enough that I'm young and can't mind link. Two strikes against me – the snake bite number three. If anything happened to Josh on my watch, I'd be out. For eternity.

Not even the demi-goddesses could raise me to a Level Two Bazmeht against the Council of Nine. Specifically, my mother. I shivered, and Josh turned down the air conditioning.

"Thank you."

"Sure."

Who hated me enough to attack the instant we landed in Miami? Someone connected to the Bazmeht. My mother had no love for me, but I'd never sensed hatred.

Natalie detested me because she adored my mother. Keket didn't like me, neither did Tefnut. Dendera was afraid of me. But would they hire someone to attack, no, kill me?

My mind, never quiet at the best of times, churned with possible suspects until the cold, gray eyes of the ninja warrior crystallized, down to the burning reptilian orbs.

It had to be her. She'd spat her hate at me before she bit me. My gut confirmed the intuition.

"Cat got your tongue?"

Startled, I immediately pushed my tongue against the back of my teeth. It was fine; not pointed or rough like during the transformation. "What?"

Josh's grin flashed across his face before disappearing. "You know, slang, for 'why are you so quiet?'"

Blushing furiously, I tapped my fingers against my knee and tried to ignore Lorelei's giggles from the back seat. "I was thinking."

"That we should have stayed to meet your 'friend'?"

I glanced at him, then looked away. "You heard that?"

"I'm not deaf. And even though you had your knee against that limo guy's throat, he didn't seem to be scared that you'd actually kill him, and you're pretty tough. I'd want you on my side if I was ever in a bar fight, if you know what I mean."

Josh paused, chewing his bottom lip. It was strange to find that we had that in common.

"Thank you," I said, trying to follow his train of thought.

"So, I'm guessing this friend really isn't your friend or we would have stayed to chat. This means…I am not the target. You are." He smacked the wheel, his grin returning to stay as he briefly met my eyes. "Am I brilliant or what?"

My stomach clenched. "I wasn't thinking brilliant." Although I had been.

He laughed. "You've probably been sent here 'cause you are like, in training or something. And you're saying that I need protection so I'll go along with it." His laughs got louder the more he cracked himself up.

Lorelei tapped the back of my seat. I had to fix this before it went any further. "The club called, and they want their comedian back."

"Ha! Admit it, I'm right."

I lowered my voice, hoping to convey the importance of what I was saying through tone as well as words. "Just because you got part of the equation right doesn't mean you know the answer. That 'limo guy' would have hurt you if he knew who you were. The good thing is that if my 'friend' doesn't know about you yet, then we have time to create a safe space. I take my duty very seriously, Joshua."

"Josh."

"Josh." I exhaled, deliberately relaxing my shoulders. "If you don't understand that what just happened is a warning of things to come, then you aren't helping yourself. You are making my job harder."

"I handled that pretty damn good." He tightened his hold on the wheel, his jaw clenched. "I got us out of there."

Diplomacy. "You did. I couldn't drive like that."

"I've known professional race car drivers who couldn't drive like that," Lorelei observed, scooting closer to the partition so she could talk to us. "I was also very impressed with your quick thinking."

He smiled and some of the tension dissipated.

𓂋𓏏𓊖𓈖𓏏𓏭 𓊪𓏏 𓍿𓏏 𓂋𓏏𓄿𓏏𓏭𓊖𓏏𓏭

All right. It seemed like we had to play to Josh's ego, which made him more pliable. I'd have to ask Bastet if this worked with all men. She's the most experienced female I know.

Studying Josh for emotional clues forced me to notice how the sunshine streaming through the window lit his hair like golden fire. I reminded myself sternly that I am not just a *girl*, but a Level One Bazmeht Bodyguard. The last thing I should notice is my client's hair.

I scooted as far away from him as the space would allow. "So," I coughed into my hand. *Duty. Duty.* "Are you ready to talk to Bastet and Sekhmet now? Hear what they have to say about your ancestry?"

Slowing so that he could take the exit from the freeway, Josh hesitated. "Uh – no, not really."

"Why? I don't understand. This is your chance to dive into your history." This opportunity should be an amateur Egyptologist's dream. Why was he fighting it so hard?

"I get that there's something going on here, but I'm not sure it's about me. I don't buy into all of the chromosome crap." He gave a dismissive shrug. "But that's science. If it's true, there will be some sort of tangible proof. No, what I'm not going for is the legacy stuff."

"Now I'm confused..." Given his attitude, chances were high that he'd agree to testing.

"That myth thing your tall, dark, and crazy boss was talkin' about."

I swallowed so hard it hurt my throat. "They told you about the Myth of M–"

"Magda, Martha – something like that. But I've studied Egypt. I know Egypt." His chin thrust forward in pure stubbornness. "What she was saying isn't real, and I quit believing in fairy tales when I was about six."

# CHAPTER EIGHT

## AMERICAN DREAM

At last, Josh pulled into a paved driveway with a huge iron gate in front of the most beautiful house I'd ever seen. The white stucco on the rounded towers bracketing a huge front porch gleamed diamond bright in the Miami sun. "You live here? It's a *castle*."

From the back seat, Lorelei laughed and Josh joined in. "You need to get out more," he said. "Besides, my uncle's mansion is bigger. You've seen it, haven't you?"

I had to remember that our medics had wiped his memory of the first night we'd met. "Yes. It's true," I agreed, trying to hold my amazement in check, "but he's the *ambassador* of Egypt."

I'd heard of the American Dream. I watched VH1. "Do you have lots of friends over? Parties?" The awe ebbed, leaving me with the glaring reality – guarding Josh by myself would be a logistical nightmare. Kegs, topless drunk girls, the police. I glanced over my shoulder at Lorelei. She gave a half shake of her head, and I immediately calmed. My mentor and best friend has that effect on lots of people. Another of her gifts.

Josh's skin flushed slightly beneath his tan. "We're pretty rich. My mom's been married a ton of times, remember?"

I frowned. "You're saying she married for mone–"

Lorelei handed me the ice bucket, cutting me off in mid sentence. "Hold this. Did the demi- uh, Bastet or Sekhmet, get back to you on the situation?"

Confused, I accepted the ice bucket and put it on the bench seat. "I texted Control, told Dahlia that I'd call in once we got settled. I haven't checked any of the messages yet. I thought I'd wait until we settled inside."

"Good." Lorelei sat back. "Good plan."

Josh unrolled the driver's side window and punched in a code, opening the huge gates. I noticed the security cameras follow our drive to the door. *Excellent.* I also noticed the path sparkled in the sunlight like pearls. "Why does the road glitter?"

"Crushed shell."

"It twinkles."

"You've seriously never left Egypt?"

Bright red hibiscus plants added color to the lush, tropical landscape. Josh slowed, then stopped, and I opened the door, stepping into the dampest heat I'd ever breathed. It was like trying to draw air through a feather pillow. I put my hand to my throat. "This is going to take some getting used to," I said to Lorelei.

Her forehead immediately dotted with perspiration. "I agree. At least we'll suffocate in beauty."

"You'll acclimatize in no time, I swear." Josh stood next to us.

"I hope so." My energy seeped from my pores, making me wish for food and a nap. "Is anybody home?" In a house this big, it seemed as if there should be a hundred people around. Why hadn't anybody come to greet him? He'd been gone for two months.

He lifted a shoulder then popped the trunk on the back of the limo. "Don't know who might be here – do you mind getting your own suitcase? We have limited staff – our housekeeper - in the summer. Especially when my mom's traveling."

Traveling? Was that a euphemism for honeymooning? "I'm not used to having *any* staff." I took my suitcase and tried to take Josh's too. "Let me get that," I said, tugging at the handle.

He yanked back. "I can do this myself, thanks."

Lorelei snickered, reaching around us to take her own carry on from the trunk. "You two are like children. Wait, you *are* children."

"I was just trying to be nice." Offended, I rolled my bag to the bottom step.

"Don't bother," Josh grumped, passing me by.

"You might want to try it," I said to his back.

He ignored me and rang the doorbell.

"You don't have a key?" I climbed the last two stairs. Not the most popular girl in the pyramid, I still had a key.

"Somebody has to be here, might just be Maria. And the house is all electronic, so we don't use keys. Mom changes the code all the time, and I never remember what it is – this is easier, trust me."

No key, no mom to greet him. It would be very easy to empathize with Josh, but I couldn't emotionally afford to be attached. For the client's own protection, a guard has to maintain a professional distance. Rule number twelve.

He rang the doorbell again and we waited in the wet heat.

Perking my ears, I finally heard shuffling footsteps behind the mammoth steel door. I prepared to wait, but Josh, looking slightly embarrassed, pulled out his cell phone. "I guess I'll have to call Mom."

I put up my hand. "Wait. Someone's coming."

Josh arched his brow. "I don't think so. Maria must be out shopping."

I picked up the soft murmur of a Spanish dialect. *Maria*. The old tones placed the woman at around seventy years old – no wonder it was taking so long. "Patience."

"You, telling someone to be patient?" Lorelei sat on her suitcase and fanned her face with her hand.

I didn't answer. It was too hot to be sarcastic. Finally, the latch clicked. Josh's shoulders relaxed, and he stuffed his cell phone into his front pocket.

Normally I don't catch emotional clues, but his nervousness spoke to me – what kind of privilege led to such insecurity? The pretty house took on a sinister quality.

I casually palmed my blade, trying to get into the correct position to guard Josh from whoever was on the other side of the door. Just in case. It's my job.

The old woman opened the door as slowly as if she was moving a rock from a tomb, but her excitement at seeing Josh made me forget the uncomfortable heat as I stepped back. No threat.

"Joshua!" The old woman's face was nothing but wrinkles, teeth, and lively, black eyes. "*Me hijo*, you're home, home at last." Her arms opened, and Josh gave her an enthusiastic, but tender, hug.

I had to look away.

Lorelei met my wandering gaze with an understanding smile. I don't do touching moments. I hadn't even said goodbye to my cat, Muu. Goodbyes are easier if you just walk away. I'd learned from the best.

Josh pulled back from the tiny woman but kept one arm around her shoulders. "Maria, I've brought some friends home."

Her black eyes sharpened as they studied both Lorelei and me. I saw what she saw as she took in Lorelei's navy blue, tailored suit and flat shoes before turning to my messed up hair, black pinstriped pants, and open jacket. Our single rolling suitcases.

"A special friend, *hijo?*" Her smile questioned without directly asking.

Josh turned bright red. "No, no," he paused, and I watched as he struggled to piece together the story we'd agreed on. "My cousin, from Egypt! Shani Nebit. She's family, Maria."

"Family?" She tossed her hands in the air, launched herself at me for a hug, and gave me loud, smacking kisses on both cheeks before I stumbled back, longing to hide in the car.

She was very...enthusiastic. Now I wore a bright, heated blush.

Lorelei quickly held out her hand. "Hello, Maria," she said crisply. "I'm Lorelei, also from Egypt, but I'm Bazmeht. I've been hired to guard the collection Zelda is loaning to the Florida museums this month. I believe someone from our company called ahead?"

Maria nodded, slipping back into the formalities of acting as hostess. "Welcome, come in, you must be tired from your journey." She tucked her arm through the crook in Josh's elbow. "We can put Miss Shani in the Yellow Room and Miss Lorelei in the Scottish Room below the dead kitties."

Lorelei and I exchanged a horrified glance, and Josh caught my hesitation to step inside.

"What?" His blue eyes sparkled.

"Dead...*kitties?*" My heart thumped in my chest. Had Zelda gone totally insane since her flight from Egypt?

"The mummy exhibit," Josh explained with a chuckle. "Maria hates it. She's always happy when Mom sends it out on tour because she can cleanse the room. Brings in candles and hocus pocus, you know?"

Lovely. We shared a home with a Spanish *bruja*. Would she sense that Lorelei and I were more than Egyptian natives? We'd have to be careful. The soft nudge in the small of my back let me know that Lorelei heard the same thing.

The foyer was cool, temperature controlled, and heaven

compared to the hot, damp mess outside. The walls were painted ivory with soft yellow accents. Ivory, gold, and crystal kept the room light. It dripped wealth.

I studied Josh. His shaggy, blond hair, scruffy cheeks, and baggy jeans. His Abercrombie t-shirt, brown leather belt, and converse tennis shoes. He didn't fit in this showplace any more than Lorelei or I did. Sad, because this was his home.

Maria led us through the room and down a meandering hallway to the rear of the house. We moved at the pace of a large, lumbering turtle, so there was plenty of time to get the layout and peek inside the rooms. I sent thanks to Mother Mafdet for my inner GPS.

As if she'd read my mind, Lorelei whispered, "I hope you've got this. That last turn did me in."

I sent her a reassuring nod. It was nice to be good at *something*.

Maria stopped at the base of a wide staircase. "Joshua, show these *senoritas* their rooms, *si*, and I will bring a tray to the sitting room upstairs." As if she couldn't help herself, she reached over and embraced Josh tightly. "It is good you are home, your *mamacita* needs you."

Josh's happiness faded. "What happened? She just got married!"

Maria clucked her teeth. "She will tell you herself, *hijo*, when she comes back from her appointments." The tiny old woman patted her hair, making it clear that Zelda was at the hairdresser.

"Mom is *here*?" Josh's voice squeaked and I hid a smile.

"*Si!*"

I saw the hurt on his face as he wondered why his own mother hadn't told him she was home, and then, I watched him quickly mask concern. He must love her, even though they didn't get along. Did I have any love left for my mother, despite her latest backstabbing at the council?

*Who cares?* I am a Bazmeht Bodyguard and I don't do soul searching.

He stared at the stairs, chewing his lip, and I couldn't stand the idea that he was hurting. It was for his own good that I deliberately dropped my suitcase to the tiled floor, making a huge bang to bring him back to the present. "Oops."

Shaking his head, he mumbled, "Sorry, uh, follow me." He led the way up the stairs, I followed him, and Lorelei stayed right on my heels. Josh took us down an incredibly long, carpeted hall, then turned left, and we were in a large room all done in plaid wallpaper and bagpipes. Lorelei laughed. "The Scottish Room? It's perfect."

"Glad you like it," Josh said. "The exhibit is up above you, and the only way to get to it is through here." He pointed to a door that I'd thought was a closet. So much for my powers of observation.

Lorelei went right to the correct closet door and set her suitcase in front of it. "I will take good care of the collection. It will be yours one day, won't it?"

Tilting my head to the side, I realized that Josh was Zelda's only child. Normally, the collection was handed down, female to female, within the family, but the Marcos' didn't have a young woman in this generation to give it to.

He shrugged. "I s'pose. I like the memorabilia in the library better. Honestly? The cat mummies creep me out."

I covered my laugh with a cough. I'd been tending cat mummies since the tender age of three, and my home was dedicated to the spirits of all the dead felines who'd been sacrificed to the goddess Bastet at Bubastis. My most sacred chore as a handmaiden to the goddesses was to change the oil lamps outside the door to the crypt of Mother Mafdet. How could he know that each Bazmeht guard had their own personal cat coffin that held their ceremonial canopic jars or that—

"Earth to Shani." Josh snapped his fingers beneath my nose. "Where'd you go?"

Shaking my head, I answered without thinking. "Egypt. I miss my home."

"You haven't even been gone a day." He angled his chin, peering close at my face. "Oh, no. You didn't want to come here." The statement was fact and I couldn't deny it. "That makes sense."

Lorelei literally leaped the four feet across the room to stand between us before I said something I might regret. "Shani is young."

I sucked in a breath. "Lorelei." Did she have to pick the same argument Josh had on the plane? Young didn't mean incompetent. I'd shown that I could protect my client, with my life, if necessary.

"Sorry. Not young, well – yes. Young. But professional. *Very professional.* She's proved that she can keep you safe from whatever dangers might befall you."

"Crazy limo drivers?" Josh crossed his arms.

"And," Lorelei continued in a rush, "it is expected that she will miss home, because this is the first time she's been away from it."

It was time to speak for myself. While I couldn't fabricate lies as quickly as my mentor – something I vowed to work on – I could be brutally honest. "I will do my duty by the Marcos family, and I am honored to be here in your home. I will protect you, with my own life if the situation calls for it," I swallowed the dark memory *that* brought to mind. Deciding he needed some buttering up, I added, "I'm looking forward to learning from you."

His shoulders lowered an inch. "What can I teach you?"

"How to drive, for one thing..." I grinned and so did he. "How to fit in and be American."

Josh paused, as if weighing his options on Ma'at's scale of truth and justice, until he accepted the idea. "I can do that, *cousin.* But only if you promise to teach me how you do that," he pinched his fingers together, "thing."

I held out my hand to shake. "We have a bargain."

Josh's gaze narrowed as he eyed me from the top of my messed up bun to the tips of my black leather boots. He scratched his chin as he looked at my compact suitcase. "You need to go shopping."

*Shopping?* I missed Egypt, and his solution was to take me shopping? "You sound like Lorelei."

Josh and Lorelei gave each other a nod of understanding.

"I might need a few things, some shorts." A pair in black and one in brown should do me for forty days.

"What about a swimming suit?"

I crossed my arms, thinking of my one-piece.

Lorelei laughed. "She needs everything."

"I'm here to work." I turned my back on Lorelei so I didn't have to see her smirk.

"I like to go to the beach."

Trying not to imagine Josh at the beach looking like a

Greek God was difficult. I shook my head.

"You'll need a few bikinis."

My ears turned hot. "I have a work uniform."

"You have to fit in. My *cousin* wouldn't wear a black suit and switchblade to the beach."

Hmm. There it was again. Blending and fitting in. "Fine. I'll get a bikini." Hoping my pale belly didn't burn within five minutes. "I'll need sunblock."

"We're making progress." Josh winked. "Did you bring a gold credit card? Save your receipts, I'm sure those insane bosses of yours will reimburse you."

"Money's not an issue." The Bazmeht paid well. I just hated to spend money on clothes that I might not ever wear again. Oh well. A guard has to be flexible, and if this job required a different dress code, then so be it.

I'd worry about where to put my switchblade later.

# CHAPTER NINE

## SETTLING IN

We made arrangements with Lorelei to meet in the upstairs sitting room, and then Josh quickly showed me to the Yellow Room. I paused at the threshold, taking it in. "It's like sunshine." Pale yellow walls a shade darker than the marble tiles, and a plush, ankle-deep, floral area rug that tempted me to take off my boots. The full sized bed was draped in yards of yellow flounces.

"*Lateef*," I whispered. "This is very nice." And so not the style of a kick-ass Bazmeht Bodyguard. Yet a part of me, the part that owns an orange iPhone and a blue disco dress, loved it on sight.

My spirits lifted immediately as I couldn't help but compare it to the hammock and plain beige walls of home. I was beginning to see the benefits of a little decoration. I'd been a tiny bit envious that Lorelei had gotten to stay in the awesome plaid tower but not anymore. "Any hidden chambers attached to this one?"

"Nope. There's a small bathroom though. T.V.'s here." He picked up a compact remote from the small bedside table and hit the red power button. The peaceful landscape painting on the wall opposite the bed turned into a flat screen television right before my eyes.

"Goddess have mercy," I whispered.

"What?"

"Mercy!" I repeated, patting my heart with my hand. "I've never seen anything like that before."

He laughed. "One of my mom's husbands was a techno junkie."

Josh tended to downplay the money at his disposal. It was another thing I liked about him. I bit my lip.

Instead of thinking of things I liked, I should be planning security measures. There was already a nice system in place, but I would search for weaknesses. Bastet and Sekhmet wanted him under guard and that was enough for me.

"Where do you sleep?" I peered out the window, noting the courtyard two stories below. Spotlights and floodlights blended with the landscaping. Probably set off with motion detectors. No shrubbery by the base of the house, which meant no place for a bad guy – or girl – to hide. Nevertheless, I knew that even with the best security money could buy, if someone was determined to break in, they would find a way.

I must never, ever forget that I was the last thing standing between danger and Josh.

"Whoa!" He grinned, a dimple appearing in his left cheek. "I told you, I have a girlfriend."

Making no effort to hide my eye roll, I set my suitcase on the lemon yellow bench on the foot of the bed and straightened my jacket. "I have a job to do," I emphasized the word job, just so he'd remember, "and you're it."

He shrugged liked he didn't care that I was all about work. "So we're not going to be pals, huh? Fine. I'm down two doors, to the right. We can have a super-secret knock – three times fast, two slow, and I'll know it's you."

Why did my first assignment have to be a guy who thought he was funny? I folded my hands in front of me and arched my brow, as I'd seen Lorelei do when she wanted to be intimidating. "Joke if you must. I still want to see what kind of system you've got."

"Locked gates, coded keys, and I live in a patrolled area. We're cool, Shani."

Trying not to frown, I reached deep for patience. It was hard, because he was rather amusing in spite of himself. "Your life is sacred."

"So now I'm the new Messiah? Can't wait to tell Mom. She's been waiting for me to turn into some kind of prodigy. So far, I've been something of a disappointment."

I turned my back on him because that joke had the bite of truth in it. I paced the marble tile floor of the room, concentrating on quieting the click of my boot heels. "I meant that your life, the *Blood of Ra*, is special to the Bazmeht. Through the centuries, our family has guarded your family and ensured that you...survived."

"That is, word for word, the crap Bastet told me."

Well, that would explain why I said it. "All right then. Did she tell you that we, the Bazmeht, wrongly assumed that you, because of your American blood, would not carry this genetic lotto? Yet you do."

"How does being a mutt put me in danger?"

"A mutt?" *Dog, dog without a pedigree.* "You are not a mutt! Just half American. There are Ura -, people, who want your special genetics extinguished."

"These mystery people want me killed over a chromosome?" Josh smirked.

"You'll have to ask the demi-, er, Bastet and Sekhmet, about that." *The client is on a need to know basis,* I reminded myself, trying to exude confidence in the face of his disbelief. *How do you teach someone to have faith?*

"I did ask. Repeatedly. And yet, somehow, I ended up with no clear answers, and you and Lorelei in my house. They *brainwashed* me." His lower lip stuck out a little as he considered that thought.

Since he was probably right, I diverted him with, "We all have a destiny."

It was his turn to roll his eyes. He grabbed the handle of his suitcase and started for the door. "Yeah. Fate. Whatever." After checking his watch, he said, "If you're quick, you have time to shower and unpack before we meet in the sitting room. Off to the right. Maria's bringing sandwiches and stuff. I'm starving."

"You don't want to talk about your destiny?"

Practically running now, he answered over his shoulder, "I don't believe in it."

I waved, smiling wide as he disappeared into his room. "And that's why you race away. Me thinks, Joshua, that you have secrets I need to uncover."

Closing the door and locking it, I quickly dialed Bastet's personal cell number, bypassing Control.

"Shani," she sang as she answered on the first ring. "What took you so long? Are you all right? Is Joshua unharmed?"

"Hello to you too, Bastet," I said, trying for professional when I wanted to launch into a litany of my miseries. "We're all fine, and we are at Josh's, Joshua's, house. His mother is home instead of in the Caribbean on her honeymoon like we thought. He has a wonderful housekeeper, Maria, but we'll have to beware, because I think she may be a witch. And this house...it could be a castle, but instead of a moat, they have a wrought iron gate and everything is electronic. Josh doesn't even have his own key. How's Muu?"

Bastet laughed so hard I heard the phone shake.

"Darling, Shani, it's been a long time since I've heard you so excited about anything other than Bazmeht. It makes me happy, my love. But don't turn too American – Egypt is your home."

Embarrassed, I took a deep breath. "As if I could forget that."

"I'm teasing. Your fat cat is in ecstasy with Dendera brushing her all day long instead of ironing my pleats. Now tell me about the limo ride. What happened? The service called back. The girl, Cadee, was stuffed into a locker. Other than scared and furious, she is fine, and she'll report to work tomorrow. How did you get away?"

I considered what I should tell her, but this was Bastet, my goddess. Nothing but the truth would do. "The false limo driver said that I was the target of the attack."

"Eh?"

"I know. We didn't stick around to find out who, exactly. I knocked the limo driver down, and Josh, who happens to be a great driver – he learned from watching NASCAR - anyway, he got us out of there and drove us home. The service will have to pick up the town car here."

"Of course. The driver's dead?"

"Injured. We put the fear of the Bazmeht into him. He'll have a bruise on his neck for days."

"What did the driver say exactly?" The warmth leaked from Bastet's voice, and she sounded like a woman headed for vengeance. Bastet, goddess of home and hearth, was fierce in the defense of them.

"That the woman who hired him said to tell me she was an old friend. I've thought about this, and he had to be talking about the ninja warrior who bit me." My stomach rolled just thinking about it. "The one who escaped from Bazmeht headquarters."

Bastet emitted a low growl, and her fury came through the phone, traveling from cell tower to cell tower across the world. I hurried to fill in the space.

"I have the limo driver's wallet." I opened it and read the name, "Gustav Colier. Florida license. It's probably as fake as his accent. I'll mail this to you first thing tomorrow. There's a thousand dollars, too."

"Drop the money off, anonymously, at the closest women's shelter."

"Of course." I loved that the demi-goddesses thought of others, but even in that, they were so different.

Bastet gave to those who needed protection, and Sekhmet chose the war wounded, those injured while doing their duty.

"Josh wants answers, Bastet. What can I tell him?"

"As little as possible. This *boy* could decide to sell our story to the tabloids, or run away, or worse – back in 1860, one of the bloodline swallowed laudanum rather than face the truth of what he was. We can't let that happen. We are few."

Josh was too vibrant to consider suicide, thank the Goddess. I knew it in my bones. "If he presses, will you talk to him?"

Bastet paused. "You should be able to handle this, Shani. You've been training to do this since you were born. Distract him. Make him fall in love with you."

Love? Josh? As part of my job description, I supposed I – no. I chewed my lip. "That might be awkward. We're cousins, remember?"

"So?" Bastet sniffed. "Making a man fall in love with you just gives you an advantage, it doesn't mean you need to love him back."

"Ooh." I would never understand Bastet's attitude. She loved men, lots of them, and rarely chose a favorite. None of them seemed to mind.

Before she got on me about not dating, I quickly changed topics. "Hey, did you know Josh was kidnapped when he was little?"

"He told you that? But how could he remember? He wasn't even two."

Two? He said he was five...unless– I used the non-committal agreement tactic from the communication chapter in the handbook. I was impressed when it worked. I said, "Hmmm." Bastet kept talking.

"Well, Zelda must have told him the story. She swore an oath to keep her silence. I suppose you can't trust a woman who has more husbands than shoes."

"Bastet?" In over my head, I needed time to think before eating sandwiches and being social. Socializing has never been my strong point, especially when I'd rather be writing notes and making a plan. "I'm supposed to meet them for food and I still have to shower."

"Have you even met Zelda?" On her own tangent, Bastet talked right over the top of me.

"Not yet." My stomach flipped a little at the prospect of meeting such a notorious figure.

"Watch yourself. I've never completely trusted her. If I could blame her for the information leak in the council, I would, but since that's one sin she can't have anything to do with, I won't waste my time. What do you think of Josh? You aren't really cousins, so if a flirtation springs to life, well..." Bastet gave a throaty chuckle.

"Bastet!" My skin heated. "I am his guard, and he is my client."

"How many times have you seen The Bodyguard? A small dalliance-" There was a crackling over the phone, and I thought we had a bad connection until Bastet snapped, "Here, Sekhmet wants to talk to you." Bastet handed the phone off with a few choice sentences about pushy behavior and being rude.

Sekhmet was her gruff self as she barked, "Shani? You keep your claws away from Joshua Sherif Johnson. He is the last male you can have a 'dalliance' with. Do you understand? He is off limits to you, no matter how 'cute' you think he is."

"I don't think-"

"Yes you do. Even I do, and I'm as old as some of these mud bricks. He is not for you, on point of banishment or perhaps even death."

"Sekhmet?" My belly coiled at the threat. Death? "I promise, I won't fall for Josh, under any circumstances. We don't even like each other."

"Good. I should have insisted you go to the jungle with your mother, but this is what I get for compromising. I have to trust you to stay distanced."

"You can!" Tears gathered at the corners of my eyes at the thought that Sekhmet might not put her faith in me. I'd worked so hard to be Bazmeht that Josh could bring me flowers and champagne and I'd smell nothing but desert sand and the Nile. That's how firmly the good of Egypt is rooted in my head.

"Good." Then Sekhmet asked, "Anything...*new*?"

I stared at the smooth skin on my hands. "Nothing. I am the same old me."

She hefted a sigh that echoed in the phone. "Blessed be the

Goddess. Forty days, Shani, forty days, and you can come home and prove to these idiots, these doubters, that you belong within the pride."

My throat ached as I held back the tears when we said our goodbyes. Guards don't cry.

# CHAPTER TEN

## MEETING ZELDA

My shower took five minutes – in, out and dried, but I still wasn't ready by the time Lorelei knocked on my door. I let her in, and she whistled as she looked at the tidy row of personal things I'd placed on the small vanity table, and my suits all hung up, the hangers facing the same direction.

"You could have gone on ahead, you must be hungry. I'll be ready in a minute."

"You make the rest of us look bad, Shani." She peered closely at my skin and sighed. "What I wouldn't give to be seventeen again."

"You are the beautiful one." Since being seventeen was the bane of my existence, I shivered. "I am eighteen in one month and ten days."

"Why are you counting down to the day?" Lorelei took a sniff of my perfume, something subtle and carnation that Bastet had given me last year.

"Because then, I will officially be an adult."

"That doesn't really matter within the Bazmeht. It's true that you are the youngest guard now, but in the past, we've chosen young guards. I was one of them, once upon a century." She uncapped my lip-gloss, then capped it and set it down next to my comb and brush. She picked up the wallet, read the license, and put it back, but not without borrowing a ten.

"I told Bastet that we'd mail the wallet tomorrow." I rolled my shoulders, uncomfortable in just a plain t-shirt and black, skinny suit pants. I'd tucked my phone in the front pocket, the ankh phone charm dangling over the embroidered pocket edge. "Should I wear my jacket?"

"And really look out of place? Goddess help you, Shani, but you need some casual clothes."

I noticed that Lorelei, who I thought to be one of the most gorgeous, with it, women in the world, was dressed to the teeth in a green and pink sheath and hot pink, low-heeled sandals. Hot pink lipstick slicked her mouth. "You don't look anything like a guard."

"That's right." She smiled. "I blend. In Florida, everybody wears Lily Pulitzer."

"Who?"

"The designer behind the green and pink."

"Oh." I shrugged, feeling hopeless. I wouldn't have picked that outfit. No place for a switchblade if it didn't have sleeves.

"Do you want to borrow one of my sundresses?"

"No!" I rubbed my arms. "I want more material, not less."

Lorelei sighed. "Relax in your modesty tonight, Shani, because tomorrow, we are going to wax, spray, and pluck you into a tanned, bikini ready body."

"Fine." I'd already agreed, so there was no point in arguing. It was all for Egypt, anyway. The smell of tuna fish sandwiches with sliced dill pickle caught my attention, and my stomach rumbled hungrily. "No jacket then. I'm starving and Maria's brought the food. She's cute, isn't she?"

"For a raisin," Lorelei scoffed. "That reminds me, when we're around people, be tactful, don't blurt out the first thing that comes to your mind. Like saying 'Zelda married for money', Josh knows that, he doesn't need to hear you say it. And Maria will be watching us, so just be careful, all right?"

"Sure." Manners and tact. Shoot me now. I led the way to the food as if it had a homing device, turning sharply into a large, open room. "Nobody will ever guess that we are different."

"Hello!" A voice, rich and smoky, floated across the room like a velvet caress to my ear, and I stopped in my tracks. It was Cairo, those deep tones, that accent. *"How* are you different?"

"Nice one," Lorelei muttered.

Josh gestured us over to where there was a cozy grouping of brown leather seats, deep enough to curl up and nap in. The colors and textures suited him much better than the overdone gilt downstairs. "Come meet my mother," he drawled. "She's anxious to greet you both."

Lorelei pressed her fingers to the small of my back in warning, and I realized Zelda might not be pleased to have us here. Why that never occurred to me, I really don't know. But who could blame this truly lovely woman, dressed in designer couture from her pedicured toes to her stylish scrap of a hat, for wanting to protect her son from strangers? What had Josh told her?

I strode forward, my hand out to shake hers. She made no move to accept it, taking in my casual clothes, and I regretted not wearing the jacket. When she got a close look at beautiful, exquisitely dressed Lorelei, the chill factor in the room increased.

My palms dampened with perspiration.

Her brown eyes narrowed as she asked, "Now, what were you saying about being different?"

Lorelei smoothly came to my rescue. Socially awkward in the best of times, being skewered by my hostess left me speechless.

"Shani's never left Egypt before, and she worried about intruding on your hospitality. The Ambassador assured her that, as family, it would be fine. I was just explaining that surely someone as gracious as Zelda would make us both feel welcome."

I groaned, knowing Lorelei had just scored a hit, when it might have been better to leave me lying in my own blood.

Zelda waved her hand at Maria, who hovered in the corner. The old maid quickly poured tea into the two empty cups. "Please," Zelda said stiffly. "Sit."

I'd heard that tone before. Not a request, but an order.

Following Lorelei's lead, I accepted a seat next to Josh, and then a cup of tea. Josh drank some kind of bubbly cola that smelled sweet. "It's Coke – want some?" He picked up the frosty glass. "Beats boring tea, hands down."

I shook my head, the idea of drinking a Coke held little appeal. Cats don't have a taste bud for sweet things, some shifters don't have it either. "I've never had one before."

Zelda laughed, a harsh unkind sound directed at me. "Of course not. Innocent *guardian* sent to spy in the name of Bazmeht." She laughed some more, and I felt Josh tense next to me as he jerked his head toward Maria.

Josh must have told his mom that Lorelei and I were *both* Bazmeht Bodyguards. She'd know I wasn't a cousin, and since she was familiar with Bazmeht history, no need to keep my duty a secret from her. She should be grateful that the demi-goddesses cared enough to send a personal guard for her son, but no. Zelda hated us on sight.

"I told Mom about Bastet and Sekhmet sending *Lorelei* to

guard the cat collection when it goes on tour. It was cool of them. Last year, we hired a private security guy, and it cost a fortune."

Sipping my tea, I waited for him to finish telling us what *else* he'd shared with his furious mother.

"Money doesn't matter," Zelda said in a clipped, cold voice. "I wouldn't have minded using the same company."

"Well. It gave me the chance to bring home my Egyptian cousin, Shani. I'm looking forward to showing her around."

"How long are you planning on staying?" Zelda glared at me over the rim of her cup. I wondered why we played the charade for Maria's sake. It was my understanding that staff knew everything. As a handmaiden to Bastet, I'd heard my share of secrets. And kept them.

Josh stretched his long legs out in front of him. "She's thinking about going to Miami U too."

"What?" Zelda's cup shook in the fine china saucer.

"He's teasing," I said before she had a heart attack. "I'm not sure how long I'll be here. As you heard, I'm missing Egypt already."

"I'll be happy to help you find an apartment, if you decide to stay and go to school."

I smiled tightly. Zelda had drawn the first line of battle in the sand, making it very clear that she didn't want us here.

"My mom was just explaining how her sixth husband didn't understand her," Josh challenged.

Zelda snapped her mouth shut and leaned over to pick up her tea. Her hands trembled, and I felt bad for her. Obviously, she would rather play nice than discuss her latest attempt at wedded bliss.

"Lorelei," she said, peering closely at my mentor. "Not a very exciting job, guarding a bunch of dust and bones. Have we met before?"

With a slow blink, Lorelei calmly finished her tea.

And lied. "No, I don't believe we have."

# CHAPTER ELEVEN

## GODDESS HELPS THOSE THAT HELP THEMSELVES

Leaving her tea unfinished, Zelda pleaded illness and left, taking Maria with her. My stomach made a rumbling noise, and I struggled to ignore the delicious sandwiches on the table in front of us.

Josh frowned. "I don't know what got into my mother, she usually isn't that rude to perfect strangers."

"Did you tell her that your life was at risk?"

He shook his head. "No, I said you were both here for the museum stuff. She thinks you're spies for Uncle Marcos to make sure the collection is in good shape."

"Why didn't you tell her the truth? Maybe she doesn't believe that the Bazmeht would send *two* guards to Miami just to protect a collection of cat sarcophagi. We're pretty well respected for what we do, you know."

"She doesn't need to worry about me with all the other crap happening. The guy she married lied about who he was, which is not cool. Said he was a Spanish Engineer, but turned out he's a gambler with a computer problem. Internet porn. It might not seem like it, but she can be freaky when she gets upset."

I had no problem believing it. "If you don't explain what is really going on, then she's left to make something up. Surely, the truth is better?" My mouth watered at the thought of flaky tuna fish melting on my tongue. *A Bazmeht Bodyguard can go without food for days. Get a grip!*

"Geez, Shani. Telling my mom I have some weird chromosome thing handed down from a pharaoh seems out there, no matter how you look at."

Lorelei laughed. "Zelda is a very strong lady. And she grew up hearing the stories of her ancestry."

"You're telling me that my mom knows all about this?" Josh crossed one leg over the other in a deceptively lax pose. "She sure didn't say anything just now when I was talking about it."

"She didn't seem too surprised, though, did she? She knows

about Bastet and Sekhmet, and that the Bazmeht are an organization of elite bodyguards." Lorelei set her cup on the saucer.

Josh scratched at the stubble on his chin. "No. Yes. Well, she was surprised that you were here, not surprised as in, it couldn't ever happen." He rubbed his flat belly. "I'm freaking starving."

*Thank the Goddess!* We can eat.

But instead of leaning forward to take one of the delicious smelling sandwiches, he said, "I don't understand why she never told me any of this."

"We don't either," Lorelei agreed. She stood, one eye drooping a little.

"Migraine?" The headaches she sometimes gets lay her flat for hours, and the only thing that helps is a pill and sleep.

"It's probably the heat and all the excitement of the last few days. If you two will excuse me, the thought of food is making me sick."

Josh, acting the gentleman - at nineteen, which was very impressive – jumped to his feet. "I'll walk you back to your room."

Lorelei waved him away. "I can find it." Her face paled. "Good night."

"Feel better!" I called after her.

"It's only five o'clock." Josh glanced at the giant, dark wood clock on the wall. "Will she be all right?"

I nodded. "Yes, she'll be good as new in the morning. Maybe your mom will be better by then too?"

Lorelei's migraines were legitimate headaches she controlled by sleep and diet, but for that matter, I could understand a little of what sickened Zelda. She'd run away from Egypt, thinking to avoid her destiny. She had to be suspicious that we, the Bazmeht, were back in her life. I wondered how she'd take the fact her son carried the Blood of Ra, the sacred DNA we needed in order to procreate.

No matter how much money the Bazmeht sank into experiments, the genetic anomaly could not be recreated within a lab, or frozen, or sealed in formaldehyde.

Zelda and Josh had to come around.

My belly growled ferociously, and I leaned forward, snagging a tuna fish sandwich off the platter. I took a small, porcelain plate as Josh sat down. "I can't wait for you anymore," I said, taking the bread off and eating the insides. Flaky, white tuna, mayonnaise and dill pickle, exploded over my taste buds.

Josh pointed at my plate and burst into laughter.

Mortified, I glanced at the bread then back at Josh. "What? Is this rude?"

"No, no, I'm sorry. I eat my sandwiches that way too. Love the tuna, hate the rye. I'm telling Maria, no more bread from now on."

"Please don't say anything. I am a guest in your home."

"Whatever." He grabbed two of the sandwiches, taking the tops off them both before handing one to me. "Sometimes, it's easier to eat it like a slice of pizza."

"I've never had pizza. I saw it on television though. It looks good."

"Never had pizza? Did you live under a rock?"

"Sort of." Lots of rocks, lots of sand. Very little time out in the real world.

"Too funny. We are ordering pizza for dinner tonight, extra large with pepperoni and sausage. You eat meat, don't you?"

I nodded, feeling like an uneducated basket weaver from the village. "Yes, I like meat. Lamb, veal, quail, chicken..."

"Chicken! I like chicken. I've never had quail."

I smiled. "It tastes like chicken."

"So you've never had Coke, you've never had pizza. Tell me you've seen movies before?"

Without thinking about it, I playfully smacked his arm. "We get movies, and the Internet, and cell phones. I've never had Coke because my training requires a very strict diet. I don't like sweets, and I usually just drink water. But pizza? That I can't wait to try." All of that melting cheese? How could millions of Pizza Hut commercials be wrong?

"Who is your favorite actor?" He was on his third pizza style sandwich. I don't think he chewed.

"American actor or Balinesian?"

"Bala what?"

"What's it like, not knowing everything?" I liked teasing him.

"This cousin thing might be fun."

He patted my arm and chuckled, which did strange things to my insides. His blond hair needed trimmed and brushed, and it was clear, from the dark shadows along his jaw, he could use a shave. But the way the tan skin around his eyes crinkled when he smiled made my stomach flip like it did after a somersault.

Sekhmet's voice echoed in my memory. Josh is forbidden. Not for me, no matter how attractive he is.

And yes, the more I got to know him, the more I liked him, it was as simple as that. From the glint in those blue-green flecked eyes, I wondered if he might be feeling something toward me too. If I scooted to the edge of my seat, and if he leaned in -

*NO!*

I jumped up, almost knocking over my teacup in my rush to avoid kissing Josh. My client. My very forbidden on pain of death duty. "I should go check on Lorelei."

Josh wore a confused expression as he got up too. "Okay, but she's probably sleeping. She said she was going to take a nap. We can hang out, if you want. Watch television, if you're tired and just wanna chill."

Suddenly, every sense I had was very aware of Joshua Johnson. His unique scent was sunshine and salt, his hair a sun-bleached blond mane that called for my fingers to run through its shaggy mess.

*What in the Goddess's breath is wrong with me?*

Blinking, I shook my head, as if that might help clear it. "I, uh, need to go running."

"In this heat? You'll pass out before you get to the road."

"Too much energy to sit still." I needed away from him, and fast. I'd always thought attraction this strong was a lie, a romantic myth.

"We have a pool."

"I need a swimsuit, remember?"

"Right. We have a gym. It's small but air-conditioned."

"I'll take it!" Anything to burn off some of the uber-awareness I had of Josh. He reached out and brushed a piece of hair from my forehead, and I could have purred. He didn't know that a cat's face is one giant erogenous zone.

*I'd promised.*

I ran to my room and changed in less than ten minutes, cooling my libido by thinking of all the ways Sekhmet might kill me. Drowning, hanging, and lethal injection were at the top of my list.

With no trouble, I located the gym by smell alone. There was a treadmill, a stationary bike, and a weight set.

And Josh, dressed in shorts and a tank top.

My breath stuck in my throat like a fish bone.

This is not my fault, I thought with a muffled groan. I am not used to being around males of *any* age, let alone one that rivaled a young Brad Pitt when he played in Thelma and Louise.

The Bazmeht promote feminine power without taking anything away from the male; we're encouraged to think as equals and warned that in the outside world, not everybody feels the same way. I went to an all-girls elementary school within Bubastis, and I skipped most of traditional high school by getting my diploma online.

I danced with a few guys at the clubs I went to, but most of my life has been solitary.

Which had to explain my gut-wrenching, mouth drying reaction to Josh's tanned, muscular body.

Not daring to talk, I kept my earbuds firmly in place and hopped onto the treadmill - it was easy enough to figure out - setting a brisk pace. I didn't stop until my leg muscles trembled and I had a side cramp.

So what if Josh kept his gaze glued to the music videos playing on the television in the corner the entire time I was working out?

He'd shown no interest in how fast I was going or how smooth my thigh muscles were in my work out shorts. Grabbing a paper towel from the roll on the counter, I patted at my face. I'd never worried if I was ugly or pretty. So long as I was in Bazmeht uniform, I was happy with a little mascara and gloss.

And my iPhone.

Thank the Goddess for music and text messaging all wrapped up in one case.

I yanked the buds from my ears, disconnecting Abba and Dancing Queen. So, did I say thank you for the work out before I left? What were the rules in an unwanted, one-sided crush? Coward that I am, I headed for the door.

"Hey!" he called to my back. "Don't forget, we're on for pizza and a movie. How do you feel about action adventure?"

I turned, still patting at my face with the paper towel to

hide my uncertainty. "Anything but romance."

"I figured you'd be the kind of girl to go for guns and dead bodies."

"Just remember that."

"Hey, Shani...how fast can you run? I mean, really run – not just on the treadmill."

My body stilled as if sensing a trick question. "I don't know. Why do you ask?"

He shrugged, as if it wasn't important, but I wasn't fooled. "I'd be interested in racing you. People say I'm fast, but I bet you could keep up." Tossing one of those dimpled grins in my direction, he turned back to the television and music videos and left me standing there with my mouth hanging open.

Had I just been challenged to a race?

I haven't lost a foot race since I was fourteen. "When do you want to go? I'm ready right now."

"Tomorrow morning, champ. We'll be good and carbed up from our pizza tonight, and if we go early, we can beat the heat. You've never run until you've run on the shores of the Atlantic at dawn."

"Be prepared to lose," I joked, knowing that I would have to let him win or else give away my heightened ability. As much as I like to win, love to win, I had to protect an older secret, that was more important than my ego. I'd make it really close though.

He switched off the television. "Girl, you have no idea the monster you've unleashed."

Josh looked so serious that I had to laugh.

"What's going on in here?" Zelda came into the gym, her nose wrinkled in distaste. "Open a window or light a candle – something. It smells like...sweat."

"This is the gym, Mom. People sweat here."

Zelda barely glanced at me as she brushed past, careful not to touch her designer clothes to my sweaty ones. "We need to talk, Joshua. Alone."

I got the hint, delivered with a sledgehammer. "I hope you're feeling better. I am on my out."

"Mom, that was rude."

"It's all right!" More than happy to escape Zelda and Josh's reunion, I'd shower the sweat off then find them and eavesdrop.

Bastet said not to trust Zelda. Eavesdropping is just one of the services a trained, super-sensitive Bazmeht bodyguard can offer the paying client, or my favorite demi-goddess.

"See you for pizza," Josh said.

"But Josh, I was hoping to go to Bella's for Pasta Alfredo."

"Shani and I are going to order pizza and watch a movie."

Zelda sighed. "I've missed you, Joshua."

"You can join us, then."

"What will you watch? A romantic comedy? I love to laugh at fools in love. And I really don't want to be alone, Josh. It's been so hard since the break up..."

Zelda could have been on Arabian Daytime Drama, she way she masterminded Josh's heartstrings. I touched her arm and watched her cringe at the contact. "We can watch whatever you want, it will be an early night for me, anyway."

It wasn't nice of me, but I turned and left Josh alone with his mother.

# CHAPTER TWELVE

## RUNNING MATE

Pizza was so much better than the commercials made it look. It was even good for breakfast. Finishing the last bite of cheese-stuffed crust, I stretched in the courtyard and waited for Josh to get up.

I'd made it halfway through some very old movie – Breakfast at Tiffany's - and halfway through a pepperoni pizza before going to bed. Lorelei had been sound asleep both times I'd checked on her – her breathing stayed even and steady, so I didn't worry.

My sleep had been deep but restless. I dream but never remember what they are about. I just wake up feeling like I've been in a battle and had my head handed to me on a platter. A run would clear the fog in my head.

*Where is that boy?*

So far as information gathering went, last night hadn't been a total loss. Josh and Zelda never had their private conversation. I know this because Josh stayed in his room until the pizza came, talking to his girlfriend on the phone.

She was in Paris, and he didn't sound like he missed her that much.

I'd done a quick search of his room as soon as he'd gone to pay the pizza driver. I wondered if it was a typical teenage guy's room, but I had nothing to compare it to. He had surf posters on the narrowest wall, overlapped so you couldn't tell what color was underneath. His window overlooked the side yard. I locked it.

He had a gigantic plasma television on the biggest wall, and two game chairs with a game system and controllers. He had a private bath, all navy blue and brown, and dark chocolate colored tile.

I think. There were a lot of clothes on the floor.

My breath quickened and I knew that Josh was awake. I've never experienced this connection with another person, and I wondered if it had to do with the Bazmeht – Blood of Ra law of attraction. I can handle myself, though. *I'm a professional.*

If I concentrated really hard, I could pick out the sounds of Josh as he left his room, his sneakers slapping against the carpeted hall as he raced for the stairs.

He took the tile steps two at a time, in such a hurry.

And then, he fell.

I heard him fall, heard him curse.

Sprinting for the slider door, I was by his side in seconds.

He sat on the floor at the foot of the stairs, still looking a bit surprised to find himself sprawled at the bottom. I dropped to my knees beside him. "Where are you hurt?" Outwardly calm, I did the five-sense body check, slipping his shoe from the injured foot and gently feeling for injury. "Pulse is fast, ankle is sprained. Back is bruised."

Josh pushed at my roaming hands. "Stop it. I'm ticklish."

"How can you joke?" I sat back on my heels and studied his pain-filled grin. "If you hadn't been running so fast down the hall, you never would have fallen down the stairs."

"How do you know how fast I was running?" His smile slipped.

I spread my hands apart. "Because you're laying at the bottom of the stairs?"

Lorelei rushed down to us, her hair in a loose brown braid, falling over her shoulder. She slept in Victoria's Secret pajamas, and it was obvious to anybody who had eyes that she was in terrific shape. Oddly enough, I didn't want Josh noticing.

"What happened?" She reached for Josh, but he scooted away.

"Dr. Fast Hands has already done her on-site medical evaluation." He sat against the wall. "I'm fine."

"Ankle's sprained, bruising on his lower back." I rubbed the spot behind my ear, which was reacting to the adrenalin rush I'd felt. No fur, please Goddess. How would I ever explain that? Someday, Josh might be willing to listen to the full story, but that day certainly wasn't today.

Had Zelda's fear of her past kept her from sharing her history with her son? Josh claimed to love all things Egypt – considering he was part Egyptian that wasn't overly surprising. But he seemed apprehensive of it too.

I glanced at Lorelei, who lifted a slim shoulder and got to

her feet. This was my assignment, and I had to make the decisions. "Let's get some ice on that ankle," I said, easily lifting him to a standing position.

He shot me a startled glance. "You're pretty strong, I'll give you that."

"Thank you. You should see me run. *I* don't fall." His weight against my body was solid, and it was clear he had strength of his own beneath the baggy t-shirt and shorts.

"Now who won't be serious? I was gonna run circles around you. Do you know where you're going?"

"Yes. The kitchen. I've already had pizza for breakfast."

"Shani!" Lorelei said, holding Josh's sneaker by two fingers. "Pizza?"

"It is so much better than granola and honey, just wait until you try some."

Josh moaned.

"Did I hurt you?"

"No but a girl who eats cold pizza for breakfast? I'm half way in love. Just tell me that you can beer-burp the National Anthem, and I'm all yours."

*American or Egyptian?* "You have a girlfriend, remember?" I set him down in a chair and leaned over to flick on the light switch. Glancing down, I looked directly into Josh's eyes. A little glazed over with pain, they still held a dangerous allure.

"She's in Paris until next week, when school starts."

"Paris? I'm impressed." I stepped away, knowing I had to ignore whatever this attraction was, and not let him know I'd eavesdropped on his conversation.

"Don't be, her dad's French. They have a house there."

I reminded myself that Josh lived in an entirely different world than I did. The slow American accent, the huge house, and the pizza, none of this was for me. Including Josh!

Lorelei sat at the table too. Since I already knew where everything was, I got her a slice of pizza, warmed it in the microwave, and brought Josh an ice bag and some coffee that I figured out how to brew from the instructions on the container.

"You read French?" Josh asked, curiosity evident in his tone.

"*Oui.*" I dipped a half-curtsy, which was slightly ridiculous in sneakers and shorts.

Lorelei wiped the cheese from her mouth with a satisfied

*mew.* "That was incredible. Better than se—" She stopped herself with a blush. "Shani also speaks several dialects of Arabic, Latin, Hebrew, Spanish, English, as well as ancient Egyptian."

Josh's mouth lost its pinched look as he laughed in spite of the pain in his ankle. "You're kidding, you're like some kind of WunderKid from Bodyguards R Us."

"Hmm?" I put the last of the dishes into the dishwasher.

"Never mind. I guess we'll have to race another day." Josh tapped his fingers against the tabletop.

"You challenged him to a race?" Lorelei wadded up her napkin and tossed it directly into the open garbage. "Shame on you."

"He challenged me, Lorelei, so don't be angry. In fact," I sent him a teasing smile, "he probably fell on purpose."

"What!"

"You didn't have to worry, Josh, I was going to let you win."

Hobbled by his injury, he couldn't get to his feet. "Not cool."

"And I was worried that you might not get along." Lorelei stood and stretched. "Let's put the injured one in front of the television, and I'll take you running." She gave me a look, which I interpreted as she had news to share with me, and then added, "Besides, we still have to go bikini shopping, and I *know* Josh can't be up for that."

"What? Let me see... Am I a red-blooded American male? That would be yes. That makes me completely fit for watching bikini try-outs, preferably while I sit in the shade with a cool beverage in one hand and my feet propped up."

"Sorry. You, sir, are benched due to injury." Lorelei clucked her teeth like she really cared. "You mentioned a shop though, do you remember the name of it? So long as you stay off of the stairs, you should be perfectly safe for a few hours."

Josh sighed, accepting that he'd lost. "Sandy's Suits on the corner of Beach and 2nd has the hugest selection of swim stuff – towels, sunglasses, everything. Hey, if you guys want, we can go to the tiki lounge tonight."

"Just get better." Lorelei waved from the door.

"What if my ankle's broken?" He lowered his eyes, as if that look would work on two Bazmeht Bodyguards.

"It's not," I assured him. "Want us to bring you back a candy bar?"

"I'm bored!"

I shut the door, still laughing. Lorelei changed into a running skirt with shorts underneath and a tank top. She had a lightweight, Nike backpack that had room for her wallet, a bottle of water, and her phone. I had my specially designed sports bra and stole a few sips of Lorelei's water. Her news had been a simple 'be strong' message from Sekhmet.

Whatever.

It turned out that we were less than three miles from the beach, which was hardly enough to get warmed up. But as Lorelei reminded me, this wasn't about the run, it was about swimwear.

She hadn't been kidding when she'd said that Miami's bikinis were works of art. Duct tape, seashells, paperclips – you name it, they made a bikini out of it.

I narrowed my eyes at the suit dangling from the hanger in my hand. "I just want something that won't disintegrate when wet. Is that really too much to ask?"

Lorelei, frustrated with my lack of enthusiasm over the coconut and palm frond two-piece, threw her hands in the air. "I am going out to call Control. When I come back, you'd better have three suits picked out and laid on the counter, or I will buy them for you, and you obviously won't like them."

She stomped out of the beachfront store and left me feeling as if I could punch somebody. I spun around when I heard a low laugh. At the very rear of the store, a girl with a black Mohawk chuckled into the sales rack.

Annoyed, I yelled, "What is so funny?"

Startled, the girl looked up, the fluorescent overhead lights glinting off her nose ring. She'd thought I couldn't hear her, little did she know. "Lover's spat?"

With huge strides, I was by the girl's side before she realized what happened. She swallowed. "Uh. Fight?"

"I am not a lesbian, and she is not my lover. We are not in a fight. Why do I have to wear a bikini? They have perfectly good one-pieces over there." I pointed to the row on the wall.

Her black Mohawk bobbing, the girl looked at me from head to toe. "Those are for lifeguards. I don't get you, you're not fat, so what's your problem? This is Miami, everybody runs around practically naked."

Crossing my arms over my waist, I didn't have an answer.

"I'm Egyptian."

With a huge sigh, the girl grabbed my arm. "I know they got beaches there. What don't you like about these suits?"

After we'd exhausted all of her questions, proving that I wasn't overly modest or poor, she asked, "Can you swim?"

My face paled and my knees wobbled.

"Crap! Here, sit down," she pushed me to a bench made from a surfboard. "K. No brainer. You can't swim, so you don't want a suit. Damn. Can you believe I only make seven bucks an hour for this? I could have my own talk show."

I lifted my head, slowly, to keep the blood from rushing out. "I can swim."

"Uh huh."

"I just don't like it. Not in the ocean."

"Well, there you go. Probably had a fatal drowning experience in a past life. Happens all the time. You just have to grab a suit and get your ass in the water. The only thing to do is face that fear and keep your nose out of the waves. You'll be fine."

# CHAPTER THIRTEEN

## LUNCH AND LIES

Shopping is hungry work, so I convinced Lorelei, with little effort, to feed me.

We stopped for lunch at an outdoor café and watched the people – all sorts of strange and wonderful people – go by. The tables were literally on the sidewalk, underneath canopy shades. "This is unlike anything I've ever seen," I said, sipping the last of my strawberry shake. "Even from MTV. Bald guys really do drive red sports cars, and girls keep iguanas on leashes! I wonder if Josh ever had a pet?"

Lorelei pointed her coffee spoon at me. "Just remember that you are here doing a job. There is nothing wrong with a harmless flirtation, but Josh is a client, and there can be no crossing the line."

"I know that." I peered at her from over my new Chanel sunglasses. "I just wondered if he had a goldfish or something. Where did you meet Zelda before?"

"Why do you think I have?"

"Because your eyes get all round when you lie, that's why, so don't even try to deny it."

"They do?"

"Yes. Now tell!"

Lorelei smoothed a strand of hair back over her ear. "Well, Zelda was just a little girl at the time, and I was guarding the collection back when her grandmother had it. Zelda has always known her history. She's expected to pass on the knowledge. That's why I'm so surprised she ran away from it all. I wonder...well, I think something must have happened to scare her."

"I can't imagine anything scaring Zelda."

"We all have our Achilles heel, Shani, don't forget that. You never know when you might need to exploit someone else's weakness for the good of all."

"That sounds so cold-hearted." I shivered in the sunshine.

Lorelei sipped the last of her mostly cream coffee. "This

coming from the girl who used a text message to wish her mother happy birthday?"

"I didn't want to bother her," I said defensively. "She has important things to do. Like save the world or something."

Lorelei rolled her eyes. "That woman – she loves you, Shani, I know that, but it would have been kinder for both of you if she'd at least taken you with her on a few of those assignments. I don't blame you for not wanting to be close."

Even though it was true, it still made me feel bad to talk about my mom.

Good friend that she is, Lorelei changed the subject. "Have you ever seen water that shade of blue?"

I looked out over the shoreline. "It isn't like the Mediterranean is it? It's vast, this makes me feel insignificant."

"Where did that come from? You are an elite bodyguard and hardly insignificant! I wish we could link minds. There are times when I know you have the most intriguing thoughts."

"Not so intriguing. Mohawk girl says my fear of the water comes from drowning in a past life."

Lorelei choked on her breath mint. "And you said?"

"Nothing. She terrified me, even after I bought three suits." I laughed then rubbed the tender spot behind my ear. "I didn't want to tell her that all cats hate the water. Well, most of them."

"Hush. You never know when people could be listening."

I looked around then leaned forward and whispered dramatically, "Our waiter is the only one staring at us. We are in the very center of weirdness. I don't think anybody would notice if we went into full shifting mode right here!"

My phone beeped, signally a text message. Sitting back, I read it. Then read it again. "Keket says that Sekhmet is really worried about Josh and I being together. She should know that no matter how strong the attraction, I would never give in to it. She threatened me with banishment, or death, for Goddess's sake."

Pinching the beginning ache between my brows, I didn't answer Keket's warning text. What could I say? I am sure the handmaiden would be thrilled if I fell from the demi-goddesses good graces.

"Sekhmet's sending you text messages? That's impressive."

"No, her handmaiden is doing it, with Sekhmet's urging, no

doubt. First you and now Keket?" I sighed heavily. The only chance I had was to sit out my forty days, protect Josh without falling in lust, and go home minus scales. Then I could accept my Level Two position within the Bazmeht.

"Lorelei, do you think my mother could somehow be involved in the Bazmeht mess?"

Lorelei arranged her bags by her feet and put on her sunglasses, as if ready to go. But I wasn't. I needed to talk about what was going on.

"What mess?"

"The demi-goddesses are worried that they are being betrayed by someone inside the Bazmeht. My mother and Natalie, are always at the base of any dissention."

My mentor's mouth tightened.

"What if Sekhmet doesn't trust me because she doesn't trust my mother? How can I let her know that she, Sekhmet, means more to me than my own mom? Would you talk to her, Lorelei, please?"

The doubts I'd been suppressing came out in a rush of breath, like a champagne fountain once the cork is popped.

"Of course, I'll talk to her, Shani, but I know that Sekhmet's concerns are coming from a different place."

"What do you mean?" My palms turned cold.

"Weellll..." Lorelei drew out the word. "It's just that you are not that experienced in the ways of love."

The tips of my ears tingled with embarrassment.

"And this is your first assignment where you are, for all intents and purposes, alone with a man. A nice looking guy, who happens to have just as nice of a personality."

I couldn't even swallow, I was so mortified.

"And all of this is compounded by the fact that Josh has the genetic code that calls directly to a Felidia – a Bazmeht, no less, who is ready to have her first taste of love. It's natural, Shani, your pheromones are answering the call of his testosterone, and with fear and duty comes heightened awareness of one another. It would be amazing if you *didn't* fall into his bed with your arms wide open."

Spluttering, I couldn't have spoken if I'd wanted to. Which I didn't.

"Bastet is all for you experiencing life, but Sekhmet is worried that you might not remember to take precautions, and if you get pregnant, the Council of Nine will never forgive you...not on top of everything else. Goddess, Shani, you look ill. Are you all right?"

"Having my non-existent sex life dissected and discussed among the council makes me feel faintly nauseas, yes." I nodded, ignoring the bleep of another text message.

Lorelei waved her hand. "It wasn't the whole council, just those of us who have a vested interest in your future. You don't need your virginity to be a guard, Goddess have mercy on us all, if that were the case," she laughed throatily. "Nobody would sign up. You just have to pick a male specimen that can't give you a Bazmeht warrior baby." She pointed to a tanned man with defined muscles, roller blading past our table. "Like him."

Stunned, I sat back and stared at her through the protective lenses of my sunglasses. "Thank you for explaining this to me. I never want to talk about it again, all right?"

"Shani," Lorelei said apologetically. "Don't let this bother you. Romance is a beautiful part of living! But when you are a Bazmeht bodyguard, darling girl, you've sworn an oath to put duty before personal feelings." She took her glasses off with a flourish. "Anything goes in the name of the Bazmeht."

Wishing I could die wouldn't make it so. "I'd rather talk about the chances of my mother being a turn-coat." I gestured to the staring waiter and pointed to my empty water glass. He poured and lingered but didn't say anything. Creepy.

As soon as he was gone, Lorelei held up her hand and bent a finger down for each point she wanted to make. "One. Someone inside Bazmeht is possibly leaking information to the Uraeli. Two. You are worried that your mother and her team might be the leak. Three. You have an entendre for Josh, but you feel it's completely under control. Four. Four- " Pausing, she asked, "How many texts have you gotten in the last two minutes?"

"Seven."

"Who wants to talk to you that bad? And why don't they call?"

"Texting is much better than talking. You can text what you need without having to take the time to personally interact." I meant it as a joke, but it was sort of true. I bent down, reading the messages. "Two from Josh, who is bored out of his mind; two from Keket, on behalf of Sekhmet; one from Dendera, Muu is fine; Bastet, insisting love is in the air; and my mother." My throat closed. "My mother?" Apprehension threaded through me as I clicked the envelope to read her text. Aloud. "Trust nobody. Sharifa."

"What?"

"Exactly. I swear the jungle is making her crazy." Still, I wondered what she meant, and why she'd take the time to warn me in such a cryptic fashion.

"This reminds me of the old days," Lorelei said with a small laugh. "Intrigue around every corner. Your mother was always good at playing her cards close to her chest."

"You and my mother were friends?" I don't know why that surprised me.

"Once upon a time, a very long time ago."

"What happened?" Why had neither of them ever mentioned it?

Lorelei put her sunglasses back on, effectively covering her eyes. "Water under the bridge, Shani, don't think of it anymore. I certainly don't."

# CHAPTER FOURTEEN

## ILLUSION

"Have you noticed the way the waiter keeps staring at us?" I picked up a large spoon, angling it so that I could see his reflection. He stood to the side of us with his arms crossed, completely focused on our small, two-person sidewalk table. "It's odd."

Lorelei sent him a wide smile and a three finger wave. "We are two beautiful women, it would be insulting if he wasn't staring."

I put the spoon down. "But he's not waiting on any of the other tables."

"Here he comes." Lorelei leaned back, her hands folded in her lap. A deceptive pose, but one that I knew put her in prime position if she had to jump up and snap someone's neck. She's quick, that Lorelei.

The waiter stopped at the edge of our table. "Dessert?"

His short, cool Asian accent brought a ripple of recognition. The scent of cantaloupe, sweet and over ripe. Somehow, I knew if I looked into his eyes, I would see death. Adrenalin kick-started my pulse, and my lips drew back in an involuntary snarl.

Lorelei heard my low growl and stood, her chair tipping over as she looked from me to him. "What? What's wrong?"

*He was Apep, the reptilian enemy of Re, and I was Mafdet, the sun god's Serpent Slayer.*

A split second instantaneous recognition between ancient foes. My right ear twitched and I gritted my teeth. His mouth changed from pink to gray, and my instincts raged.

Shoving Lorelei behind me, I leveraged the table into the waiter's waist. His eyes narrowed, and I saw the fangs of his eyeteeth as he bared an evil smile. "Shani Nebit," he hissed. He leaped over the table at me, pulling me into the street, his nails digging into my wrist.

Lorelei grabbed my arm, yanking me back, but she lost her grip. Waiter guy and I circled one another, primal enemies. I used the fork I'd clutched in my fist to stab into his shoulder, once, twice, until he let me go. He screamed like a girl and I smiled.

He didn't know who he'd decided to attack today, he had my name, but not my game. I rolled my shoulders and balanced on my toes.

Traffic stalled around us, and I was vaguely aware of Lorelei pacing behind me. Her impotent fury crackled in the thick, salty air. Cars honked impatiently as the waiter and I faced each other like American cowboys in the street. Me, an Egyptian female in black running shorts and a white t-shirt, staring down a slim Asian waiter, also dressed in black and white, with a red blood stain blossoming over his collarbone.

No doubt, the surrounding crowd assumed we were filming the next Hollywood blockbuster.

If morphing in front of one human was against the rules, what would Sekhmet say about this? As much as I wanted to claw his head from his neck, I couldn't do it here.

"I drew first blood. Tell *her* that." Why wouldn't Ninja meet me face to face? "Why does she keep sending her minions?" I threw the fork down at his feet as a black town car raced for us. Neither one of us wanted the fight to end. The car kept coming, and at the very last instant, the waiter jumped out of the way.

Leaving me on the other side of car. The rear door opened, and Josh pulled me in. Lorelei, laden down with our bags, hopped in right after me. In the back were two bench seats, facing each other. Lorelei and Josh sat with their backs to the driver, me opposite them.

"What is going on?" Lorelei demanded. "Who is driving? Where did you get this car?"

Josh grinned past the worry etched around his eyes. "You're welcome. You two sure get into a lot of brawls. You might as well admit you need me to bail your asses out. Meet Cadee, our original driver."

"Nice to meet you," I said automatically, my pulse slowing to a manageable beat.

"She's almost as good a driver as me," Josh admitted with a shrug.

I couldn't stop the giggle that turned into a belly laugh. What a wonderfully ridiculous thing to say. "How are you, Cadee, after your ordeal in the locker? I'm surprised you want to work with us at all."

"You mean, am I still all cramped up after spending eight hours with my knees folded to me chin? Nay, it's fine, I feel, only raging mad and thirsting for revenge."

"Then you're in the right car," I said with a glance at Lorelei, who looked truly furious.

"I'm Lorelei," she said to the black-haired, pale Irish stunner behind the wheel. Cadee wore tightly fitted leather gloves, so new that they still had that great leather smell, like the inside of a Lexus. I noticed they'd been made to fit her hands exactly. The hand stitching was practically invisible. I was stricken with glove envy.

"And the fork-wielder is Shani. Bless you for breaking up the street fight. Now what in the hell was that about?"

I almost melted under the glare Lorelei sent my way. "You can't be mad at me." I tapped my chest just to be sure.

"If you ever push me out of the way again, as if I'm a child, I will personally kick your ass!" Lorelei leaned forward, her eyes blazing coals from her face.

"Whoa, girls, girls..." Josh said in attempt to lighten the tension.

I vaguely remembered doing something like that. Caught in the moment, life or death. "I'm sorry."

"I trained you! You should have warned me of the danger-"

"As soon as I noticed his freakishness, I did. You flirted with him and called him over to the table for dessert!"

She paled and I immediately regretted my words. "I'm sorry. It's just that he was strange, and he kept staring. I-" *I'd started to change.* My instincts took over, but I couldn't tell her any of that in the present company.

I grabbed her hand. "Don't be angry with me. You trained me, and you trained me well. It was like, like I went outside of myself. Instinct."

Exhaling, Lorelei's fingers flexed in my palm. "Damn, but you are so fast, Shani. I hadn't realized how quick your reflexes are. You stabbed him with a fork, and I never even saw you pick it up."

"You said that we had to use the weapons at hand." Worried that I'd somehow upset her beyond repair, I bowed my head.

She lifted my chin before gently pushing me back to my seat. "Well. You did that. I just couldn't believe it when you were in the street, it was-"

"A showdown! You each needed guns, *pow pow.*" Josh blew the imaginary smoke from his imaginary pistols. I looked closer and saw the worry in his eyes. He was joking to cover his concern. I turned sarcastic, he made bad jokes. You'd think I'd picked up an emotional clue.

"Guns would have been nice," I agreed. "Too messy though. Remember, no cops." Light tone, breezy. Kidding for Cadee. What an impression to make on our first meet. I hadn't thought to bring my switchblade with my jogging bra. Not a mistake I'd make again.

Josh and Lorelei leaned in so that we could talk to each other without being over heard by our new driver. Didn't want to freak her out any more than what she already witnessed.

"So that guy was totally after you? *Not me.*" Josh tapped my knee to keep my attention.

"He probably wanted you and made do with me." Josh had to believe he needed me.

"No, that can't be right, because you said that you pushed Lorelei out of the way. Lorelei is the target, then." He touched Lorelei's arm.

"He wasn't actually making a move toward me. I didn't know anything was wrong until suddenly he and Shani were going at it." Lorelei stared at me thoughtfully. "He just asked if we wanted dessert."

"Cantaloupe." I rubbed the tip of my nose.

"He didn't say," Lorelei said.

"I smelled it. But that doesn't matter, does it? He just looked suspicious, and then he was...there." Sighing, I added, "Maybe this particular attack had nothing to do with Josh at all. Random. We didn't decide to shop until this morning, and lunch at that restaurant? Not planned."

"I don't believe in coincidence." Lorelei looked at Josh. "How did you know where we were?"

"Not coincidence, that's for sure. Shani texted me where you were eating. I was bored, so when Cadee showed up with the new car, it seemed like a nice thing to do, you know, to save you both a walk back to the house. Got me out of the house too. And we totally got there just in time – didn't you say you didn't want to involve the cops? I heard sirens coming."

"Hmm." Lorelei sat back and stared at Cadee. She raised her

voice. "And you showed up at the house why?"

"No need to give me the evil eye, Miss Lorelei," Cadee answered with wink. "I get my worksheet every mornin', and Joshua Johnson was on it. Eleven thirty, sharp. I'm never late. Unless I get stuck in a locker."

"Who called in the order?" I asked, curious now myself. After yesterday's misunderstanding, I wanted every detail signed twice.

"My boss will know, Miss Shani. I can call in as soon as we get back to the house. You'll see everything is on the up and up. Unless you want to stop at the grocery store? Are you stocked for the storm?"

"What storm?" I peered out the window, but the skies outside were clear and blue. Just as they'd been all day.

"It's nothing," Josh said dismissively. "We'll get a little wind, that's all. Newscasters always try to make a tropical storm into a Category Five hurricane."

"Hurricane?" My ears perked.

Lorelei turned to Cadee for the facts. "What is Josh not telling us?"

"Tropical storm Fern, who names a storm Fern, I ask? Well, she's due to make hurricane status by tomorrow, and she's headed right for us within the next 2 days."

"A Cat One at the most," Josh said with a shake of his head. "No worries."

"Cat One?" That didn't sound so bad. "The dangerous storms are Four and Five, right?"

"If you don't have a roof on account of the last little storm." Cadee sniffed. "A Category One could really do you in. Not all people live in the land of milk and honey. Speaking of which, Mr. Josh, we're home."

I laughed at the sorry look on Josh's face as he stammered, "I didn't mean, I was just kidding, ah..."

Cadee turned and smiled, her eyes as green as grass. "Never you mind, now, I was speaking out, as usual. Didn't mean to offend you, sir."

Pushing a button from somewhere on the dash, Cadee waited as the gates opened, then she pulled the car in front of the house. Zelda waited on the stairs. Her pretty face looked concerned until Josh hobbled out of the back.

"Josh! I was wondering where you'd gone to, you didn't

leave a note."

"I never leave a note." His shoulders slumped, and he shoved his hands in his front jeans pockets – put-upon teenager instead of the hero he'd just been. "Since when do you care where I go?"

"Josh!" Zelda covered her mouth with her hand.

Cadee cleared her throat. "Excuse me, but I'm on call for you, all day. Mr. Josh has my number, if you want to go anywhere. I'll just be in the car. Waiting." She tipped her hat over her eyes.

Lorelei and I exchanged a quick look. "We don't need to go anywhere," I said. "Please, don't stay here because of us."

Josh pulled his wallet from his back pocket. "How much do we owe?"

"It's all been paid. I, uh, peeked ahead at the schedule, and I'm on call for the next 39 days."

Lorelei smacked her forehead. "Bastet. Sekhmet. Now I get it. I told you they'd take care of everything, didn't I?"

"True, Bastet said that Cadee would be back at work today, she just didn't specify for us." It made me feel a lot better knowing that the demi-goddesses were behind the car and driver. "Do you at least live nearby, so you can go home and take a nap? Do laundry? Something besides sit?"

Cadee nodded. "I'm ten short minutes away. You don't mind then? My kids get a kick out of it when I pick them up from school like this."

She gave us each her card then left with a jaunty wave. "I like her," I said. "Makes me feel even worse that she was stuffed in a locker."

"What? Who stuffed that poor girl into a locker?"

I'd forgotten that Zelda was there. "Uh."

"Never mind, Mom. Let's go inside. I could use a Coke."

"The news says that we're going to get a hurricane. We need to put the shutters up! I have water, canned food, and batteries."

"Mom, chill out. The glass is shatter proof, the shutters crank down, and the front door is solid steel. We are safe, okay?"

We went to the kitchen where Maria had set out a large pitcher of iced tea and sliced lemons, plus a tray of lemon cookies. The television droned from the corner, the news giving bulleted lists of everything that a Miami resident needed to survive the storm in comfort.

Josh didn't look at all worried, so I wasn't going to worry either. However, my attention kept pulling to the graphics of the approaching storm. *Not that I was worried.*

Zelda sat down at the table with us, avoiding Lorelei, which I thought strange after her near recognition last night. Unless Lorelei kept her away with mind power?

There were times when I really regretted not getting that gift from the Mother Goddess, even if I *could* hear better than any of the other guards.

"Shani, a box came for you today, and you too, Lorelei." Zelda waved her hand toward Lorelei. "They were heavy, so I had the delivery man take them to each of your rooms."

A box? "That was fast. Bastet said she would ship my personal items, things that couldn't fit in my small suitcase."

"Bastet also sent something for me, something that she said I should share with all of you."

"What is it?" In the last two days, I have not gotten better at being patient.

Josh pulled at the hunk of hair over his eye. "What did that crazy woman send to you? A bomb? A mummified cat for the collection? Those ladies are loco."

Zelda laughed with surprise. "Yes, I agree. They are both slightly insane. However, they've also been very good to me over the years."

Intentional or not, all three of us stared at her with rapt attention.

"How so, Mom?"

"Well," she busied herself by refreshing her glass of tea. "As you know, your uncle, while *fond* of me," she sipped then set the glass down with shaking fingers. "Has been...disappointed...in my choices. My," she cleared her throat, "husbands."

*She thought her brother had sent us to spy on her.* I focused on the table and the snag in the linen tablecloth, instead of seeing Zelda's pain. I'm an emotional wuss no matter who is doing the suffering. Except for Ninja – that's one woman I can't wait to make suffer.

Lorelei kicked me under the table, so I knew to pay close attention.

"Bastet and Sekhmet would each send me news clippings

and articles of the family. In this day, with the Internet, it's not so important. But I used to be starved for news of home. To see my brother's face, my nephews." She sniffed delicately. "They've grown up without me. Without you, Josh, in their lives."

"Ah, Mom. Don't cry." Josh hunched forward over the table.

"I will if I want to. Pass me that napkin."

One thing was certain, Zelda had spunk.

Forgetting the part about being a quiet guard, I asked, "Why didn't you go back if you missed them so much?"

Zelda exhaled heavily. "I had my reasons."

Into the strained silence, Josh said, "This probably isn't the best time, Mom, but somebody tried to kidnap Ramy, and maybe me, while I was there."

She slammed her hand against the table. "Why didn't you call me?"

"You were on a cruise ship somewhere on your honeymoon. Remember? Anyway, these Bazmeht chicks stopped the bad guys, and now they're here because they seem to think that I have some kind of pumped up DNA."

Groaning, Zelda looked into my eyes. "No."

I swallowed. "Yes."

Zelda knew what we were. Whether she wanted to admit it to herself or not, she knew. "We aren't here to spy on you. Lorelei will guard your collection, that's true. But Bastet sent me to guard Josh, in the event someone finds out about his, er, special genetics."

She closed her eyes as if she could wish us away. "I never wanted this."

Josh reached over to poke his mom in the arm, his tone one of stunned disbelief. "You can't believe this. It's not *rational*."

Lorelei spoke, calmly and slowly, and I knew she used her mind powers to talk to Zelda without spooking the woman even more. "It is a good thing we are here. In your home. To protect your family. Your heritage."

Zelda snapped her fingers, breaking the connection. "Do you think I give a damn about that heritage? It has been a load on my back from the time I was born. My mother believed, my grandmother believed, but once I grew up, I wanted proof. *Proof!* Who could believe such outrageous stories?"

"Yeah." Josh folded his arms over his chest and nodded firmly.

Lorelei reached out, putting her hand on Zelda's forearm to calm her. "Josh knows that we are an elite bodyguard service and that he is descended from the true Egyptian blood line. He doesn't believe or want to know, *any more than that.*"

It was like someone let the air out of Zelda, and she deflated. Now she understood that Josh remained innocent of what we are, and what he means to us. I shifted, uncertain.

Shape shifters belong in movies, not real life. Perhaps the knowledge we exist is what pushed Zelda away from Egypt all those years ago.

Josh sat on the edge of his chair. "Mom, what are they talking about? What heritage? The cat sarcophagi? The old memorabilia in the library?"

Defeated, she lifted her glass. "All of it, Josh. That is all going to be yours someday. It is who we are."

"If it's who we are, then why won't you ever go back to Egypt? I know it calls to you, I've seen you sitting in that room in the dark." He paused, then confessed, "It calls to me, in my dreams. My nightmares."

"Nightmares? You have *nightmares* about Egypt? This is horrible. You never mentioned it." Zelda stared at her son, her mouth twisting before she buried her head in her arms. Huge sobs racked her body as she gave into deep sorrow. "I wanted to save you. I thought I could change things for you. No, no. It can't be."

Brushing past us, Maria went to Zelda and folded her into a soothing hug.

It sounded like she was singing a Spanish lullaby. My chest ached, and I stared at the ceiling. Could I leave? Would it be rude? Was it even *more* rude to witness this woman's anguish?

Lorelei pulled at my sleeve, a signal to stay put.

For the record, I thought this very unfair. There was nothing about staying for a nervous breakdown in the handbook, and that is all I am going to say about *that.*

# ⟨HAPTER FIFTEEN

## The Truth Will Always Tell

It took a glass of wine and moving into the downstairs living room before Zelda spoke again. Josh perched next to her on the ivory and gold brocade couch while I sat cross-legged on the floor opposite them. Lorelei sank into the heavily cushioned chair in front of the window. Maria brought in the package from Bastet and left it on the coffee table where we could all see it before she headed back to the kitchen.

Zelda sighed and pointed to the package. "You ladies probably already know the Myth of Mafdet by heart."

My blood zinged at hearing the ancient Mother's name, and I bowed my head in a quick prayer.

"But Josh hasn't, not since he was a baby." Zelda turned toward her son. "I stopped telling the stories after you were kidnapped."

Josh propped his feet on the spindle legged coffee table and swiped his hair off his forehead. "Mom. I was fine with Pierre. You sent my Xbox."

Draining her glass, Zelda admitted, "That was, perhaps, not a shining moment of motherhood for me. I..." She swallowed hard. "As I look back, there are quite a few of those. Believe it or not, Joshua darling, all I ever wanted was to be the best mother to you."

I could practically hear Josh think, 'What happened?' but he didn't say it out loud. Another thing to admire about him.

"That wasn't the first time you were kidnapped," Zelda admitted in a monotone. "When you were two, you were stolen from me, straight from your nursery."

Lorelei and I exchanged glances, but then I reverted my attention back to what happened on the couch. Seated next to Zelda, Josh paled.

"Your father...he wasn't home a lot. Not that evening either. The nanny was sick, so you and I were together. I'd bathed you, sang to you, put you to bed with kisses and hugs. My heart burst with love for you. And in the morning, you were gone."

"Oh, Zelda. I never knew." Lorelei hugged her knees to her chest.

We might as well have been invisible. Zelda spoke in a small voice to Josh and Josh alone. "Your father blamed me, told me and anybody who listened that it was my fault someone broke into our home, stole you from your tiny bed. He blamed my crazy family. And after two days, he walked out for good. I didn't care. I contacted Bastet and Sekhmet, Bazmeht Guardians linked to our family by blood."

Josh took his mother's hand, and Zelda gratefully curled her fingers around his. A pinch of pain bracketed Josh's mouth and eyes, but I was powerless to offer comfort. Not that I even knew how.

"They came. The demi-goddesses."

"Who?" Josh looked from his mother to me, to Lorelei. We kept silent. This was not our story to tell. Our job is to protect and guard from harm. Not blab.

"The demi-goddesses, Bastet and Sekhmet. They came to me in my hour of need, no questions or repercussions for running away from Egypt."

Zelda flicked her gaze toward me. "And I did run. Scared for my life, you see. Sekhmet helped me then too, though I swore her to secrecy and promised her mine."

Secrets. So many of them, and now they were going to tumble out like angry wasps from a nest.

I wanted to escape to the safety of the Yellow Room with its floral carpet that reminded me of Bastet's summer garden. I looked longingly toward the kitchen. Escape.

Lorelei mouthed the word 'coward' at me and I shrugged. It was the truth. Not always, but in this instance, absolutely. Give me something I could shoot, knife, or tackle, and I'd be fine. An outpouring of emotion made me want to bolt.

"Demi-goddesses. Are you freaking kidding me? Did they brainwash you, Mom? What the hell are you talking 'bout?"

"Shh. Listen to me, Joshua Sherif Johnson. You have ancient Egyptian blood in your veins, and I should have been brave enough to drag you back to Egypt and demand our places in my brother's life, but I was terrified. Stupid with it, and once I made the first mistake, I felt trapped and compelled to make them over and over again."

"I don't get you, Mom." Josh pulled his hand from hers and sat with his back to the couch, arms crossed in front of him.

I sit that way a lot when I'm nervous. He said he'd had nightmares...I wondered what they were about. Did he wake up feeling beat up and battle worn too?

"Bastet and Sekhmet sent their guardians and the Bazmeht scoured the world. They found you, Josh, within a week. You were," she coughed and wiped tears from her cheeks, "hungry. Scared. Angry. But not a bruise on you. Not a scrape. Somebody had taken you, for no reason, no ransom note – and left you in a cold, dirty warehouse in Kansas." She drew in a ragged breath. The urge to crawl from the room before I joined the poor woman in tears flooded my body.

And I don't cry.

*I am a Level One Bazmeht Bodyguard trained to kick ass...*Lorelei dabbed her eyes with a tissue, and I chewed my lower lip.

"You never told me any of this!"

Josh sounded mad, and I thought I understood. It is much safer to be angry than wounded.

"Why would I?" Zelda answered with a bite. "And have you scared to death? I was terrified enough for both of us, and when Pierre took you from me when you were little, I couldn't stand it. I couldn't see you, I would have killed him and smothered you with my fear."

"So you ran off and got married again." Josh's lip curled.

"Yes. I'm sorry."

Looking at me across the expanse of living room, Josh scratched the back of his neck, confusion and old hurt on his expressive face. I kept mine a mask. *Don't let people know they can harm you.*

I wanted to tell him that, to warn him to hide his vulnerability. I was supposed to protect him from harm, yet he was emotionally bleeding out in front of me. I got to my feet. "Do you want a Coke? With ice?"

Josh nodded gratefully. "Yeah. Do you mind?"

"Not at all." I practically ran from the room.

Maria watched the tropical storm update on the news. Having already memorized the layout of the kitchen, I got a tray, ice, Cokes, and wine. And a few bottles of water too. Maria smiled at me and went to a drawer. "Ice tongs."

"Thank you."

"How is the senora?"

"Fine. Am I right in assuming that she doesn't normally have these emotional outbursts?"

"No, no, the regular way is..." Maria made a zipping motion over her mouth.

Our arrival, the package from the demi goddesses, had provoked a meltdown. I took the tray to the sitting room, carefully moving the package out of the way before setting it on the table.

The drinks brought a short reprieve. Josh fixed his cola, and Zelda hopped right back into reliving the past. "I was afraid to be a mother to you, believing what your father had said – it was my fault that you'd been taken. To this day I don't know why. I thought that if I could just find the right father figure for you, then you'd be safe. Instead, I married badly and often when I should have swallowed my pride and gone home to my brother."

Josh, paying more attention than I thought, asked, "Why did you leave Egypt in the first place? You said you were scared. Did your brother hurt you? Your dad?"

"My dad, your grandfather, died when I was a young girl. My brother is a prince among men! You've met him – can you imagine him being cruel? No, it was my own foolish choices that made me afraid for my life. I was not," a small smile played at the edges of her mouth, "unattractive. I dated, flaunting my family's name, money, and heritage in the face of Fate. A," she glanced from us to Josh, "a bad man seduced me – not that he had to work so hard. Then he threatened to tell my family what he'd done. Ruined me. My brother's political aspirations would be over."

Josh raised his brows.

"I went to Sekhmet and made her a deal. She helped me, and I – I agreed that when the time came, I would keep my heritage safe and pass it down to my daughter. You were a boy, so I took it as a sign from the Goddess. I was not worthy of my heritage. I didn't have more children, on purpose."

Shaking his head, Josh leaned forward, his elbow on his knee.

"Pride is an ugly thing." Zelda took a healthy swallow from her glass of wine. "I ran to America with my tail between my legs and married the first man who had enough money to make me feel secure. Six years ago, when my mother passed away, the cat memorabilia came to me. I took them in, just as I'd promised. I'd had this house made specially to hold the ancient Egyptian treasures. I'm sure my brother is furious with me, that they are out of Egypt where they belong. But I can't go back there, and I made Sekhmet a vow to take them."

Josh sighed. "No wonder you're so cranky."

The observation surprised a laugh out of Zelda, and she visibly relaxed.

"Let me finish. I still have to read the Myth of Mafdet – Bastet wrote that she thought it was important for me to read it out loud? Josh, this might be very confusing for you, but I promise to answer any questions you have when this is over. I should have told you all of this before. This is your birth right. I didn't want you tormented by doubt and lack of faith, as I was. I should have given you the choice."

"Now you tell me. How can I stay pissed when you're being so cool now?"

Re help me, but my heart swelled with pride in Joshua Sherif Johnson.

Zelda's lower lip trembled, but she didn't cry, thank the Goddess. "I love you, Joshua." She coughed into her hand, re-crossed her legs, and picked up the package from Bastet.

Pulling the scroll from the envelope, she cleared her throat and began to read the translated script.

"The world began in the celestial waters of Nu. Re, the All God, created gods and man so he would not be alone. This is the story of Mafdet, the first feline goddess. She was known as the Warrior of Justice, the Slayer of Serpents, the Lady of the Mansion of Life."

"I remember Bastet reading this to us," I whispered to Lorelei. "When we were training as handmaidens."

"Shh!" Lorelei held a finger to her lips.

"Many, many thousands of years ago, when Egypt, *Khemet*, was new, Mafdet was created to care for the first king and all who came after him. Her people were the Felidia, cat shifters, and her role was to protect the pharaoh and his chambers, from the multitude of enemies a powerful man-god had. Mafdet took on the head of a panther, with speed of the lynx. She brought the decapitated heads of the king's enemies and dropped them at his feet. She alone had the ability to heal a snake bite or a scorpion sting."

Zelda met our eyes, a natural born storyteller, her familiarity with her heritage giving the story life.

"The pharaoh gifted her, his greatest champion, with slaves and gold. The kingdom grew peaceful under her watch, and the pharaoh sent her farther and farther from home to bring back more gold and more slaves. More power. The pharaoh's greed grew. The Uraeli, snake people descended from Apep, used this opportunity to whisper secrets and lies into the pharaoh's ear, because they wanted the king's power for themselves."

I looked at Josh, so caught up that he hadn't moved. Zelda's reading was almost as captivating as Bastet's.

"One day when Mafdet returned from battle, victorious, she was met with cold distrust from her king. Years passed as Mafdet fought to regain his regard. He sent her away without explanation. The Uraeli took more and more until the land died. The people were on the verge of a great rebellion before they starved. At last, Mafdet gave a monumental sacrifice to Re, begging him to give her magic to fight the greedy Uraeli so she could save her pharaoh from dishonor and shame. Re, unhappy with the pharaoh's lack of interest in his land or people, answered Mafdet's prayer."

She paused theatrically, her head bent over the scroll.

"At the Ceremony of the Sun, Mafdet shared her passion with the pharaoh, and in time, she bore nine children. Re promised that each of them would be gifted with nine lives, so long as they swore to protect the Egyptian bloodline of the pharaoh, who carried the Blood of Ra, as did all the early kings of Egypt. Re decreed that only those males with the Blood of Ra could impregnate a Felidia female and create a shifter. Mafdet did her duty with pride, and once again, Egypt flourished."

Zelda took a quick sip of Josh's Coke. "A thousand years went by, and the Uraeli fostered a coup to put their own king on the throne. They cunningly overtook the Pharaoh and his family, killing all but three. Mafdet and her army, taken by surprise, brutally fought to the brink of death and hid the three survivors among the Egyptian people. Sorely wounded, she called together the remnants of her army, reminding them of their oath to Re. She stoked the flames of their fury so they would never forget their hatred of the Uraeli."

Taking a deep breath, Zelda continued, "That night, as

Mafdet warred the fever raging through her, an evil Black Cobra slithered into her room, attempting to suck the life force from her body and infect hers with his poison. Mafdet is the only cat-shifter to survive the poisonous snake venom and she killed him, slashing his neck with her claws."

I was on my knees, leaning in to hear, even though I knew what happened next.

"Less than twenty warriors remained, and they gathered around Mafdet's side as her life force ebbed. Mafdet bargained with Re to spare her eternal death, which would surely land her in Duat instead of the heavenly Field of Reeds, until there came a time when her death would serve the purpose she'd been created for. Her last breath in exchange for that of a pharaoh's. Re agreed, giving Mafdet enough time on earth to appoint Bastet, a maternal and peaceful Felidia warrior, to joint rule with Sekhmet, who feared nothing in the defense of justice, before seeking her resting place. The Bazmeht and the Council of Nine were charged with serving the Blood of Egypt, first and foremost, and then to tend Mafdet's underground crypt as the ancient mother's ka waits in limbo to reunite with her body. When the time comes, the key will be found and she will save us all."

Lorelei and I exhaled twin sighs of delight.

"I forgot how lovely that is," my mentor said.

"There's a post script from Bastet. She writes that Sekhmet located an addendum to the myth in a museum in Spain." Zelda narrowed her eyes. "Spain? Hmm. They think it could be a clue regarding the key to the crypt."

I couldn't even look at Lorelei, but I wished we could mind link so we could have the conversation I so desperately needed to have. I discreetly sent her a text.

*OMG. Do you believe it? The key to the crypt is real?*

Lorelei didn't move. She didn't blink. *She didn't have her cell phone.*

Zelda shrugged delicately. "You both are welcome to search the cat memorabilia in the library – there might be something there. I haven't read those books since I was a girl." She set the scroll on the coffee table.

I was so excited, so pumped by the idea that in my lifetime I might discover the mystery of the crypt that I could barely sit still. I chewed my lower lip, wondering if the Bazmeht council would welcome me back with open arms if I found a clue to resurrect the ancient Mother.

Lorelei, oddly silent, sent me a searching look that I couldn't decipher. Josh spoiled the mood in the room. Standing, his expressive face annoyed, he said, "This is a load of Grade A bullshit, Mom. No wonder you ran away."

# CHAPTER SIXTEEN

## FOUR HEADS OF HORUS

Deflated, I excused myself and walked to my room. Like his mother, Josh preferred not to face what was right in front of him. Would he too suffer through life until he finally acknowledged the truth?

*Goddess grant me strength.* Less than forty days, and I was out of here anyway.

Opening the door, the first thing I noticed was the box in the middle of the bed. I didn't remember having anything so big that it needed a computer box. It was a sad truth that most my clothes fit in my carry on, and I had my laptop in my bag.

Curious, I took the nail file off the small vanity table and slit through the tape. A sandalwood scented note from Sekhmet greeted me immediately. Longing for home, I clutched it to my chest and sat on the edge of the bed to read it.

"A Bazmeht Guard does her duty without regard to personal sacrifice. I've sent your sarcophagus, in the event you need to find strength without the backbone of the Bazmeht to hold you steady. There is no shame in weakness, so long as you fight through it. Keket sends her regards, Sekhmet."

Keket sent her regards? I found that difficult to believe. I stood, remembering that I'd just asked the Goddess for strength, and here Sekhmet had sent me the root of my power.

No warm, tender feelings, just fact. And the sarcophagus that I'd created with my own two hands. While I awaited rebirth, it was home to my Ka, as my shadow spirit wandered the cosmos.

Sekhmet had wrapped the ceremonial coffin in enough bubble wrap to protect bone china during an earthquake. I pulled it from the box, my fingers trembling slightly at what the casket represented.

Nine lives, if the Bazmeht warrior proved worthy.

Canopic jars of limestone and ivory, filled with desert sand, mud from the Nile, fur from my first change. One jar remained empty for my ashes. Instead of the traditional Four Sons of Horus heads the jackal, the baboon, the human, and the falcon - my jars had a cheetah, a lion, a panther, and a lynx.

According to legend, my entire body had the ability to change into one of these felines. Not just my head, hands and tail, but the whole thing. I'd never seen it happen, although Bastet said it was true. Sekhmet swore Mafdet and her warriors had once eaten an entire army while in lion and panther form.

I shivered, staring at my hands. Earlier today, while fighting the Asian waiter, I'd felt my fingers elongate and grow, and my claws started to spring free. I'd had to struggle internally to stop the change from happening right there in the street.

The idea that I couldn't control my power, something that I'd been trained to do since I'd hit puberty, terrified me. I couldn't help but wonder if the snake bite that should have killed me had somehow –

*Goddess's spear.* I sank to the floor, landing with a *thud* on the cushy rug as the line in the Myth of Mafdet came back to me, as if someone was saying it directly into my ear.

"Mafdet survived snake venom..."

I stared at my coffin, decorated with hieroglyphics, ankhs, and battle scenes. What did the fact that I'd survived, like the Ancient Mother, mean? Had Bastet sent the myth to jolt my memory that I was not the only Felidia to survive a bite? Such news guaranteed the council's hate. How dare I have anything in common with the Greatest Warrior of All Time? My unintentional audacity could prompt them to demand my death.

Rationally, I realized that the reason I probably hadn't remembered the line before now was because *before* I'd been bitten, it hadn't seemed overly important. It was common knowledge that a snake bite killed a Felidia, Bazmeht Bodyguard or not.

Warned as children to stay inside the pyramid gates, to stay away from the desert dunes and rubble from broken statues, away from deadly snakes.

Before I could change my mind, I texted Bastet.

*Is it true that nobody since Mafdet has survived a snake bite?*

I stared at my phone, waiting for her to answer. After five minutes of holding my breath and staring at the wallpaper, I realized I was just making myself crazy.

I finished unpacking my box.

My sarcophagus told the story of how, from the beginning of time, real cats were mummified and buried – some had their own tombs, some shared with their owners. I traced the hieroglyphic of Mafdet that I'd put in the lower corner. For the Felidia, cat coffins are ceremonial, until our last death, when we get cremated and our ashes placed in the last canopic jar. No evidence of our Re-given powers can remain for scientists to examine. We take great care to protect what we are.

I judged my casket to be about as wide as a small kite, and a little deeper than a shoebox. The best place to store it would be beneath the bed. And hope that Maria wasn't *too* dedicated of a maid. Carefully opening the lid, I looked at some of the treasures inside. Lapis lazuli, turquoise, my first peridot necklace. I picked up the bronze ring in the shape of a cat and slipped it on my pinky finger. The tail wrapped around my finger twice, and I recalled exactly when I'd found it.

I'd been about ten and knee deep in the mint garden, pulling weeds for Bastet and Sekhmet. It had been so hot that day. I'd sat down to rest a minute, annoyed when I'd landed on something hard. Figuring it was just a rock, I was thrilled to find the dirt-encrusted ring. *Treasure.*

Laughing, I remember thinking that I'd found the equivalent of an afternoon off from chores, but Bastet had surprised me by telling me to cherish the ring, as it was a gift from the Ancient Mother. And to get back to my duties.

The memory warmed me. There are so many things I can't do, like mind link. But I hear better than any other guard, and the Goddess sent me a ring. I'd survived the poisonous bite of a snake, but then been banished by the Council of Nine. No wonder I'm confused.

My phone bleeped and I jumped to snatch it from the bed where I'd left it.

Bastet. *It is true. You are special. Just as the oracle predicted. You will be a great warrior and lead the Bazmeht into a new millennia. Have you had any problems?*

*Problems?* They weighed me down, yet Bastet thinks I'll be a great warrior, even though I got killed on my first assignment. I'm attracted to my off-limits client. Threatened by the Uraeli.

I calmed down and rubbed the spot behind my ear.

Just the facts.

*Well. There was this waiter.*

*Cadee already called me. Why didn't you?*

Shocked, I took a second to form my answer before sending it. *I was listening to Zelda have a nervous breakdown. You never told me about Josh's kidnapping as a baby. I think we need to work on our communication.*

Her answer was immediate. *He was two, I told you that. Besides, you are on a need to know basis.*

Silly me, I thought I should know everything!

I wondered how much I could get away with via text. If I were in front of her, that answer would be the end of discussion. But here, safely out of the range of her disapproval, and on my own in a situation that kept getting trickier, I might push farther. With one eye closed I texted, *I need to know more.*

She didn't answer me back.

Guilt washed through me. The demi-goddesses love me, which is why they provoke such reactions. I feared their disapproval more than a write up. How could I ever be the greatest Bazmeht if I kept getting into trouble? Maternal Bastet probably told *all* of her guards that we were special.

I heard a quick tap on my door, then Lorelei rushed in. "Did you get – oh, yes, Sekhmet sent mine too. Normally, she only sends them when the mission will be a long one, full of danger."

My unease returned with all the subtlety of a water buffalo splashing across the Nile.

"Sorry." She put her hand on my arm, sending calming thoughts. "I should have worded that differently."

"No. I'm a warrior. I can take it. Forty days isn't that long for a mission, is it?"

Lorelei shook her head.

"Which means," I put my hand over my stomach, "that we must be in more danger than we thought. Cadee, the driver Bastet hired for us, called in, to report to Bastet what happened this morning. Before I could."

"Oooh. Well." She walked over to the window overlooking the courtyard below.

"Is it normal to have someone watching every move you make? Or is it because they really don't trust me? Are they expecting me to turn into a snake? Just tell me, Lorelei, if that's the truth."

Lorelei's laugh wasn't as comforting as usual. "No, Shani. They don't expect you to turn into a snake."

"I hope not, I couldn't take it." I paced the room. "Did you hear the line in the Myth of Mafdet? The one where SHE is the only cat shifter who ever survived a snake bite? She could heal people who'd been bitten?" My pulse leaped erratically.

"I heard, and I'd completely forgotten about that before now. It made me wonder..."

"Wonder what? I'm a monster. I almost morphed today in the middle of the street. There was a part of me that knew the waiter was Uraeli, without *me* knowing it." I stopped, on the verge of screaming with frustration.

"You aren't a monster. Sekhmet said the bite was not responsible for your death because you were already dying of the knife wound. Josh pulled the ninja off you before very much poison got into your system. You are lucky, Shani. Blessed by the Goddess. It's obvious that Mother Mafdet wants you to be Bazmeht." She shrugged. "Don't over-think it. Listen to your gut."

I thought about what she said, however, I also remembered the sharp sting of the snake's fangs enter my sensitive skin, the poison coursing through my veins, burning the entire way.

But I wouldn't argue with Sekhmet's not-quite-true explanation, not if it allowed the rest of the Bazmeht to accept me back into the fold. "Thank the Goddess, then, for that."

Lorelei patted my hand. "I'm curious as to why Bastet sent the scroll to Zelda. If she wanted us to know that Sekhmet believes there is more to the myth, then she should have sent the information directly to us."

"Maybe she wanted Josh to hear it from his mom. He hasn't heard the history before, and if he's going to be brought into the Bazmeht circle, he needs to know."

"I'm not sure he should be brought in."

My ears perked. "Why not?"

"He's not pure Egyptian, for one thing. Don't tell me you've forgotten the oath? To protect the true Blood of Ra? When was the last time you saw a blond Pharaoh?" She laughed, and I joined her, hiding my disappointment.

There was no denying that Josh was only *half* Egyptian. "Well, he claims an interest in Egyptology, so maybe our half is winning."

"Hmm. Perhaps he just picked something that he thought would make Zelda mad. Those two have an odd relationship." She looked at the sarcophagus. "I wonder if the danger Sekhmet senses toward us comes from Zelda? She seemed awfully mysterious about why she left Egypt in the first place, over twenty years ago. Sekhmet doesn't help anyone without a purpose."

Lorelei's observation surprised me, but I had to admit it held truth. Sekhmet had the heart of a single-minded warrior. I wanted to be just like her.

"And what happened to Josh for the week he was kidnapped?" She walked the square of my room, her brow furrowed as she tapped her lower lip. "Why was he found in Kansas? He was two, which is how old our children were when the Uraeli attacked."

"What are you talking about?" The hair on the nape of my neck rose to attention.

"Fifteen years ago, the Uraeli were trying desperately to get one of our children. They got four before we figured out what was going on."

"What do you mean?" I spoke slowly, making sure that I understood what she was saying. "They got four."

Lorelei stared at me, her brown eyes hard. "I always thought it was a mistake, not talking about it...four of our children died, bitten by the Uraeli."

*The children of Bubastis.* "What did Bastet and Sekhmet do?" My chest tightened and it hurt to breathe.

"Bastet cried, sent prayers to the Mother Goddess, and Sekhmet went on a rampage, wiping out any Uraeli within a hundred miles. The rules got tougher, and we realized we couldn't be so...relaxed, even within the Bubastis compound."

I felt sick. "I thought the stories about snakes outside the gates were meant to scare us into good behavior. Four kids died? Whose?"

She lifted a shoulder. "It doesn't matter."

Children were so special. It mattered. "It might explain why the council is so angry I survived a Uraeli attack."

Lorelei sighed. "Maybe. You might be right. Tefnut is one of the women who lost a child. You know how hard it is to be chosen to carry a baby, and she was certainly bitter over the loss."

She hated me and always had. "Who were the others? Felidia children as well as Bazmeht?"

"Two of them were Felidia, a boy and a girl."

My belly cramped, and I suddenly had a very bad feeling. "Who was the fourth child?"

Lorelei wouldn't look at me.

"Tell me." I clenched my fists.

"She was *my* child, Shani. And the Uraeli bastards killed her."

"Goddess have mercy! Lorelei, I am so sorry. How? Why didn't you ever mention it?" The inverted pyramid at Bubastis has a huge underground network, and the only time we'd been allowed to play above ground was with intense supervision or on the training grounds.

"I've often wanted to know that myself. But your mother was on guard, and she says she doesn't remember."

My stomach knotted. *No.*

I guess that would explain why the two women were no longer friends. Not remembering what happened when your friend's precious child died on your watch would certainly put a wet blanket on the friendship.

"It was right after that Sekhmet started sending Sharifa around the world. I've always wondered if it was some kind of punishment."

Lorelei fists clenched so hard on the windowsill that it cracked the wood. "No offense meant to you, Shani, but if that is the truth? The punishment wasn't nearly harsh enough."

# CHAPTER SEVENTEEN

## IN SEARCH OF ANSWERS

Josh knocked on my door, and I hurried to answer it. Even though I was disappointed in his reaction to the Myth of Mafdet, I would have welcomed Set himself rather than try and comfort my friend.

I didn't know how. *What could I possibly say?*

Waving a bunch of printed computer pages in my face, Josh barged in and started talking so fast I wasn't sure he spoke English.

"I did a Google search on Mafdet and she's listed as the oldest feline deity, first kingdom, or even earlier – no pictures of her though, other than some fragment on a vase. She has a panther head, like that story said. But then again, some sites list her as Bastet's mother, which doesn't match what you have at all."

"Interested, in spite of the Grade A baloney?" I grabbed a sheet of paper from his hand and read the sites he'd visited. "None of these are even accredited sites! Your mom probably has more accurate information in her collection."

He took it back, finally noticing Lorelei, who was – thank the Goddess - rewrapping my stuff in bubble wrap to hide it from Josh. "Hey," he said with a rushed smile. "Didn't see you there."

She laughed, tucking the last item into the box and closing the top. "You seem very excited about what you found. Are you willing to believe?"

"No. I'm not that gullible. But I'll give you guys credit, there's just enough truth in your story to make it plausible. Except for the cat shape shifting, claw killing, snakes parts."

I cleared my throat, unable to look at Lorelei for fear of laughing. "So, what about the fact your mom *admitted* your family has been entwined with the Bazmeht? That traditionally, our families are bound, and they have been for thousands of years."

"I'll totally believe that we've been holding onto the cat

stuff. That's cool. But to think there's been a family that has been guarding us and protecting this Blood of Ra thing? That's beyond ridiculous. From what I got out of that old story, my genetic specialty has more to do with," he turned a painful shade of red, "my fathering other kids like me. For what reason? To perpetuate the myth?"

I bit the inside of my cheek to keep from cracking a smile. "Calm down. It isn't that bad."

"You don't know." Josh jerked his chin at me. "What's in *your* DNA?"

I blinked, surprised.

"That makes you 'special'. God this is ridiculous." He self-consciously swiped at his hair.

"You mentioned that." What was I supposed to do here? I almost handed him my phone and told him to call Bastet. Even better, Sekhmet – she wouldn't worry about his tender feelings, she'd give it to him straight.

Lorelei stepped in to save me from myself. "Well, we have superior strength, speed, reflexes, sight, and hearing. We are genetically bred to be bodyguards."

Josh's jaw dropped a little. "I was just kidding. You're kidding, right?"

My mentor, who I vowed to emulate, pointed a finger into his chest. "No, Josh, I am not kidding. What nature hasn't granted us in the way of muscular enhancement, we work for; push-ups, sit-ups, running, weight lifting. Shooting at the range, sky diving,"

"I haven't been sky diving," I interjected before Josh wanted to know where to sign up. "But I've got 99 percent accuracy with my Glock."

Shrugging a slim shoulder, Lorelei asked, "Any questions?" She was practically daring him to show a lack of faith so she could prove him wrong.

"I'll get back to you," he answered, lowering the pages to his side.

Smart boy. He must have remembered the sleeper hold I'd done on him. And I know he saw how fast I could run, even if it was only on the treadmill.

"So. Do you want to look through the memorabilia your mother has? Or are you afraid that we might be telling the truth?" I crossed my arms over my chest.

"You have a gun. A Glock." Josh backed up two steps. "But...where is it now? I haven't seen it."

I couldn't exactly tell him I was on probation, not after Lorelei had just built us up as Super Guards. "We didn't feel this job needed it."

"Who decides that?" His brow furrowed together.

"Bastet and Sekhmet," Lorelei and I said in unison.

"Those two are in everybody's biz. Well, I don't want them in mine."

"Too late," I said. "They've been involved since before you were born."

I saw from the way his gaze narrowed that I'd said something wrong.

"True. I've met Bastet and Sekhmet. If Sekhmet helped my mom twenty years ago, or more than that...she shouldn't look like she's only thirty now."

I bit my lip. Bastet had to be at least a thousand years old, but Josh wouldn't appreciate knowing that.

"They are both older than they look," I answered truthfully. "They have excellent genes."

"Excellent plastic surgeons, you mean. And Bastet? She's hot."

"They haven't had plastic surgery!" Lorelei sounded offended by the idea.

"That's it though, what makes us special," I nodded, going with the flow. "Our 'DNA', it slows the aging process."

"You could bottle that and make a fortune."

I tossed my hands up in frustration. "Why would we do that? We keep the true nature of our organization a secret. It keeps everybody safe that way." His attitude made me angry. "You don't need to worry about what you find on the Internet. Listen to *us*, learn from us, we will tell you the truth."

He snorted. "You haven't told me the truth since we met. There is nothing that you can tell me or show me, that will make me believe in all of this ancient bloodline crap."

Annoyed, I stepped forward, and he jumped back, holding his chin to his shoulder to protect his neck. "Don't touch me."

"I don't go around knocking out my clients-" I held my hands up, even though I wanted to shake some sense into his stubborn head. I could tell he wasn't really afraid of me – fear gives off an unmistakable scent, but he was concerned. If the

Uraeli got to him, he would need to be very concerned.

"Bad for repeat business." Josh turned the knob of the bedroom door. "I don't care what's in the collection. Probably nothing. But I'm going when you are because I don't want you stealing anything."

My eyes flashed, I could feel it, and from the way Josh's face paled, he'd caught it too. "That is *insulting*. Even from you."

"Tempers, tempers," Lorelei chided. "This has been a very high-emotion day. Maybe we should wait until tomorrow to search for clues to what Sekhmet was talking about."

"I'm not waiting," I said at the same time Josh nodded. "Good idea."

He knew I wanted in that room, and he was being a jerk. Why? "The library is locked," he said.

As if that could keep me out?

Lorelei put a restraining hand on my arm. "We can wait until the morning. Things always look better after a good night's sleep."

Who was she kidding? A cat shifter might prefer to sleep fourteen hours a day, but a guard just needed three solid hours in a row to be in prime fighting form. Lorelei usually got results, so I kept my mouth shut to question her methods later.

I glared at Josh, wondering how I'd ever thought that angled chin was charming. Or that annoying lock of hair on his forehead was cute. Hormones, schmormones. I was so *over* my crush.

He wadded the papers he'd printed and threw them in the general direction of the wastebasket before leaving, slamming the door behind him.

Lorelei held a finger to her lips before I started yelling. "Shh. You can help me catalogue the cat mummies against the master sheet. Shani, you tend to be single-minded in your pursuit of something. Right now, you are focused on the memorabilia that Zelda has in the library. There might not be anything in there, and it isn't worth fighting with Josh over it."

"He accused us of wanting to steal from his family – that would be like stealing from...from ourselves."

"When people feel out of control, sometimes they want to control whatever they can. I'm sure he will be more rational in the morning."

"Rational?" My blood boiled. "Well, if he's not, I'm just

going to go and search that room anyway."

"You won't either, Shani Nebit, not after he told you not to."

"He's not the boss – Bastet and Sekhmet are!"

"His house. Calm down, now. I'm glad you'll help me. It will make the time go by much faster. The last time I saw the collection was, well, forty years ago." She smiled, rubbing her brow. "I'm looking forward to revisiting some of my favorites."

I have nothing against hard work, or cat coffins, or honoring the dead spirits of the felines who've moved on to walk eternity with Re. But the exchange with Josh left me shaking with repressed anger, and all I wanted was to challenge him to a wrestling match and solve our differences in the Bazmeht way.

No blood, no foul.

I'd lunge for his shoulders, hike a foot around his calf, and *wham*! Down he'd go before he knew what hit him. I'd straddle his chest, my knees pinning him to the floor. I'd feel the heaving of his breath, the strength of his torso beneath me, the heat of his eyes as he stared into mine...my cheeks flushed and I shook my head in disgust – what in the Goddess's name was I thinking?

There was wrestling and there was *wrestling*.

Changing into jeans and a dirt-brown t-shirt, I followed Lorelei to her room. "We don't have to dress for dinner, do we? Last night was casual. Pizza. I can always run out and get one of those. Extra sausage?" My stomach rumbled. Like the other guards on active duty, I never have to worry about being fat. My body needs more calories than the average person just because of my revved metabolism.

"You're not running anywhere." She rolled her eyes. "There is nothing the matter with cheese and bread in our rooms. We don't need a three course meal."

"But it would be nice..."

"I have peanut butter crackers in my bag."

"Now that's appetizing." I followed her into her room, struck again by the décor. Green, blue, and red plaid and the tartan over the bed made me think of Scottish caramel and black show dogs. I haven't gotten out much.

"Take it or leave it. I want to finish at least half the room before we break for dinner."

I checked my iPhone, which automatically changed to the correct time no matter what time zone we were in. "I can't believe it's six thirty. Where did the day go?"

"Playing nurse, shopping, attacking a Uraeli waiter, Myth of Mafdet, and emotional overload."

"Oh yeah." She summed it up nicely, although she'd left out the part about the Bazmeht compound being compromised and four dead Felidia children. Since one of them had been hers, I wasn't going to remind her. How would it be, to lose a child? Even my hard heart couldn't imagine the anguish.

Children were precious but especially within the Felidia community where pregnancies were so rare a happening. Males with the Blood of Ra few and far between, Felidia females not so fertile. Re's idea of population control, perhaps.

Bazmeht warriors were fortunate to be gifted one child in all their years of service to Mafdet. Depending on the span of their lives, it could be one hundred years or one thousand. Multiple births and twins seemed a blessing, though rare.

Lorelei tossed me the peanut butter crackers. "Stop pouting and eat. Where did I put that key to the room upstairs?"

Even though the house had electronic keypads, the tower room had double precautions.

She looked through the jumble on her desk. Opened one drawer and then another. "Hmm." Then she snapped her fingers and pulled the desk away from the wall. "Here it is!" Lorelei unlocked the closet-looking door and switched on the light.

Nothing happened.

"Light bulb's burned out." Shrugging, she went up a few stairs. I stayed on her heels. We can see in the light or dark, it doesn't matter. It took a moment for our eyes to adjust to semi-night vision.

Thirty-six stairs led to the top of the room, where she had to unlock another door. Lorelei and I stayed quiet, as if something about the dark unknown required silence. She stepped over the threshold and turned left. I went right. We kept our backs to the wall and searched the room.

Awe filled my soul as I took in the rows and rows of cat sarcophagi. Some the size of mine; some were smaller chests made of stone. I felt instantly connected to the past. "Breathtaking," I murmured.

"Just as I remembered it," Lorelei agreed. "When it was in

the mansion in Egypt."

"How many are there?"

"Oh, I forgot my tablet downstairs. But over a hundred. I'll be right back."

I walked past each row, using my sensitive fingertips to trail over each foot of the sarcophagi. Faded paint in blues and greens gave an old patina to a few, while others looked newly designed. I preferred the older ones with personality.

As a child, I'd made up stories for each of the coffins within the crypt that I tended. I called to each one by name, if the names were listed. If they weren't, I dubbed them *Merit*, which is Egyptian for beloved.

I learned to hide that silly romantic streak by the time I was eleven and realized that I wasn't like the other girls. I wanted to be Bazmeht, a warrior like my mother. Dreams were for girls who weren't good enough to make the team. What else did they have, poor things?

I put my shoulders back and continued circling the room, noting the temperature control panel and the clear plexi glass over the oldest of the coffins, even in this vault-like chamber. Zelda might not have wanted to believe in her heritage, but she certainly protected it well.

I sent a quick text to Sekhmet, praising Zelda's efforts.

To my surprise, she texted back right away. *Where is Josh?*

I should have let sleeping lioness' lie, I thought with a shudder. *He went to bed early. Not feeling well.*

*What's wrong? Is he ill? Does he need a food taster?*

I laughed. She showed her true age with a question like that. *He doesn't believe in Mafdet.*

*Make him believe.*

As if it were that simple. *I will try in the morning.*

*Now!*

An order. Sighing, I went downstairs and apologized to Lorelei. "You will do anything to get out of paperwork, won't you?" She trudged up the stairs, her tablet in hand.

"I would rather be with you."

"Go."

I went to Josh's room and knocked on the door.

There was no answer.

"Josh." I knocked again. "Open up the door."

"Miss Shani?"

I whirled around, my hand to the pulse beating in my throat. Maria, clad in a white, fluffy robe and pink bunny slippers, said, "Joshua went running."

"Now?" Goddess have mercy, I was the worst guard in Bazmeht history. Josh left without my knowledge, and Maria had just snuck up behind me.

Her wrinkled face held extra lines of worry as she explained, "He runs when he is upset, *pobrecito*. And tonight," she shrugged. "Very upsetting for everyone. Ms. Zelda is in bed with a compress, and I was just on my way to tell you there is soup in the refrigerator for when you grow *hambre*." She patted her tummy.

I didn't have time to think about soup. I had to get my feet on the road. "Does Josh run on the beach?" I could find the beach, no problem.

"*Si*. Are you going out?" Maria clucked her teeth. "It will be dark soon. It's dangerous for a *senorita* at night."

"I'll be fine."

I turned toward my room to grab my sneakers instead of wearing my black leather flats, and I listened as Maria shuffled away. She made plenty of noise, which meant that I had been so focused on getting Josh's attention that I hadn't been *paying* attention.

I blamed it the casual setting. Posing as Josh's cousin instead of a bodyguard messed with my codes of behavior. Wearing my black suit, I was a guard, first and foremost. This area of mine obviously needed immediate work.

Starting now, I would be a guard all of the time.

As I launched myself over the twelve-foot, wrought iron fence, I prayed I would find Josh before he ended up in trouble.

# CHAPTER EIGHTEEN

## LEARNING NEW TRICKS

*Too late.* Using my very refined preternatural hearing, I'd run two miles in three minutes until I'd picked up the sonic timber of Josh's deep voice.

I also heard the breathing of three adult males.

"I told you, I don't have any money, man. I was just out for a run." Josh didn't have the good sense to sound afraid.

Fear for him enveloped me, an odd sensation that I chose to bury rather than examine. He wasn't far away now, close to the beach road where Lorelei and I ate lunch. Where the Uraeli waiter tried to take me on.

Goddess! Please give wings to my feet run – faster than lightning, faster than sound. Faster than my fear for Josh. Leaning forward, I rejoiced in the stretch and burn of my muscles.

Feet pounding pavement, I turned the corner and there he was. Night dropped fast in Miami, but the streetlights illuminated the scene like a photograph. Dressed in baggy running shorts and a sweaty t-shirt, Josh didn't look worth robbing. Yet, three men held a knife to his throat and once again, I'd left the house without my switchblade.

It didn't matter. They surrounded him like jackals and my nose twitched. I turned on my super sensory powers and strode into the middle of battle as if armed in steel. I wanted one of the three junked up druggies to take me on – my body craved the release of adrenalin a good fight brought. I'd take all three at once.

My hair had long ago fallen out of its bun, and I brushed the waving strands off my face. "Hey." I walked into the middle of the circle with a sway of hips as old as time. *My name is Shani Nebit. I'm a Level One Bazmeht Bodyguard, highly trained to kick ass.* "Can I join the party?"

Batting my eyelashes, I kept my flashing pupils away from Josh's stunned face. I made sure that each one of the morons threatening my charge knew what he was getting into. Serious freaking hurt.

The first one launched himself at me, and within moments of punching, kicking and maiming, the three rogues groaned on the ground, begging for mercy.

I didn't want to give them mercy but I had to. It was part of the Bazmeht code.

Dialing 911 from my untraceable cell phone, I said that I'd been mugged and that the bad guys were still around. Squinting, I made out the faded address on a building a few doors down. I begged them to hurry, disconnected, and turned to give Josh a piece of my mind.

He yelled at me. *Yelled* at *me*. "What in the hell do you think you're doing?"

I pointed to the bad guys tied up with plastic bags that had littered the street. Wrists, ankles, sleeper hold. They were slumped together like the three amigos.

Josh's entire body tensed, an expression of confusion; he wasn't afraid *of* me. But *for* me.

"What was all that," he wind-milled his arms and tossed a few air punches, "you were doing? Where did you learn that, cause I sure don't think they teach that in the women's defense classes down at the Y."

"Y?" My heart, which had beat steadily throughout the fight, chose that moment to skip.

"A women's shelter – never mind. All I'm saying is that is some seriously freaky shit you do, and I don't like it."

He didn't like it? I kicked the three knives to the center of the street where the police would be sure to see them. No fingerprints. I didn't like that he'd gone out without me.

I tapped my toe, telling myself that Sekhmet would kill me if I so much as harmed one hair on his egotistical head. "Fine. We must leave before the police come."

"Oooh. So you don't have to answer any questions? Questions the cops are sure to have after getting a call from a woman who claims to have been mugged, and yet, the guys that did it are all passed out in a heap of blood and broken bones."

Sirens that Josh couldn't hear yet sounded from a mile away. "Can we talk about this as we walk? Are you hurt? I understand if you are so overwhelmed with gratitude that you can't thank me right now. I can wait." I strode toward the street, turning my back on him.

He jogged to keep up with me. "I want to finish my run."

"Your ankle?"

"Totally fine. I always heal fast."

I wanted to run circles around him, Goddess help me, but it was the truth. I wanted his regard, his respect. His admiration. And there was a horrible part of me that wanted him to know I was holding back. "A slow jog," I agreed, rolling my shoulders. "What were you thinking, leaving the house without telling me? How am I supposed to guard you if you act as sneaky as a ...a *snake?*"

"I had the situation completely under control, before you barged in acting like some mythological Amazon."

My cheeks burned in the breezy night air. "I could tell. They were just showing you their knives to be kind?" The idea of Josh bleeding or – I rubbed the spot on my chest where the ninja had knifed me – dying, made my stomach churn. "Let me guess. They wanted to be friends, and I was witnessing a primal ritual where you were going to join their gang."

I remembered an episode – I forgot the name of the show – where some guy had to kill a random stranger to get into the gang he wanted.

"Those weren't gangsters," Josh snorted, his lip curled. "They were doped up, strung out, I could have taken the knives away any time I'd wanted to."

"Really?" I reached out and snagged his iPod, nowhere near as wonderful as my iPhone, and dangled it out of his reach.

"Hey!" Josh lunged for it, but I kept it out of the way as I danced backward. "Give that back!"

The next thing I knew, I was running as if the hounds of hell were on my heels, Josh's iPod clutched in my fist. The slap of my soles against the cement echoed perfectly as he kept the pace.

I ran a little faster – and so did he. My heart actually accelerated, and I risked a glance over my shoulder. Josh grinned and waved, not even out of breath.

So I added more steam. The beach road was in sight, and I told myself that I'd stop at the street and give Josh a chance to save face.

The jerk passed me.

I forgot everything I'd ever been taught about not giving ordinary people a chance to see that I am more than a young woman in a bland suit.

With a startled laugh, I ran. He went toward the sandy beach, which was hard to run on until we hit the wet stuff where the waves lapped up and back again. I crunched shells beneath my feet and breathed in salt water. The moon, low in the newly dark night, shone with muted comfort in the distance. The sound of my heart beating in tandem with Josh's as we sprinted toward the pier made me giggle like an idiot.

I'd stumbled into heaven.

Unprepared for the feelings that overwhelmed me, I sped up, determined to show him that I was faster. That I was in charge...Re must have decided to teach me a lesson in humility because I never saw the rogue wave that hit me like a wall of concrete.

I don't care for water, and it doesn't think much of me either. The wave pulled me out and into a rip current that left me with aching lungs as I fought to stay in control.

There's a chapter at the end of the Bazmeht handbook that focuses on thinking outside a tough situation. I concentrated on saying the alphabet in Russian instead of panicking at the real prospect of drowning.

Bastet might not be so forgiving if I died again so soon!

I squeezed my eyes shut in denial. My body changed and flexed as I rolled along the bottom of the ocean floor. What would happen to my Ka if a Great White Shark ate my body, bones and all?

My phone! *But wait.* Who in the Goddess's stone crypt was I going to text from here?

*Think.*

What would Lorelei do in this situation? You can't shoot a wave into submission, or, like Bastet did, love an ocean until it fell under your spell. Sekhmet, queen of all chaos and defender of justice, would wrestle a turtle and ride it bareback to shore.

My head pounded for want of air and it was harder to struggle for control. The battle wore me down.

*Mafdet.*

An image of a tall woman with a panther for a head and scorpion tails in her hair shimmered before me. She held a crude spear that she poked at me. Hard.

"Get up! What kind of warrior accepts death? For Re's sake, stop sniveling and get up!" She poked me again and instinctively, I put my feet down in the defensive bodyguard stance and touched the ocean's murky bottom. I bent my knees, pointed my hand straight upward, and pushed off with all of my might. Depleted and out of breath, I somehow managed to break the surface, spitting salt water and curses into the night.

A strong hand grabbed my arm, hauling me sputtering through the choppy waves on my back, a forearm under my neck so that my head was tucked against a bare, masculine chest.

I tried to talk, but each time I opened my mouth, I choked on more water. In my defense, I'd never taken to swimming. Not in the calm of the rivers or the chlorine-scented pools. Every guard had to be efficient – whether they liked it or not – so I managed the required laps and simple dives. I wasn't the only cat-shifter who eyed complete submersion with distaste. Boat rides were fine, and the water of the Nile was a life-giving blessing. I preferred to give thanks from the shore.

Choking, I attempted to get loose of the vise around my body, but whoever had me in their grasp was determined to save me. The minute I could touch, I dragged my feet, forcing my lifeguard to stop.

"Wait," I fought for balance on the movable sand, waves hitting the back of my calves.

"You're stubborn." Josh's voice was deep and hoarse as he croaked the observation.

"I've heard that before." My voice, salt-seared, dropped an octave or more. I barely recognized it. I stood there, trying to find a way to make everything stay still for just a moment. "How do you turn this thing off?"

"The ocean? You want me to turn off the *ocean*?" He reached out, searching my face and scalp. "How hard did you hit your head?"

"I don't know. Mafdet saved my life."

"I saved your life." Josh slid his arm around me and I realized I shivered violently.

"No. Mafdet, she poked me with her spear." My teeth chattered and clicked. Could I be in shock? "I am a lousy bodyguard."

"No you're not," Josh said, lying through his concerned smile. "I thought you'd been pulled to sea. Gone. Then suddenly your head popped up from nowhere and it was as if the moon shone right where you were. Your eyes were all gold, like headlights."

*Great.* "Told you-"

"Mafdet poked you with her spear. I heard." He led the way toward the dark shore.

"I w – wanted to win." I fell forward, hit by a curl of water. Josh held me, stopping me from going down and under again.

"You would have. I couldn't keep up that pace anymore. Brutal. I was sort of hoping you'd fall or something. Now I feel bad. If you would have...well, it would have been my bad vibes that did you in. Karma, man. I'm sorry."

Dry sand. I dropped to my knees wondering if it would be too tacky to kiss the ground. I did it anyway then wiped the sand from my face with the back of my hand, effectively smearing it over my wet cheeks.

"You're making a mess," Josh said. He picked up his shirt, wadded in a soggy ball, and patted the sand and dirt from my face. As caring as a lover.

I rolled over, sick to my stomach – which was filled with salty ocean water that tasted like old fish poop and dirt. Heaving it out helped but it worsened the embarrassment factor. Josh rubbed my back and I felt fur sprout along the back of my ear. No!

"Water," I mumbled into the sand. "Fresh water." *Go away!*

"Good idea. I'll be right back." He had to be exhausted, yet he raced down the beach toward the lights at the far end of the road. "Don't go anywhere," he shouted over his shoulder, his feet literally flying.

Funny boy, that Joshua Johnson. I edged away from where I'd spewed ocean water, and lay down on the dry sand. I faced the waves, keeping my back to the dark protection of the trees.

On my side, I stared at the mysterious waters. If not for my vision of Mafdet, I'd be dead. I should call somebody, I thought with all the life force drained from me. Who?

Lorelei.

She'd yell at me, but just maybe she wouldn't see a reason to share this little mishap with the demi goddesses. I reached for the special pocket in my bra for my phone, worried I'd ruined it beyond repair.

*It wasn't there.*

My breath came in great big gulps as I glared at the murky

ocean water that had tried to kill me without the shield of my phone. Phones allowed for constant contact; in a world that left me stranded without the ability to mind link, my phone was the great equalizer. It was gone.

*I am really, truly alone.*

The ocean seemed darker, more menacing, as the moon slid behind a smoky gray cloud. Texting allowed me to keep in touch without having to make myself emotionally vulnerable...I sent group messages, telling my mom and cyber friends that I was fine or having a great time, when instead, I was lonely and ostracized by my peers.

The gritty sand scraped my skin, and the salt stung in the cuts I'd gotten in my fight with Death. I imagined a picnic full of fire ants, and I was the cous cous salad. *Ignore the pain.*

I'd get a new phone. A better phone. This was America! I could have a phone first thing in the morning. My skin itched, and I rubbed at the inch thick growth of fur striped down my neck. It had to go away before Josh got back.

*Happy thoughts.* Kittens, balls of yarn, shooting a bullet right through the forehead of Poseidon. I calmed myself, bit by bit.

At first, I thought I heard the heavy *thump* of my overworked heart, but then realized it was Josh's heart as he ran along the sand, worried. I sat up, dizzy, focusing on body control management until my fur receded into my skin and I was me again. Wet, battered and bloody, but me.

Without my phone.

Josh ran toward me, his relief palpable. "I couldn't see you."

"I laid down." *Morphing in and out, don't mind me.*

"You have sand on your cheek." He handed me a large plastic bottle of water and a wad of paper towels. "Mints. For your stomach. Cadee called, and she's on her way to pick us up. Just had an idea we might need a ride. Didn't seem to mind the late hour, she didn't even ask questions."

I'd forgotten about our Irish limo driver – and the limo. I wanted my friend, my mentor. "Lorelei could have come."

Josh kicked at the sand. "Here's the thing. I know you've gotta be dying for a shower and some Tylenol, but I – I have some questions. It's just you and me, Shani, and you can tell me the truth. Before anyone else is around."

I sighed, hating that word. Truth. So many truths.

"You were under water for fifteen minutes. I know." He held up his rubber, waterproof watch with the green glowing numbers.

My flesh chilled. I hadn't realized that cat shifters had the ability to hold their breath so long. Bastet and Sekhmet hadn't mentioned it, but maybe they didn't know about it? Who would need to know that? We protected Egyptians in a sea of sand.

I shrugged, bathing my face with the cool, fresh water. I gargled, spit, and then took a throat-soothing swallow that made me sigh. "Thank you. A shower sounds fabulous. I don't think I'll ever get the sand out my...er...parts." I somehow ignored the discomfort my shorts were giving me in favor of pretending I had water in my ear.

"Wedgie?" Josh asked sympathetically.

I rolled my eyes, jiggling the other ear.

"I told Cadee we'd meet her on the road by the pier. Can you walk?"

"Since I was one," I snipped. "Can't we talk after I have a shower?

"I asked Cadee to drive us to the hospital. I didn't think you'd want Lorelei to know about what happened tonight, so I figured if we went with Cadee, nobody else has to know."

*Except Bastet, who Cadee told everything to.* Josh was too nice. The moon chose that instant to come out of hiding and lent its silvery sheen to Josh's blond hair. "You have a halo."

"What? Nobody, not even my mother, has ever said that before. Besides, if we don't tell anyone about you almost drowning, then we don't have to mention the druggies who wanted my tennis shoes for crack."

Ah. I understood an ulterior motive better than flat out kindness.

"The salt is drying to me. It is incredibly uncomfortable." I heard my whining and tried to stop by sounding forceful. "I won't go to the hospital. I hate doctors."

"Your head is bleeding. What if you have a concussion?"

"I never go to the hospital. Never. And I'm too hard-headed for a concussion."

He scratched his chin. "True. Never? What if you were gushing blood and needed stitches?"

"Steri-strips do just as good of a job."

"Listen, if I'm ever bleeding? Take me to the hospital. Steri-strips. I sorta thought you were going to tell me crazy glue."

"When you are done being a comedian, will you listen? I want to go to your house, take a hot shower, and go to bed."

I had some serious praying and thanks-giving to do.

"We have to talk."

"I agree." My head pounded as if there were a million little demons with hammers inside it.

"You are a very fast runner, Shani."

It hurt too much to nod. I grunted.

"But I kept up with you. Don't you think that's totally freaky? I'm super fast, but I've never run that fast in my life – I didn't know I could."

There were a lot of 'totally freaky' things going on, all right. I'd have to assimilate his running as fast as a lion later. "Josh-"

"What? Oh, shee-yit, what's – you're bleeding from your eyes. Damn, we *are* going to the hospital!"

I heard the fear in his voice and it helped banish mine. A film of red clouded my vision and my hearing grew so acute I heard the lizard's claws scratch against the trunk of a palm tree. And Cadee, she searched for us. Worried. Competent, with her flashlight and blanket.

"Cadee's coming."

"No she's not. I told you we'd meet her at the street. Sit down, Shani, before you fall down."

"No." If I sat down, I might not be able to get back up. The pounding in my head increased and it was as if my whole body wanted to convulse – and change. Goddess, help me. Forget fire ants, piranhas tore me apart fleshy bite by fleshy bite.

My wet hair covered my nape and ears, but I could feel my jawbone click as my bones tried to shift into feline form. I bit the inside of my cheek, tasting flesh, blood, and sand. The pain halted the uncontrollable urge, but I knew I couldn't look at Josh or else he'd see I was different.

My eyes, normally brown, would be glowing gold, the irises diagonal. He'd be scared to death, and since he only had one life to give, I had to keep my pupils to myself.

*Hurry Cadee.*

*I am.*

Surprised that she'd heard me, I almost squealed. Nobody ever hears me, and I certainly *never* hear them!

I wobbled from side to side.

Was the snake venom responsible for my mind opening? Or had it been watery near death experience?

*Who cares? You'll need to learn to block it, love, or else anybody will pop in and have a listen.*

She was a dot on the horizon, her flashlight a beam of hope that things might turn out well. I knew nothing about deliberately putting up a shield for my thoughts, since I'd only ever wanted to bring the barriers down. I remember searching that section of our training for clues to get past the wall but nothing worked.

I imagined building a new wall to keep unwanted visitors out. Blood dripped from my eyes and nose to puddle in the sand at my feet.

"You are scaring the hell out of me," Josh whispered against my hair.

When had he cuddled me close? Why was it so cold?

I couldn't feel the weight of his arm over my shoulders, although I saw that he had it there. My bare feet...my bare feet? I'd lost my shoes to the ocean wench.

I should push him away, but I was as powerless as a kitten. It didn't feel like I was dying – and I knew the difference. Desperately ill, I called out for Bastet and Lorelei, but doubted they heard.

Josh rocked me back and forth, as if I were a child in need of comfort. The motion made me nauseas, but the ability to speak out loud had disappeared. I could barely concentrate on keeping my head down and my hair over my ears.

I tore the wall in my mind down, mud brick by mud brick.

*Cadee.*

*Yes?*

*You can't take me to the hospital... cover my face and head with the blanket you have and take me straight to Lorelei. Have I your promise?*

There was a scary silence but she agreed, her lilting tones hesitant. *Sure. You're a strange one. But the Bazmeht pay well, so I'll do as you say.*

*Josh can't see my face.*

*All right, love.*

Like a switch flipped, my mind went black at the same time my knees gave out. I heard Josh calling my name, then even that disappeared into the dark.

## ANOTHER DAY, ANOTHER DRAMA

My mind jumbled, chaos, although there was a lingering image of Josh leaning over me. He'd seen me die twice – only last night, I hadn't died. Had I?

"Thank the Goddess...how do you feel, Shani?" Lorelei's grip on my palm crushed the fine bones of my hand, but I didn't complain. Her worry settled across her face, though she normally mastered her emotions.

"Raw," I croaked, my lips cracked and stinging.

Lorelei released my hand and brought an aloe-scented sponge to my mouth. "I've been out of my mind. And before you scream that you were violated, it was only me trying to break into that brain of yours to find out what happened. As usual, I got nothing."

"Is that why I can't think a straight thought?" The red ball of my childhood bounced around my head like a frog. A rabbit? Mmm. My stomach rumbled.

"I heard that, I'll run to the kitchen in a minute. Nobody made any sense last night, and Cadee is worth ten times her skinny weight in jewels and gold. Josh wouldn't let go of you, but she made sure your head was covered and your eyes. You were bloody and half changed! Did Josh see that? How would you know? You were out like - well, I thought you might be dead. Yes, dead."

Tears fell down her cheeks and my eyes watered, filming with red.

"Stop that. I just got your face cleaned, no crying until we figure out what in Re's name happened to you." She dabbed gently at the corners of my eyes with a fine cotton handkerchief. "I have to call the demi-goddesses now that you are awake. Bastet wanted to come immediately, but Sekhmet said that she felt you would be all right. I was beside myself, Shani, just sick." She put her knuckles to her mouth. "I almost called your mother."

"No." My pulse skipped.

"Shh. I didn't. But only because – what would I say? Sekhmet counseled patience, so I prayed. All night, in between aloe vera sponge baths. Maria brought me two plants worth, and I used them both."

My head hurt. A combination of Lorelei's uninvited probing and drowning and bleeding profusely. "The bleeding's stopped, yes?"

"Yes. Cadee kept her eyes averted and helped me as much as I could let her. Once you stopped shifting, then Maria and even Zelda helped. Josh has been furiously pacing the hall, but, shifting aside, you are naked as the day you were born, and modesty called for privacy."

Thank the goddess for that! I looked down, noticing that even the fine silk sheet that covered me felt heavy on my tender flesh.

"Salt water is an exfoliant. I've been thinking and thinking, it has to be that our skin is so sensitive already that the salt water acted as acid or something." She tucked a strand of hair behind her ear. "I don't know, but it's the best conjecture I've got."

"Thank you, Lorelei, for sitting with me. You look exhausted."

"I tried to absorb as much of your pain as I could, but you are stubborn, even passed out like a drunken reveler after a party on Bastet's barge."

"It isn't nice to call your grateful patient names." Why had Cadee been able to read me, and not Lorelei, who I trusted with my heart, soul and life?

She slumped forward, bent at the waist, and rested her forehead on my mattress. "If you only knew the language I used last night..."

"Lorelei," I said with an uncomfortable laugh.

"I love you, like the daughter I never got to raise. There wasn't an opportunity for a son."

Without thinking, I touched her hand. "I'm sorry." In our culture, a girl stays with the Bazmeht mother, but a boy lived in the world, away from the Bazmeht, once he turned seven. The mother would see him, of course, but the inverted pyramid of the Bazmeht was for women – the demi-goddesses, the handmaidens, and the warriors.

She smiled tightly. "I longed for children, but the Goddess

will give what she does and no more." She smoothed the sheet at my side. "And then take it away...I loved being a mother, even for such a short period of time. With my daughter dead, there was no one to follow in my footsteps. With Sharifa gone so much of the time, you were a daughter without a mother and just what my sore heart needed. I hope you don't mind that I took such an interest in your well being."

I sat up, ignoring the pain in every inch of my body. "Mind? It was always my secret wish that you were my mother, in truth." My heart swelled and banged against my chest. I was surprised she couldn't hear it. "I love you too."

"I thought that we would be able to mind link, the two of us. But it's not important. What *is* important is that you are alive and on the way to well."

*A mother.* Someone who sat by my side, nursing me through some strange attack on my skin. But as I looked at Lorelei's light brown hair and beautiful smile, my mother's auburn waves and assessing gaze came to mind.

I pushed the image away, blaming my confusion on the pain. "Thank the Goddess that we heal fast. I'm ready to get up, check on Josh – he was so nice last night. I don't want him to worry more than he already has."

"Oh?" Lorelei stood, her brow arched. "I thought you'd want to stay in bed all day. Watch television or read. You know?" She tapped her lower lip in thought. "Josh never said why you two had gone out last night."

"Get that look off your face, Lorelei." I took a sip of water from the glass by my bed. "Josh went out for a run, and I joined him." Somehow, I managed to remember his wish to keep his near stabbing quiet. "I want to tell him thank you too."

"Well. We can get you in a robe and untangle your hair. You really need to brush the sand from your teeth." Lorelei moved in short, efficient bursts around my room. "And keep the ankh beneath your pillow. It promotes healing of the mind." She walked to the window and opened the shades a fraction of an inch. "Does the light hurt your eyes?"

I carefully shook my head no.

"You're lying."

"Yes. But I need the sun."

Laughing, Lorelei opened the blinds all of the way. "There you are. Want your sunglasses?" She walked to my vanity top as sunlight flashed over crystallized bling.

"Is that – my phone?" My adrenalin sped up to a charge and I pushed the sheet back.

"Yes it is and lay back down." Lorelei took my robe from the hook on the bathroom door and tossed it to me. "Cadee says she found it in the sand last night. You must have dropped it during your run."

I didn't care. I slipped my arms into the sleeves of the soft cotton robe that had been a gift from Lorelei. "Let me see it?"

No matter how many flaws in my character this phone, sand-encrusted and missing a few charms, pointed out, I couldn't have been happier.

The mom-moment with Lorelei had been nice, but this – I clutched it to my cheek, not caring that the screen was black and cracked or that most of the crystals were gone. This was therapy. Maybe the battery was dead. I started to take the back off, but Lorelei smacked her forehead and snatched it from my hand.

"I forgot to charge it for you. Let me plug it in. And hey, if you're feeling spry enough to jump from the bed, then you need to call in to the goddesses. You know that Bastet has probably yelled at poor Dendera all night long and worn a new path in the granite stone, pacing and praying for you."

I lay back down, tucking the sheet around my waist. "I'm *exhausted*."

Lorelei tucked my phone into her pocket with an evil chuckle. "That's what I thought. I'll run to the kitchen and get you some food, then go to my room and call in for you – how's that?"

"My thanks, Lorelei."

She blew me a kiss and left me to my thoughts. Which remained a mess, no matter how tidy I tried to make them. I forgave Lorelei's intrusion, though, certain I'd have done the same thing if our situations had been reversed. Reading another person's thoughts without their permission was *huge* on the 'do not' list. I couldn't remember the exact number of the infraction. At the moment, I didn't care.

A knock sounded at the door – three taps, then two longer ones, and I grinned. Josh slipped inside, as furtive as a cat trapping the canary.

He looked me over from head to toe. "You look terrible."

The comment stung. "It's all your fault."

"Mine?"

Pleating the sheet at my waist, I nodded. "Yes. Yours. If I hadn't had to save you from those druggies last night, after you ran out without your guard – me – then..."

"You didn't tell my mom that, did you?"

"Who knows what I said in my delirium?"

"Your hair is sticking up on one side and you have reddish brown stuff on you. Ew," he peered closer at me. "Is that blood? Nasty."

I now felt as attractive as molded cheese. The green furry kind. "If you can't be nice, you have to leave."

"That's cool." He sat down across the room, probably so he didn't have to see me up close and personal. "How do you feel?"

"Now that you've shredded my appearance? Fabulous. Thank you for asking."

"We're pals, Shani. I don't care what you look like."

Romance seemed as impossible as – as – it wasn't important. Wishing I'd taken the time to brush my teeth wouldn't make it so. "I'm not sure what to say to that." Pals? It felt like getting third place in an archery contest. Last night, his worry for me had been intense. Obviously, he was over it. Well. *I am a professional.* "I could have beaten you last night."

Mortified, I couldn't believe that those words fell from my mouth. Professional? How could a Bazmeht with the mentality of a toddler be professional?

"Ha!" His expression smug, he added, "I knew you'd still be fuming about that this morning. Fact is, I was winning."

"And then I got sucked out to sea – hardly a fair race." I folded my arms over my chest. Yes, a three-year old.

Josh's blue eyes narrowed and all traces of teasing disappeared. "Exactly. So what in the hell was that about?"

"What?" I shrugged.

"Fifteen minutes you were under. Then you started spouting more blood than a George Romero movie. Your eyes did this weird flickering that scared me to death, and you know what was freakiest of all that? It felt like déjà vu."

He pinned me with those eyes of his, and I instinctively shielded my thoughts. Could he read me? Did he even realize what he was trying to do? *He'd had a flashback to the first night he'd tried to protect me.*

I just couldn't be a professional with scrungie teeth and bed-head. And for whatever reason, I was acutely aware of the fact that while Josh was fully clothed in clean jeans and a t-shirt, I was practically naked.

My stomach tensed, and I cleared my throat as heat traveled from my toes to my scalp. "You're right. We need to talk. I just need five – fifteen – minutes to shower." And shave my legs.

When had I turned into such a *girl?* "We can meet in the library. Kill two birds with one stone, as the saying goes."

"What is it with you and killing stuff?"

"I am not even going to smile at that stupid attempt at humor. Now go, or you are going to get another eyeful of my unkempt self and you'll be scarred for life."

"Not so fast. For the record, I totally didn't need your help last night."

I sighed. "You didn't need my help against the bad guys, and you were going to win the race on the beach. Fine. Your ego is safe with me."

His sigh was both deeper and louder than mine had been, yet he wore a crafty expression that I mistrusted immediately. "Well, you can make it up to me by teaching me how to do that pinch thing."

Ah...the real reason he was in my room and annoying me. "You want me to teach you how to do the sleeper hold so you can go out and defend yourself against druggies in the middle of the night. Do I look like an idiot?" I held up one hand. "Don't answer that."

"I saved you. You owe me."

"I don't owe you anything." Mafdet saved me, I was certain of it. But what could giving Josh a form of self-defense hurt? It wasn't like the sleeper hold was an ancient Bazmeht secret. "You have to promise that you won't use it as a parlor trick."

"Parlor trick? Oh – *party* trick. As in toppling the quarterback after he beer bongs a six-pack and before he takes home the hottest cheerleader on the squad so that I have a chance? 'K. I promise."

"Give me fifteen minutes." Josh. Cheerleaders and parties with beer bongs – not that I knew what that was. No wonder he wanted to be just 'pals' with me. Feeling sorry for myself, I tossed the silk sheet back, grateful that my robe covered all of my parts to my knees.

Josh ruined a perfectly good pity party when I caught him staring at my bare feet, then my calves. His gaze stopped at the hem of my robe. His voice was husky as he said, "Shani – I happen to dig girls who look like they've kicked ass and taken names." He left with a wink that knocked my pulse into overdrive. "See you in the library."

Tugging at my hem, I decided that there was something to say about a guy who knows how to make an exit.

# CHAPTER TWENTY

## IN THE LIBRARY WITH THE LIPSTICK

Before showering, I checked myself in the full-length mirror. My body is leanly muscled and my skin, minus fuzz, has a golden tone. Being tan was never a high priority – who had time to worry about things like that? I recalled Natalie splashing with some of the handmaidens in the fountains during a hot summer day. Laughing and having fun, while I did another hundred squats.

My fast rise through the ranks had been worth it. Frowning, I reminded myself that focus and hard work would get me out of this mission with my pride in place. No flirting, no remembering how wonderful Josh's chest had felt beneath my cheek.

*None of that!*

I turned, noting the scrapes on the back of my thighs and spine from where I'd bounced along the ocean's floor. Fifteen minutes. I'd have to ask the demi-goddesses about being able to spend so much time without air. I showered off the film of dried aloe paste, letting the refreshing clear water clean my pores and hydrate my thirsty skin from the outside.

As I shampooed small shells from my hair, I gave thanks again to Mafdet for her spear to my side. I had no doubt that the ancient mother had looked out for me last night.

I applied chamomile and carnation lotion to my skin, sealing in the moisture. Keeping my make-up minimal and scraping my hair back into a no fuss bun, helped me arrive three minutes early to the library.

Call it cheating, but I knew Josh waited for me. His unique scent of sunshine and salt was now imprinted on my sensory glands.

I wore my Bazmeht Guard uniform – including the jacket – as a reminder to my awakening libido that Josh was off limits. I'd skipped my sunglasses, because even I had to admit that wearing them inside seemed over the top.

Inhaling, tossing my shoulders back into procedural posture, I strode inside the library like a Roman soldier.

If I was the soldier, then Josh was the furious Caesar, shrouded in betrayal.

I looked around the room, noting the high wood shelves alongside two walls filled with books. Another wall housed antiques. My eye zoomed in on a lone canopic jar of limestone, topped with a faded gold cat head. Where were the other three jars? It was bad karma to separate them.

The fourth wall was mostly glass, something filtered to keep out the UV rays for protection of the treasures inside the room, while allowing natural light.

Piles of books and opened scrolls lay scattered over the floor. I looked closer, thinking someone had been interrupted while reading.

"What is the matter?" I asked in a neutral tone, hoping to keep emotion out of the equation. Josh was so angry I wouldn't have been surprised if steam came from his ears.

"What's the matter? *What is the matter?* Don't you see this mess?"

Clutter, certainly, but mess? "Perhaps your mother was reading?"

"My mother would never spill anything and leave it to sop into the carpet-" he pointed to an area behind a chair, that in my defense, I couldn't see. Hands loose at my sides, I walked around and saw the glass.

"Would you like me to get a towel?"

He glared at me. "Where is Lorelei?"

"She went to her room to make some phone calls."

"I bet she did."

"What is the problem here?" Chills landed at the base of my spine as I realized where Josh was going in his line of questioning.

"Note the lipstick on the glass?" Josh shoved it with his toe so it rolled to my boot.

It was hard to miss Lorelei's hot shade of Flamingo Pink by Jet. "Maybe she was reading, got sick, and had to..." I couldn't think of a good excuse for my mentor to rush out of the library – when she wasn't supposed to be in it in the first place. "Puke."

"I would buy that lame excuse, except there's a page torn out of this book." He picked up an old, leather-bound tome and shook it at me. "It isn't the only book destroyed in this room. The problem is, I don't know enough about what was in here to say what was taken or why."

Didn't take a Master's Degree to answer that question, I thought with a very bad feeling. I wished I had my phone, so I could text Lorelei a warning. But since she had it, it was as much wishful thinking as mind linking.

When would Lorelei have had time to break into the normally locked library, drink water, ruin antique books, and leave a mess as if interrupted? "I don't believe what I'm seeing."

"So now you're calling me a liar?" Josh raked back his messy blond hair.

"Of course not!" Exasperated, I closed my eyes, searching for my center – the place I go so I can open all of my senses completely. I needed to find a smell or a visual clue that I might have overlooked when walking in.

"What are you doing?"

"Working." I kept my eyes closed, concentrating on retracing each of my steps.

"Napping." Josh snorted.

"Shh."

Finding my center required blocking annoying pests, like someone talking to you about a lawsuit.

I dove deeper into my subconscious. I'd noted the windows, the books, Josh's face, the chair, the spread of books across the floor – someone had definitely been searching for something. If pages were missing, they must have found it.

I inhaled slowly, breaking apart each individual scent as it reached my nose. Leather – old bindings. New leather – a familiar smell, one that nagged at my memory.

Lorelei's lipstick on the tipped over glass. A deliberate clue, pointing at Lorelei. "Where's Maria?" I shook myself to full awareness.

"You're kidding me."

"No."

"Why would she destroy our property? That doesn't make sense!"

"You are the one that said she didn't like the 'dead kitties' and she heard the Myth of Mafdet. What if she's trying to protect you and your mom from something she thinks might be bad?"

"It *is* bad." Josh scowled at me, blame on his face.

"*I* didn't do it."

"Lorelei did – the evidence is right there, and you are covering for her."

"Set up. Too easy." Had the Uraeli set it up? I paced the room. "Nobody could get inside of here, it's as tight as the Bazmeht compound. Maybe your mom kept the library locked because she knew Maria wouldn't tolerate the myth or the old gods and goddesses? You said Maria is into hocus pocus."

"Ridiculous. We lock the library to protect the valuable items in here. Maria has a key to everything in this house. It had to be Lorelei, just face it." Josh looked at the cover of the book then showed it to me. "A history of Bastet. Has an entire ten pages gone." He brushed his hair back. "She could have photocopied them instead of destroying the book."

Josh sounded very shook up – over history. The guy had potential to be an Egyptologist after all.

"When do you go back to college?"

"Don't try to change the subject. Lorelei is guilty as sin."

I kept my mouth tightly closed and stared at him until he answered. "I was supposed to start Friday, but thanks to the storm coming our way, they emailed saying classes won't start until next week. Why?"

So much happened in the past three days, my forty days should be paid in full.

"Lorelei would never treat an old text like that. She just wouldn't. We've spent too much of our time taking care of historical objects to be so careless. It had to be Maria, she's the only one left in the house. Unless your mom has Flamingo Pink lipstick? I've only seen her wear red."

"Neither Maria or my mother would do this."

I shrugged. Trust was a hot commodity, and in my experience, hard to hold on to. What if Maria had a family back home that needed money for a surgery or some other emergency?

"I should call the cops."

Right. Very bad idea – at least until I figured out what had been taken. "How about we go through each book and write down the titles of what's been ruined? That should give us a clue where to search next. You know that I didn't do it."

"I guess," Josh relented a little. "But some of these are in different languages or hieroglyphics."

"Lucky for you, I read heiro."

"Tell me speed reading is one of your super powers."

I unbuttoned my jacket and sat on the floor in the middle of the chaos. "I wish." But wishing doesn't make it so.

# ⟨HAPTER TWENTY-ONE⟩

## SECRETS REVEALED

"You are a freaking robot."

I let the accusation bounce off my professional shoulders, the same way I'd ignored being called 'impossible' and 'slave driver'.

"We've been at this for four hours. Lorelei was pretty damn insistent that we were in here."

I tapped the side of my nose. "She was right, and she knew it. You are the one that didn't want to let her in."

"What if she's the one responsible for all this? She probably had some excuse all lined up." He crossed his arms.

He sounded very unsure of himself, which suited me fine. "Lorelei didn't do this." A scent memory teased my mind, but I couldn't place it.

"You are being ridiculous. I agree that this stuff is intriguing as hell. Shape shifting, cannibalism, a grab for power. Lower Egypt, Upper Egypt. All I know is I'm freaking starving. You can't tell me you aren't hungry...I'd kiss you for a Coke."

That got my attention away from the Isis and Osiris legend, where Mafdet cut off Osiris's penis with her teeth.

"What makes you think that I'd let you kiss me?" *For a Coke?* It took all of my willpower not to imagine his lips pressed to mine...it helped picturing Sekhmet's sword of justice separating us at the mouth. Or maybe she'd only be satisfied with decapitation? Sekhmet, like Mafdet, believed that the ends always justified the means.

He looked shocked by my, yes, *over*reaction.

"What? Am I so repugnant that kissing me is the worst thing you can think of doing for a caffeine fix?"

Blue eyes wide, Josh sat back on his heels. "Whatever. It's just a saying. I was seeing if you were really listening to me." He grinned. "Guess you were. Wanna kiss? C'mon," he teased. "I'm thirsty and bored and-"

"Does your Parisian girlfriend know that you go around kissing women for soda?"

I swear on my honor that I was trying to tease back. I don't know why the sentence came out so judgmental. I'm not jealous. I'm not the type.

*Josh is not for me.*

"We're on a break."

"I knew it! How long have you been broken up?"

"Well. We agreed to a trial separation before I went to Egypt for the summer. Which was supposed to be fun, and I wasn't going to Paris with her, like she wanted me to. She was kinda clingy, you know? Like we were going to get married or something. At nineteen? Who does that anymore?"

"Does what? Get married? Or be nineteen?" He had *lied* about the girlfriend situation. I thought about what Lorelei had said regarding control issues. When someone doesn't have any control, they will grab what they can.

"Haha. You're right. You're not funny."

"You, Joshua, are a hypocrite."

"How so?"

"You accuse us, the Bazmeht, of lying to you about everything, but you lied too. I could never be your girlfriend."

He snorted. "No worries, you are so not my type. I like blonds with...curves."

I touched my multi-colored, straight, shoulder length hair. "Most of those curves can be bought in Brazil at a *discount*." I liked my lean muscles. I did.

"Why are we arguing about this, cuz?"

"I am not arguing. You and I are like oil and water, *dude*."

"You know what your problem is? You don't think for yourself. The Weird Sisters have you all brainwashed into believing some bizzarro stuff. Yeah. You were raised in a cult."

"A cult?" My anger built to a crescendo – combining Josh's disregard for me on a personal level – which I didn't know how to handle, so I was going to ignore it – with his lack of respect for the Bazmeht, and the demi-goddesses. "The Weird Sisters? You are going too far, Josh."

I jumped to my feet, letting my inner ferocity play up and down my spine. No changing, of course, but there's an aura of power that surrounded me. I felt it to my fingertips.

From the way Josh started crawling backward, he did too. "Uh. Sorry?"

Only, I could see that he wasn't at all sorry. He'd been

trying to get under my skin. To push my buttons, as he liked to say. His eyes dazzled with green flecks and he effortlessly got to his feet.

I walked toward him, stalking him like prey. *He would get a taste of my anger. But anger wasn't what I really wanted to taste.*

I moistened my lips with a quick flick of my tongue. Josh swallowed, never dropping his gaze from mine – we were locked together as he challenged me. Welcomed me. Dared me.

To do what? *I was in.*

The sexual energy jumped between the two of us like an electric current, as hot and sizzling as lightning.

*What is this?*

My skin, hot then cold, while my body trembled with something indefinable.

His chin angled to the left, his jaw clenched, and he braced his feet apart. I could run the two feet left between us and lock my mouth to his, and maybe the burn in my belly would catch the rest of my body on fire.

Lorelei said I was naïve in the ways of love, but this had nothing to do with love – I don't think. This was the urge to...*mate.* Hot, sweaty, powerful. My body melting with a need I didn't care if I understood. What was death to the fiery embrace Josh was offering?

*No.*

Sekhmet forbid it. Being Bazmeht had to come before hormones and mind-numbing pleasure. I closed my eyes, breaking the tension, then turned, giving him my back. I counted to ten in steady breaths until my heartbeat regulated and I could talk without panting like an obscene phone call.

"You're right. We need a breather." I sounded calm. *I didn't feel calm.* How was I supposed to control this? I couldn't confess to Lorelei that my body betrayed me just as they'd all predicted. I wanted the council to be proud of me. I had to fight Josh's appeal on my own.

I was in trouble.

"A break, yeah, and a cold shower. I don't suppose you're going to explain what *that* was all about?"

Keeping my flushed face down, I shook my head. "I'm not withholding information," I whispered to the books on the floor. "I don't know either."

He exhaled and I imagined him yanking the hair off his forehead. "Right. I'm hungry," Josh said, mercifully changing the subject. "We can meet back here in an hour. I still don't think you should tell Lorelei what we found. See if she asks you any questions. That will prove she's guilty, you know? Sleuth 101 stuff."

While I appreciated Josh's sense of humor, I wasn't in the mood. I brushed by him, my skin still so sensitive that it hurt, and headed for my room without saying a word. I'd forgotten about being hungry, and now I craved sunshine more than food. Sunbathing by the pool didn't require swimming and it would sooth my jumbled nerves.

Confused as I've ever been, I changed into one of the new bikinis I'd bought – black on black, no big surprise there – then grabbed my iPhone, which Lorelei had left on my pillow with headphones and a note to call her.

A little Egyptian drumming to remind me of home, while soaking up the sun's healing and empowering rays. The drained pool held no fear. I laid my towel on lounger, and within five minutes, relaxed without a single thought of Josh. I would give him the definition of going on a break!

I sensed him coming by the third song, and showed no surprise when he pulled off my headphones.

"How do you do that?"

"Listen?" I reached my hand out until he dropped the earbuds back into my palm.

"Fine. Be that way. I brought iced tea with lemon, so you don't have to worry about getting scurvy. Dang, you really got banged up!"

"Scurvy?" Self-conscious, I flipped the edge of the towel over a huge bruise on my thigh. "Isn't that for pirates?"

"Lack of vitamin C, baby." Josh dragged a lounge chair within a foot of mine, wedging a tiny table between the two then placing a tray with two teas with lemon, on top. "Don't make any sudden moves. It could spill. You did notice there's no water in the pool? Drained for the hurricane."

"I am in no hurry to go swimming." I kept my sunglasses on, shading my eyes from sharing anything more than I wanted.

"Guess that's true. I'm wearing my lifeguard shorts, though, just in case you want to run through the sprinklers later. Cool off."

"Lifeguard shorts?" Unable to stop myself, I leaned over on one elbow to look at what he was wearing and almost swallowed my tongue. Goddess have mercy, but Re couldn't have made a finer physique.

Josh's broad shoulders – surfer's shoulders -- tapered to slim hips and muscular legs. Brown hair, bleached wheat by the sun, glinted in the light. Brown hair? I took off my sunglasses, blinking for clear vision. Yes, checking out Josh's chest hair was purely professional. Light brown chest hair, dark blond brows? I'd assumed, and I know that Lorelei had too, that it was natural golden blond hair on the top of his head.

"You are not a true blond."

Grinning with that dangerous left dimple, he said, "This is Miami, Shani. Everybody highlights."

"Highlights?"

"So I have a lot. The sun does the rest."

My mind circled itself, trying to add this newest piece of the puzzle. Zelda's chestnut hair wasn't so different from Josh's sun-bleached, highlighted *brown* hair. So much for the blond Pharaoh theory. I wondered what Josh's dad looked like. "What ever happened to your dad? Is he still around?"

"Nope. In the immortal words of Green Day – Good Riddance."

"Who?"

"A great nineties band. Practically vintage. Anyway, it doesn't matter. I figured out a long time ago that my mom, as crazy as she is, is the one steady parental unit in my life. Scary, I know, but she's all I got. And since she's so freaky about her past, I decided to learn about it through family over the summer – totally got screwed there – and college."

His deep voice resonated within me and I lay back, closing my eyes as he spoke. Was it the mutual recognition of our body's centuries bred DNA that called him to me, and me to him? He carried the Blood of Ra. He could give me, a Felidia, a baby.

If I wanted one, which Goddess knows, I don't. Just the thought of diapers made me shiver in the heat.

I was starting to think my heart could be involved and *that* terrified me more than my sudden desire for hot, no strings attached sex.

With Joshua Sherif Johnson – the one man that is

completely off limits.

"Tell me about your nightmares. I think I have them, but I don't remember details. The Oracle says my psyche is protecting me from some deep hidden secret."

"The who?"

"Oracle...uh...Shem-tet." I tried to think of a different way to describe her. "She's more than a fortune teller, she reads the stars too."

"Sure she does."

I chose not to get mad. What did he know, anyway? "Do you remember your nightmares?"

"Unfortunately." He took a drink, loudly setting his glass back down. "I always end up dying."

I kept my body very still at this revelation.

"I read this dream book once, totally lame, by the way. It said that death signified new beginning – duh – and possibly good fortune. I always thought that you were supposed to wake up before you actually died, but not me. I die every time."

"How?" Intrigued, I almost sat up. But instinctively I knew Josh would tell more if it seemed like I wasn't really listening. Oh, but I was.

"Different ways, different time periods. Really strange. Sometimes, I know I'm in ancient Egypt, and I know where everything is. I speak fluently in whatever language we're speaking. Sometimes, I'm in China, or the Mayan Jungle. I'm a sacrifice to the Jaguar god in that one."

"Amazing." Amazing didn't even begin to cover it. Josh dreamed his past lives, whether he knew it or not. "Do you believe in reincarnation?"

"Well." He paused. "Do you?"

"Yes." And the glory of nine lives, if a guard was worthy.

"I sometimes wonder," he hesitated, as if embarrassed. "If I was a king. I know, nobody's ever a peasant or a slave in a past life, but in the dreams I feel...royal."

Just saying, we'd been telling him that for over a month now. I played it smooth. "Hmm. Past lives. The girl selling swimsuits told me I'd drowned in a past life, and to keep my nose out of the water. Good advice, considering." I stayed on my back, sunglasses in place. The warm sun occasionally dipped behind a black cloud – Josh said thunderstorms happened almost daily during the summer – but it always returned.

The sun, *Re*, replenished my energy as nothing else could. Renewed in spirit, I promised to find answers to all of the questions available while keeping Josh safe from the Uraeli.

"Drowning – that's nothing. I've died by fire, in war, and by dismemberment."

"Ew!"

"Tell me about it. Scorpion sting and snake bite."

He sounded so proud of his dream injuries that I sat up to look. "Where?"

Josh pointed to the vein above his collarbone. "There. Every time, no matter how hard I try to change direction of the dream, I die."

"No, no – I meant where were you? What era? Egypt?"

"Oh, uh, most of them are in Egypt. Really ancient, primitive times. They end so bad. But there's one that I love." He finished his tea then drained mine. "Where I'm powerful. Instead of being a sacrifice or just too stupid to live, I'm running across the desert and pretty soon I'm running so fast that I turn into a huge lion."

*Holy Mother Mafdet.* My breath caught somewhere in my esophagus. I pulled my emotions very close to the chest.

Josh ran as fast as me.

His reflexes were super quick.

He healed fast.

Most importantly, he'd had the dream.

Which was a familiar one – *if you were a member of the Felidia.*

"Cool." Careful to keep the tremor from my voice, I rose and wrapped the towel around my shaking body. Adrenalin, energy, a blast of sheer power at Josh's casual revelation shook me to the core. "I supposed we should get back to work. I'll change, and we can meet back in the library. I still have to show you the sleeper hold trick." I tried not to stare at his features, to search for other clues. "I'm really sorry about the destruction. Did you ask Maria about being in there this morning?"

"No. She's not around. But I'm telling you, Shani, it wasn't the housekeeper." His mouth thinned.

"All right. Let's not argue about it. I'm going to stop in the kitchen for something to nibble."

"I'll bring some cheese and crackers," Josh offered.

"I promise not to spill." I crossed my racing heart. If the

culprit wasn't Lorelei, and it wasn't Maria, that left Ninja as the wanton page thief.

"Fine. See you in a few."

"Take your time..." I ran to my room and locked the door behind me, whipping out my phone and pressing speed dial. My blood pumped as if I'd run a marathon.

"Bastet? Is Sekhmet with you? Put me on speaker so you both can hear me. We need to find Josh's dad. His real dad! Josh isn't a natural blond-"

"Shani!" Sekhmet bellowed.

"-and the proof was in the DNA. Zelda's got so many secrets, but the biggest one? Josh's dad must be a member of the Felidia."

# CHAPTER TWENTY-TWO

By the time I finished telling them about my near death experience (and I found out that with each rebirth it gets harder to die, which explained my fifteen minute underwater marathon) the break in at the library, and the oncoming hurricane, Bastet was ready to send her private plane. "Come home. It is too dangerous for you there!"

"I am a Bazmeht bodyguard, Bastet, you can't call me home like I'm a child."

"You're only seventeen," Bastet said in her maternal tones.

I interrupted her like a typical teen. "My age didn't matter when I aced all my tests. And I'm practically eighteen. Only one month-"

"Let her do her job!" Sekhmet volleyed into the conversation. "The only reason to bring a guard home is if she feels she can't do her duty. Are you capable of protecting Joshua with your life?"

"Of course." I answered immediately.

"Then stay."

"Hold on to something solid."

I laughed. "Bastet, Josh says it will be a little wind, not to worry."

"Your primary duty is to protect Joshua. Your secondary job is to search the library for clues to the Myth of Mafdet." Sekhmet lowered her voice. "Who was foolish enough to break in and steal the pages we might need? All the signs point to the End Time, and we must be prepared for war."

"The oracle agrees, change is coming, Shani. If we can wake Mother Mafdet, then we can bring Egypt back to its full glory!"

*War? As in death and destruction?* "I'm looking, but so was someone else, it has to be Ninja, but what does she care about the Myth of Mafdet? And if she was inside the house, why didn't she attack Josh?" I paced back and forth as I spoke. "At first, I thought that Maria, the maid with the voo doo, might have had something to do with it, but Josh is adamant that she wouldn't destroy the family property. I defended Lorelei, but there *is* the glass with her lipstick on it."

"As if she'd make such an obvious mistake. Find the idiot stupid enough to enter a house under Bazmeht protection and make them pay with their life! We must be ready for the mother. She has to wake." Sekhmet sighed. "Keep your jars safe, no matter what."

"You sent Shani her canopic jars? Her sarcophagus? Why? Sekhmet, I never approved of that! They are safest here, at the pyramid."

"I sent Lorelei's too, so be angry at me for that as well. I am following my instincts, Bastet, and I can't always listen to your weak, 'well-meaning' feelings. This could be *war*."

"You are so bloodthirsty. Our duty is to protect the bloodline and guard the mother's crypt. Shani, for over two thousand years, Sekhmet has claimed war was coming, and she's been wrong for most of them. Shem-tet says a time of *change* is coming, not death."

"I'll not be caught unprepared because you want to suckle the world like some monstrous barn cat!"

"Sekhmet, you are going too far. We lead the Bazmeht together. Not separately. I want to know everything that you've done behind my back!"

"No, Bastet, I don't think you do. Shani, find any scrap you can in relation to the Myth of Mafdet and fax it over. Email, text it, I don't care. Send it and find the stolen pages."

With that, the connection ended. Chills broke out over my skin like individual pinpricks of fear and fur sprang behind my ear without warning. *This was real.* The threat to my world, to my way of life, real. With fresh determination, I slipped on a pair of comfortable black jeans, tucked my phone into the front pocket, and chose a brown t-shirt and brown leather flip-flops.

"Lorelei!" I smacked my forehead, remembering her anger when I'd accidentally left her from the loop before. I tried calling her but it went directly to voice mail. I ran to her room, shaking the locked knob. With my ear to the wood, I heard her tight breathing. *Migraine.* Poor darling. "Anything I can do?" I asked in a whisper.

"Nothing." Her reply came in a pain-filled voice. "I took some medicine."

I put my hand against the door. "Lorelei? Were you in the library earlier?"

"No. You wouldn't let me in." Her tone turned frosty. "Go, Shani. I need sleep."

Being helpless after she'd stayed with me all night didn't set well, and now I'd hurt her feelings. I'd have to mend the rift later, possibly with a dish of her favorite cheese soup. "Take care."

*Home*. Before things fell irreparably apart. Sekhmet and Bastet argued all the time, but I'd never heard real anger in their voices before. In order to help, I had to be in Egypt. The sooner the better.

I'd be away from Josh and this insane attraction that had nothing to do with either of us as people, just our hormones wanting to be horizontal. Not due to youth, as Lorelei said, but our DNA.

Reaching the library, I twisted the knob. Locked, too. That meant nothing to me – a Level One Bazmeht. Bypassing the electronic code completely, I used my preternatural strength and applied the perfect amount of pressure to loosen the mechanics of the lock until it popped open.

I blew on my fingers like I was James Bond and walked in. Zelda whirled around, the glass with the lipstick on it in her manicured hand.

"Where is that woman? She deserves the firing squad! A Bazmeht Bodyguard knows better than to leave this kind of mess, and we don't eat in the library. I keep this room locked for a reason. How did you get in here? Did you steal the code from Maria?"

Zelda looked divinely mad. Her hair was styled in a curled bob that accentuated her large brown eyes, rimmed with as much black eyeliner as I put on Bastet for ceremonies. Her dress, a sleeveless sheath in purple, perfectly matched her pumps, which added three inches to her height. An ivory winter scarf draped loose around her neck. Gorgeous, if slightly crazy.

"Lorelei is sleeping. She has a migraine." I wished I'd waited for Josh. I turned toward the open door. Obviously, Zelda didn't know about the damaged scrolls just yet. Did I tell her? By the pitch of her shriek, I surmised it was too late.

I slowly shifted around. She picked up one of the scrolls, which had a corner torn off as if it had been a gum wrapper.

Speechless, her face drained of color, and I ran to protect her head from bouncing off the floor as she fainted.

"Nice catch," Josh said from the doorway, his hands filled with a tray of food. "I guess she saw the damage? She always complained that this stuff was a burden, but she took it pretty seriously." He set the tray on the high sofa table. "Either that, or she noticed I had chips in here." He looked down at his mom's pale face, his eyes twinkling mischievously. "It's against the rules."

My heart fluttered. *So are you.*

"Ooh," Zelda moaned, and I tried to make her more comfortable by laying her flat.

"Mom, are you all right?" Josh knelt at her other side.

"I can get up," she said, pushing at my arms.

"Let me help you."

"You've done enough. These things are irreplaceable, how could you? I never would have given you my permission to view them if I thought you'd ruin them. How will I explain to Bastet and Sekhmet? To my brother? I've let the family down. Josh?"

"They'll understand, Mom. Here, have some water."

She took the glass and sipped. "You just don't know," she said, shaking her head. Curls bobbed against her pale cheeks. "I came in here, looking for Maria. She always cleans the library on Wednesdays. You know the hurricane is coming straight for us?"

"Mom,"

"If you tell me it's just a little wind, Joshua, I swear I'll never speak to you again."

"I was gonna say that we have an up to code house, if it were a cat 5 we'd be safe."

"That's not true. But I had the tower room fortified to withstand two hundred mile an hour winds. We need to move what is left," she sniffed, "of the treasure, your heritage, into that room." Zelda looked down her beautiful nose at me. "You will help, of course."

"Of course! When is the hurricane coming?"

"Tomorrow, or the next day."

"Lorelei is sleeping right now, she gets awful migraines. Can we wait to move things until the morning?"

"It will take us that long just to go through all of this." She put the back of her hand to her forehead.

"I'll do it, you don't have to help." I felt guilty and I *knew* I was innocent.

"If you think I'm letting you touch these priceless items, think again. I'll have to document the damage, and," Zelda held her hands up and shook an imaginary throat. "When I see that woman, by God, I'll know why she-"

"Lorelei didn't do it. She would never vandalize something, especially something so important." I tried putting my hand on her arm, thinking calming thoughts.

"Stop touching me!" Zelda got up, standing on wobbly legs before regaining her composure.

I still had so much to learn...

"Josh, we will start at this end of the room, the one with the most damage. I will call out an item, leaf through it, and see if anything is missing or ruined."

"I know you're upset, Mom. But Shani and I already wrote down all the damaged titles. *Whoever* did this," he met my gaze and I smiled gratefully, "is looking for the same thing we are – the Myth of Mafdet. Clues to the key."

"What? Well, let's call the police, if we've been robbed-"

"Nothing else is missing. The police won't do anything about a few pieces of paper. Hey, Mom, did anybody come to the door yesterday? Were you home all day?"

"I was home. Nobody came around here, not until last night when this strange girl almost drowned." She jerked her thumb at me. "Who goes swimming in the ocean at night?" Zelda clucked her teeth. "Josh could have been hurt trying to save you, and you're supposed to be a guardian." Glaring in my direction, she shared her opinion of me. "Sekhmet and Bastet must not have much to choose from, if you're one of the best."

Ouch? I couldn't even think about defending myself, she was right on all counts.

"Cadee!" I snapped my fingers.

"The limo driver?" Josh gnawed at his lower lip. "What on earth would she want with anything in the library? How'd she get the key? Why would she wear Lorelei's lipstick? Totally wrong color for her. Besides, she was a real trooper last night. I wouldn't have been able to get you home without her."

"True." Not to mention that if the demi-goddesses had hired her, she'd passed a very strenuous background check. We'd had a connection, Cadee and I. Taking out my phone, I punched in her number.

"Cadee speaking."

"Hello, Cadee – It's Shani. I wanted to say thank you for all of your help last night."

"How are you feelin'? In between hanging hurricane shutters," she laughed in her throaty way, "I've been worried sick about you. The kids are making me crazy, celebratin' that they don't have school, when I'm on call for the next month. I don't suppose you'll need a driver during the worst of the storm?"

"I'm so grateful for your help. I think you should take the next few days off with pay." Bastet would agree that it was the right thing to do.

"Thank you, thank you! I'll get the little darlin's fresh batteries for the Gameboys. I can do without electricity so long as they've got triple A's for a week."

I laughed. Kids sounded like a pain in the behind. "Oh, and thanks for finding my phone. I think I focused more on losing that than losing blood. Now, if you could just find Lorelei's lipstick, everybody would be happy."

"Glad to help," she said without missing a beat that might signify guilt. "I'll be going out to the market one more time before the stores all close tomorrow, so if you need me to drop anything by, just pick up the phone! Or," she waited a second before saying, "you could try the other thing."

"Hmm." I scratched my nose, sending her a 'thank you' thought. She didn't say anything. "I think it's on the fritz. Be safe, all right?"

I hit end, and pocketed my phone. My mind linking abilities sucked – always had. Maybe Cadee could teach me a few things. The Irish were notorious for their gift of sight. Goddess knows I'd devoured stories about regular people able to do all sorts of paranormal tricks, wishing I could master telepathy.

"Cadee says that she's going to make one more store run, if we need anything?"

"My mom's stocked for a two-year depression." Josh tossed a potato chip at her.

Zelda picked it up between two fingers as if it was a bug. "Joshua, you know better than to bring food into this library." She smiled though, and he smiled back.

It was sweet and I looked away. Even if Josh's mom was

crazy, at least he had one. Mine was somewhere in the jungle doing Goddess only knows what.

With Natalie – her hands down favorite.

I sighed and got to work, using my phone to take pictures of the damaged books, which I emailed to Sekhmet. Zelda could read fluent Italian and German; I had pretty much everything else except for the texts in Japanese. "Sekhmet wants anything flagged that is in relation to Mafdet, no matter how small. We can send her the titles to go with the pictures in case she can find another copy somewhere. It's amazing what's on ebay these days."

"Ebay?" Zelda shuddered. "I prefer Craig's List."

"Mom, what are *you* doing, discount shopping?" Josh looked adorable with his dimpled grin and sexy five o'clock shadow along his jaw.

"How do you think I keep my money?" Zelda lifted her nose in the air. "Why pay full price for Chanel if you don't have to?"

We worked companionably, getting halfway through the library before Josh got up and stretched his back. I did the same, and I noticed Zelda discreetly try to stretch her butt muscles. She was something else.

"Listen, I'm willing to work for another hour, but then I gotta get out and blow off some steam, you know? Have some fun. And Shani needs to see Miami before it gets blown away." Josh winked at me and I knew I'd better stay safely at home. Locked in my room. Under the bed. *Nowhere near a bed.*

"We have more to do," I said as primly as a vestal virgin. I'd packed my peacock blue disco dress, the only thing I had that was 'fun'. "Many hands make light work, or something like that."

"Your work involves protecting me. I'm going out. You can look like a Men In Black dork if you want, but I'd pick something else. Anything else. What you are wearing right now would be preferable to that damn black jacket."

I stared at my feet, encased in flip-flops. What was the matter with my jacket?

"Joshua!" Zelda flattened her lips into a disapproving line.

"I'm nineteen, Mom. You can't stop me."

"I wouldn't dream of it." She gestured to the mess in the room. "By all means, choose drinking beer at the beach over protecting your heritage."

Finally, Josh would listen to reason. I picked up the list of titles, checking to see where I'd left off.

"The only beer I'm drinking is the root kind, I promise. I'll be fresh as a daisy in the morning and I'll even carry the really fragile stuff to the tower myself. Don't worry, Mom."

"Well...will you be back by midnight?"

*Midnight?* Temptation danced just out of reach.

"One," Josh negotiated smoothly. I was reluctantly impressed. He looked at me and held his hands out. "We have to be back by one, so don't nag at me to take you out for breakfast, got it?"

*Dear Goddess.* Keep my nose above the waves.

# CHAPTER TWENTY-THREE

## FUN – MIAMI STYLE

He didn't want me to look like a dork? Well...I'd do as Lorelei insisted and blend with the crowd. I pulled my blue dress out of the closet and shook it free of wrinkles. The iridescent cloth was pure magic. Never needed ironing, and moved as if it had a life of its own. It even managed to give me curves.

I flung my head forward and counted one hundred strokes with my brush so when I popped back up again, not only did I see spots before my eyes, I had extra bounce in my multi colored strands.

*Not a date.*

I was protecting Josh against the nightlife of Miami, which everyone said got wild. My pulse leaped with excitement.

My low-heeled blue sandals had crystals along the straps. I chose vanilla lip-gloss for shine and smudged my eye shadow to create what Lorelei's Cosmo magazine called 'allure'.

Was I blending to fit in or wanting to look pretty for Josh? My pulse sped up a little, and my tummy did flip after flip.

Purely professional, I decided, even if I did look more like a pop tart. My switchblade fit neatly into the strap of my super bra, every girl should have one with pockets. Maybe when I retire, I'll design an entire line of Bodyguard undergarments...blinking, I brought myself back to the present. My cell phone fit into the other strap, and leaving my hands free to protect Josh, as necessary.

"No shifting, no losing control, no rogue waves, and no Uraeli – not tonight. One night of teenager fun with no emergencies is not too much to ask, is it?"

My reflection didn't share any words of wisdom, so I left. Josh waited at the bottom of the stairs, his eyes sparking with appreciation as he took my ensemble. He whistled.

Blushing, I got to the bottom step and twirled. "Dork enough for you?"

"That would be dork-*y*, Ms. Egypt." He clasped my hand

and bowed over the fingers. "And yeah. You got the look." We walked across the foyer and out the front door, down the steps. "I heard you gave Cadee the night off, so I called a cab. Driving Mom's car and parking on the strip is out of the question - and walking down to the beach in heels is never a good idea. What else do you have in that closet of yours, Shani Nebit?"

Warm bubbles of happiness threatened my composure, so I reminded myself that I was guard, not a girl. Opening the door to the cab, I peered inside to make sure it was safe before letting him in. He stared at me and I gave a small shrug. "Habit."

"Take tonight off, would you?" He gave the driver the address to the restaurant. "You're a beautiful woman of mystery, and we're going to enjoy Miami like natives."

His compliments tasted as rich as hot chocolate made from cream and I guiltily drank them up. "It doesn't work like that. I am...what I am."

"Another clear statement from the Bazmeht corner. Just promise me that you'll lighten up a little and enjoy the night. I've seen glimpses of a fun streak in you."

I bit my lip. Who doesn't have a secret part of their life that belongs to them alone? Mine had the occasional disco ball in it, never a client. Perhaps relaxing, a little, might be nice. To push the boundaries that I'd put in place – for my own good.

"Well?"

I wrinkled my nose. I supposed that lifting a few of the rules, for tonight, might not be horrible. I patted my phone, safely tucked into my bra strap.

If there was trouble, I could always call for help.

I was never really alone.

"All right. I will try and have fun."

Josh groaned. "Do you have to sound like you're dying?"

I smiled.

He shook his head. "Too many teeth, you could be trying to eat me."

Nibbling on him held great appeal. I relaxed my mouth.

Rubbing his chin, he pretended to think about it. "Better, but..."

I stuck my tongue out at him and started to laugh.

"That's it!" He nudged my leg with his. "First, dinner at the Waverunner, where we can people watch. Tons of fun. Especially as the night stalkers come out of their caves. Like vampires!" He hissed, showing his human, not scary at all, eyeteeth.

I gave him a courtesy laugh.

"What, not a vampire fan?" He put his hand over his heart. "Quentin Tarantino from Dusk 'til Dawn – it's a classic."

There were a lot of things ten times scarier than fake vampires. Someday, maybe he'd come around to accepting his fate and then vampires would cease to fascinate him.

I couldn't wait to tell him about Ammut, demon of the underworld. The Swallower of Souls ate the hearts of those who weren't worthy to move on to the Field of Rushes or Paradise. The Beast of Destiny had the head of a crocodile, the body of a lion and haunches of a hippo. I shivered. Talk about scary.

"Here we are." The cab let us off on the busy strip, and the driver gave Josh his card for when we wanted to go home. I slipped out as Josh paid the man and held the door against the crush of people walking in the road.

Miami, Ocean Drive, equaled chaos, and my blood sang to dance along the edges. Josh flattened his lips at me, noting how I stayed to his left. "Relax."

Impossible.

The restaurant had a crowd of tables in front of it, and the smells of freshly baked rolls and garlic, cheese, and wine and even lamb, teased my nostrils.

Josh, the perfect gentleman, impeded my attempts to guard him. I went for the front door, just as he went for the door, which ended up in a power struggle. With a twist of my heel on his toe, I won, and we stumbled into the dark interior of the restaurant.

"Dude!" The young maître de at the podium slapped hands with Josh, at my side, in a high five. He looked me over, grinned, and he and Josh engaged in another round of hand smacking.

"Male bonding ritual," Josh whispered with a smile that zinged down my spine and back up again. "This is Kurt. We graduated high school together." His breath was warm against my cheek as I scanned the candle lit tables for any signs of danger.

"I got you the best seat in the house, if you want to follow me?" Kurt grabbed two menus, and I saw Josh slip him cash, which he pocketed so fast I almost doubted myself.

Bribery, I smiled proudly at Josh. Some things were global.

He led us outside to the corner table, where it wasn't so crowded. I sat with my back to the wall so I had a clear view of three sides. Josh sat to my left, and on my right was a half wrought iron, decorative fence to separate the diners from the walkers.

"Outdoor dining, at its finest," Kurt bowed. He took our drink order – a Coke for Josh, and a Perrier for me – and left. I like the bubbles.

The menu didn't have prices, which meant the food should be first rate. I made a note to pay the bill, this wasn't a date, and Bastet and Sekhmet could easily afford to cover Josh's meal.

The cars drove by at a snail's pace, showing off for those of us watching. Vipers, Lamborghini's, Porches, Ferraris – the automobile as gorgeous as the people driving them.

"Do you have a car?" The way he drove, he probably had ten.

He ducked his head. "No."

"Why not?"

"Speeding issues."

I laughed, taken by surprise. "Maybe NASCAR is missing out on a driver..."

Two men in mini-skirts and purple feather boas walked by, making me smile. The dark-skinned man had real crystals glued to his cheekbones. He waved, and I waved back. It was a never-ending floorshow, and Josh and I had front row seats.

"This isn't too weird for you?"

"It's like a carnival. Cairo has spots like this."

Kurt returned and I ordered the fish of the day in a creamy dill sauce, and Josh ordered steak, medium rare. We shared mashed potatoes and French fries and laughed hysterically at the parade of humanity.

Two hours later, I waved my white napkin in surrender. "I'm stuffed."

"Want coffee? Dessert?"

"I have no room, and I'm not crazy about sweets."

"Lucky for you," Josh said.

"It's genetic. Besides, I prefer water."

"You *are* a purist." He shook his head, pushing his glass of iced water toward me. Mine was already empty, and the bottle of Perrier long gone.

"I like to take care of my body. It has to last me a while." I sucked on a lemon slice, enjoying the sour tartness.

"Well," he leaned forward with a strawberry dipped in whipped cream, waving it beneath my nose. "From a purely technical, non-emotional point of view, it's a nice body to take care of."

"I thought you liked curves."

"I like you." He teased my lower lip with the strawberry, and I opened my mouth for a small bite. I knew I was in over my head, I'd known from the minute he'd wanted to go out tonight but it didn't stop me from licking the whipped cream off the tip of his thumb.

I wanted him to kiss me. Heat surged through my body, and I marveled at the energy we created.

Groaning, he dropped the strawberry to the table and stood, putting a disappointing but appropriate amount of distance between us. "I can't do this again, let's get out of here. I need to walk. Fresh air. I don't think you understand what you do to me. If you did, you'd be dangerous."

"I *am* dangerous." Embarrassed that he'd so easily rejected my wish for a kiss, I pushed the chair back and followed him out of the noisy, crowded restaurant. "I have one hundred percent accuracy-"

"I wasn't talking about the Bazmeht, Shani. I was talking about you, as a female."

Stunned, I didn't know what to do or say as he walked away from me and out of the restaurant.

He saw me as a beautiful *woman*. Not a warrior. I buried my confusion and fell back on what I knew – my training as a guard. I hadn't learned how to be anything else.

# ⟨HAPTER TWENTY-FOUR

## OLD HABITS

Out of habit rather than a hint of danger, I glanced left, then right. My gaze hooked by the milling bodies around the bar section of the restaurant. The lights flashed in neon colors, and the bartenders busily called drinks and took money. It reminded me of the disco back home.

A woman with spiky black hair laughed, the sound familiar. She shouted for another round, and I almost turned back to see her, but Josh was already out the front door. Uneasy, I hurried after him, stopping at the podium to ask after the bill.

"It's taken care of," Kurt grinned.

Josh had treated me as if we'd been on a date.

Mouth dry, I went outside.

"Some bodyguard," Josh teased, already back to his normal, easy-going ways. I envied his ability to forgive and forget. "I beat you out the door. What if there'd been a sniper waiting for me?"

"Then you'd be dead, and I – I'd be fired." Worse, I'd be banished from the Bazmeht. The idea of Josh lying prone and bleeding on the sidewalk spurred me into grabbing his arm and shoving him against the building. "Let's go home." I could tuck him into bed and jog back to the bar in under an hour. I'd face my nemesis once and for all.

The mask slipped, and I could see he was still upset with me by the way he tightened his jaw. "You promised to try to have fun."

Wishing I could smooth the confusion between us wouldn't make it so. I turned my head away. Going back inside wasn't an option. On the other hand, if the spiky hair and guttural laugh belonged to who I thought it might, then Josh's ass was on the line anyway. Making the next few decisions about damage control.

"But if you can't bring yourself to let go, fine. I'll call the cab."

I swallowed. Josh's courtesy proved his upbringing as a

gentleman, despite his surfer dude shell. The question remained, did Ninja know we'd been eating dinner, or had I been gifted a lucky break?

Opportunity beckoned. I'd slip in, pretend to go to the bathroom, and instead check out the woman at the bar. Confirm identity and track her down *after* midnight, er, one, while Josh waited safely on the sidewalk.

"Let me just make a trip to the ladies room, and I'll be ready to party."

"That I'd like to see." Josh stuffed his hands into his front pockets and relaxed against the building. "Shani, I'm sorry if I came on too strong in there. I get that you, well, you aren't like the girls from around here."

He was so wonderful my ears wiggled. "I'm not like most girls, actually, and I am having fun. I just have to remember that above all, my job is to protect you. I know you don't believe it, but there's a real chance someone might want to hurt you. I have to make sure that doesn't happen."

"Don't go all Charlie's Angels on me." Shrugging, he nudged me with his elbow. "Go do your thing, and then we'll walk down to the park. We can see the ocean without you drowning. There's always some people hanging out, listening to local bands. It will be a good time."

I wasn't here to have a good time. Underneath my blue dress, I was all Bazmeht. "All right." My conscious flip-flopped over whether or not he could follow a simple instruction. My experiences so far didn't give me much confidence. "You'll stay right here?"

"Sure."

I stared at him some more, knowing it would do no good to make him promise on the Goddess. If he wanted to wander, he would. "Please."

"Hurry up!" He did that thing he does, brushing his hair off his face when he's irritated, that I find adorable.

Almost irresistible. "I'll be right back."

I went inside, sticking to the shadows. My pretty blue dress provided excellent camouflage as I made my way between the tables, my gaze focused on where I'd heard *that* voice.

Smoky and deep, it brought an image of gray eyes and pointed fangs to mind. My pulse sped and it took all I had to walk – not run – and snap her head off.

The bitch owed me a life, and I wanted hers.

I knew it was her, just as surely as I knew my own name. The ninja, or Uraeli warrior, had branded me with her venom and ruined my reputation. Because of her, I wasn't trusted within my own community, and I'd been banished to Miami while everybody waited to see if I'd grow scales.

Righteous anger consumed me. *I am bred from the lioness, the lynx, the panther, the cheetah, and the All-God Re. I am stealthy and powerful. My jaws designed to decapitate the snake in a single crushing bite.*

Just one picture.

I took out my trusted iPhone, pressing the camera icon, and pointed it toward the direction of fruity perfume covering the woman's cunning lack of scent. Because Re felt the need to toss a scrap to the Uraeli traitors, cat shifters, who have an incredible sensory palette, can't smell their enemy the snake. It was nice that Ninja favored sweet perfume so I could pick her out of a crowd.

In war, what difference did fair make? But long, long ago, Mafdet, on Re's behalf, threw vengeance like a mace and almost annihilated the Uraeli race. To keep balance, He gave the rebel Uraelis a few tricks of their own.

Slightly flaring my nostrils, I almost choked on the scent of cantaloupe. I'd never eat it again.

Tiny Ninja was dressed to kill in a silver sequined sheath that cut off at her knees. Her feet clad in silver stilettos, her nails painted black. Her skin dazzled white against the tan of her admirers; her teeth glowed in the neon glare.

I watched her enthrall those around her. It appeared that she'd come alone, but she had a seat tipped forward, as if she was saving it for someone.

Who?

What would happen if I showed my face to her here, in the middle of all of these innocent people?

This wasn't the place. Our time would come to battle again, I had no doubt about that. I pushed the thought to the front of my mind, sending her a promise.

*We'll meet again, soon.*

Her head swiveled around to where I crouched in the shadows. Her gray eyes sparkled with malice, I could see venom reflecting in the oily orbs. She couldn't see me, but I had a sickening feeling that she'd heard my intent loud and clear.

I took her picture then with swift feet, sliding from my place against the wall to hide beneath a table just as she ran toward the spot I'd been. My heart drummed in my chest in an ancient tempo I hoped she couldn't hear. Peeking around the tablecloth, I saw her sniff the air and search the shadows for me.

I kept my mind shielded tightly until I heard her mutter beneath her breath, "I'll find you."

Not until I want you to, I promised. She returned to her stool at the bar, and I slipped into the bathroom, grateful for the flexibility of my spine as I fit through the bathroom window. I couldn't take the chance that she'd be watching the front door.

Dropping to the alley, I went around the block to the front of the restaurant. Josh waited right where I'd left him. With Cadee.

"Look who I found!" Josh said with a grin. "She was giving me hell for not calling her to drive us around tonight."

"Hello," Cadee smiled. Beautiful enough to grace the cover of a magazine, her skin glowed with health, and her shoulder-length hair held the shine of an oil slick. She wore a short, leather mini-skirt, knee boots, and a crocheted, black, sleeveless blouse. Her black gloves peeked from her crocheted bag. "You should've called, Shani. Your boss pays me well."

"Bastet says that gold in the right palm eases the way to happiness."

Josh tilted his head and chewed his lip instead of laughing at me.

"She's the nice one, eh? Sekhmet, she's a firecracker, that one." Cadee's eyes invited confidences, and I decided that she had a gift, like Lorelei, to put people at ease. She'd saved my life and stopped Josh from seeing the horror that I'd been. My shoulders relaxed. "It was a last minute decision. Josh wanted to…what did you say, live a little? Before we were trapped inside the house by the storm."

Cadee laughed, no sign of a grudge in her expression. "I don't know if you've ever been locked inside a house for three days but it does seem like you're trapped."

Living in an underground pyramid has given me an appreciation for the sun and blue sky. But I'm all right for a few weeks without it. I brushed my hair out of my eyes. "Did you get the batteries?"

Her brow furrowed. "Hmm?"

"For your kids – the video games."

"Oh – aye," she twisted her mouth into a pout that didn't diminish her beauty. "I bought the last few packs the store had. Are you ready, then? For your first hurricane?"

Josh and I exchanged a glance. "We anticipate a little wind," I said with a straight face.

"Don't listen to this charmer, he's liable to land you into trouble." Cadee elbowed Josh. "Anyway," she laughed, "I'm meeting up with some friends. Would you care to join us?"

"No, but thanks for asking. I'm taking Shani to the park to listen to music."

"Josh, you be a *good* boy, do you hear me?" Cadee teasingly wagged her finger at him, while I, virgin guard that I am, blushed at the innuendo.

"We should get going." I straightened my shoulders and lifted my chin, which was formidable in my guard uniform but probably made me look like a girl playing make believe in my blue disco dress.

Cadee saluted me before heading down the crowded street, passing the entrance to the restaurant we'd just left.

"Stop chewing your lip," Josh said.

Stung, I pointed at his mouth. "You do it too."

"When I'm nervous. What have you got to be nervous about?"

Ninja. What would happen if I told Josh about my enemy? No. I couldn't, not until he accepted his destiny. He wouldn't understand the war between the Bazmeht and the Uraeli.

"Anything specific you want to share?" His voice held a sharp edge.

"No."

His brow flew upward, and I realized I'd better come up with a better answer.

Opting for deflection, I tossed my hair. "You imagine a conspiracy to keep you uninformed. I don't know any more than you what will happen next." Which was true, if vague.

"All you do is worry. Life is too short to go around with a wrinkled forehead." Josh reached forward, lightly touching the aching spot between my eyes. "Give me an hour of freedom, and then I promise to let you lock me up at home for the rest of the night."

"Oooh, lucky guy," a man in a leather vest said as he passed by.

"Josh!" Self-conscious, I pushed him toward the throng of people in the street. What if Ninja had spies watching for me? What if – I put us in the middle, surrounded by colorful decoys.

He pulled me forward, saying, "I know you don't want to be here but you are. Enjoy. You're not hurting anybody, and you'll be at my side the entire time, guarding me with your life."

He made it sound much hotter than anything in the Bazmeht handbook suggested.

Once we crossed the street, I tugged him to the side beneath the shadows of a Banyan tree. I'd send the picture of Ninja to Sekhmet so she could put our enemies face into the data bank at control. "Let me call in. It will only take a minute." I turned, discreetly, untucking my phone from its strap.

"You have some cool tricks," Josh said, rubbing his chin and staring at the front of my dress. "Wait!" He grabbed my phone before I knew what he was doing, and I gaped at him. Nobody's done that to me since my first week of training.

"Give that back." I held my hand out, palm up.

"Hear me out," he said. "If you call to check in, they're gonna tell you to keep me under wraps – those meddling ladies can't help it. They don't know the situation, hell, I don't know the situation – but Lorelei said you're one of the best guards they have. They should trust you to make the right judgment. I trust you to totally keep me safe. I doubt that whoever vandalized the stuff in the library is looking to pop me on the street, you know?"

He didn't know Ninja, and thanks to the mind sweep we'd done on him, he wouldn't recognize her if she stood in front of him and introduced her nasty self.

But he had a point. At his side, I'd keep him from harm. My honor, my duty.

I didn't want to argue with Bastet or Sekhmet, who would both go out of their minds knowing that I'd seen Ninja – who somehow managed to escape Bazmeht security. Her and her companion. The inside traitor.

Confused, I wanted to prove I could handle myself. Running to Bastet every time there was a glitch didn't make me seem very competent. And Sekhmet wouldn't understand Josh needing to 'live a little' instead of work toward finding clues to the riddle within the Myth of Mafdet.

Sighing, I decided I'd talk to Lorelei about it as soon as we got home, even if I had to wake her.

"What are you thinking inside that beautiful head of yours?" Josh put his hand on my elbow and guided me down the street.

"You win. But if I see anything at all out of the ordinary, we are leaving."

He burst into laughter as a woman roller-blading with a smoking monkey on her shoulder passed by. "Who gets to define 'out of the ordinary'?"

# CHAPTER TWENTY-FIVE

## KISSING COUSINS

As Josh led us through the steady stream of people – a lot of them loudly feeling the effects of too much alcohol – I kept my eyes sharp and my ears fine-tuned. Words jumped from the middle of conversations, creating a convoluted story of Miami at night.

"-but he's dead!"

"-she still has sex with him-"

"-for the money, she's loaded-"

"-I heard he's got a big-"

"-meth addiction-"

"-I'll only be gone two weeks-"

I shook my head, concentrating on anything familiar, familiar to me might mean danger for Josh. Voices with European accents, plots to kill, that sort of thing.

We turned into a well-lit park surrounded with benches. In the center was a stage where a band took a break.

"Rock and roll," I said with a nod. "I like it." My iPhone held a mix of Euro hits and American music like Three Days Grace.

Josh grinned, but I sensed something darker beneath his smile. "Want to meet the band?"

I don't know how it happened, but I went from being a Level One Bazmeht guard to a groupie, a term I was well familiar with, thanks to Rock of Love. "Yes!"

"They're called Third Time's The Charm, alternative stuff. The songs use a recurring theme of good versus evil. Spooky." Josh made a 'bwah ha haha' sound, designed to scare me.

I assured him it didn't. "I have faith that good will triumph over evil in the end." We walked toward the stage, side by side.

"You would." Josh shook his head in mock-disgust, stopping before a guitar wielding, tall blond. Highlights? Now I'd always wonder. "Mark, meet Shani, my uh, cousin from Cairo."

I didn't like the cousin story any more.

"Josh – you're back." Mark bobbed his head. I noticed his

hand wasn't out for me to shake, so I kept mine loose by my side too. "Shani from Egypt. Came just in time for the hurricane. How long you staying?"

"Depends on how well I like it here," I said, keeping my tone as dry as his. I sensed an undercurrent between he and Josh, and I couldn't tell if they were friends.

Mark snorted. "Good answer."

A short guy with olive skin and dark hair came over with the bassist and lead singer. The short guy tapped Josh on the shoulder with his drumsticks. I didn't like it and took a step forward. Josh blocked me before I broke his drumsticks over his head.

"Dude! 'Bout time you got back. Wanna work your magic tonight, man?" He flipped the sticks in the air, handing them to Josh, who handed them right back.

"Nope. This is the Cabo show, now, we're here to listen, that's all."

Cabo sucked in his lower lip and pointed a drumstick at me. "Your cuz here is a freaking genius. Crazy brilliant, man. We're on in ten. Want a beer?"

Josh used to be the drummer for this band? I remembered to what seemed like ten lifetimes ago to the night at the ambassador's mansion. Abhar had shown Josh the Egyptian drums, which Josh played.

"Go ahead, Josh." My mouth dried at the thought of Josh on stage, working his 'magic' on the drums. Working his magic on me.

"Another time, Shani."

He sounded angry, so I didn't push. But I was disappointed.

A pretty, blond girl in a bikini with a thin sarong tied around her hips swayed toward us. "Parker," she batted her eyes at the lead singer, "will you sing Isis next? It's my favorite."

"Isis?" Intrigued, I asked, "The Egyptian goddess?"

"Yeah." Parker slouched his shoulders, his eyebrow piercings winking in the amp lights. "Chicks dig it. Josh wrote it before he quit. Loser." Parker slid a dark, malicious look over Josh. "Ready to come back?"

"No." Josh didn't drop his gaze. "I told you, I'm just here to be a fan."

He wrote? I remembered the scribbled writings I'd found in the locked case in his room. Maybe not love letters, or angry poetry but lyrics? I'd heard his dismissive conversations with his ex Parisian girlfriend, and he hadn't seemed anguished enough to write what I'd read. Lyrics made more sense.

"You can sit with us, Josh," the girl offered. "We've got room." She gave me a distracted but friendly smile. "I'm Tiff."

She led us away from a confrontation to a giant blanket that had a cooler on one corner and couples in various stages of making out on the other three. "Sit anywhere," she said with an airy wave. "There's vodka and Red Bull, help yourself." She wandered off before I could say thank you.

"Tiff's always been a little out there," Josh said without apology. "She's cool though."

"She seems...nice." Like a half-naked butterfly, she fluttered around, greeting her many friends.

"Yeah. We dated in high school."

He hadn't been kidding when he said he liked blonds with curves. "She's pretty," I choked past unwanted jealousy.

"It was tenth grade. She dumped me for a trumpet player." He went to the cooler and pulled out two Red Bull's. "Here. It'll give you wings."

I put my hands up. "The last thing I need is wings, trust me."

"It's just an energy drink – no vodka, Mom."

"You are *funny*. I have plenty of energy. Is there a water bottle in there?" No way would I take any chances and try something new when Josh needed me clear headed. While he bent over digging through the ice for a water, I snuck my phone from his back pocket and gave a sigh of relief the instant my fingers felt the orange plastic.

Giving it a quick kiss, I hid it away. I'd promised to try to have a good time, but all I could think about was Ninja. In the same restaurant as us, but unless I'd read the situation wrong, she'd been surprised I was there. I wish I knew where the Bazmeht leak came from, so I'd know who to trust. How long had Josh and Tiff dated?

"Shani! Stop worrying." He handed me a dripping wet water bottle with the label half slipping off. "We're safe here, no matter what you might think. Nobody is going to want to hurt us in the middle of a crowd."

As if that would make me relax my vigil...my mother, hateful as she was, hadn't raised an idiot. "Josh, why didn't you tell me you were in a band?" Visions of Bret Michaels danced through my head. "Did you wear a red bandana? Biker boots?" I bit my lower lip. "Do you have any piercings?"

"Freak." He sat cross-legged on the blanket, so I did too. Our knees touched and I liked the casual, yet forbidden, contact. "You heard Parker. I quit. Now be quiet, 'cause they're starting."

"But,"

"Shh." He watched the band get ready as the lights dimmed. The crowd hushed in a wave of silence, and the stage went dark.

By the Goddess, this was way more exciting than television. My stomach tensed, and I found myself holding my breath as I waited for the show to start.

A single strum sounded into the night and then the entire stage lit up like fireworks as the band dove into Tiff's favorite song. Isis.

Parker's voice was deep and dangerous, his lean body whipped around stage as if possessed by Isis herself. He sang of her power, her passion, and her devastation as Seth killed her husband Osiris. Seth and Osiris were brothers and this murderous act sentenced Osiris to the Underworld. Pain resonated through the ballad parts of the song and *thrummed* with danger during some of the faster sections.

I was stunned that Josh had written such a powerful song. Each lyric, each note was heavy with Egyptian history – our shared past. When it was over, the stage went dark, and the crowd burst into applause. I clapped so hard my hands stung.

The lights came back on and Parker pumped his fist into the air. "Third Time's the Charm, baby!"

Josh got to his feet, pale beneath his tan. "Let's get out of here."

"What is wrong? Are you sick?"

Pulling me toward a dark side exit of the park, Josh stumbled over blankets, coolers, and a few prone bodies before breaking free of the park enclosure. A trail led to the dunes and the mostly secluded beach. Lights were forbidden because of the nesting sea turtles, leaving the only illumination to the moon and stars. Waves crashed against the sand with ferocious thunder.

Very mysterious.

Thanks to my night vision, the huge expanse of midnight

black water seemed crystal clear. "This is close enough." I yanked backward and he stopped.

"Sorry. Let's sit on the dunes then."

I eyed the distance between the beach and the small bank of sand. "All right."

"I thought I could handle taking you there, you know, show off my cool friends." Josh plopped into the sand with a heavy thud.

I chose to sit with a little less enthusiasm, saving my already bruised behind from more injury. "You did not want to show me you had 'cool' friends. You wanted me to hear the song you wrote. It was brilliant, haunting, and true to the original legend."

"You would think of that."

"I thought you didn't know any of the history?"

"How could I not have picked something up? I live in an Egyptian exhibit for Christ's sake."

He had a very good point there.

"But that song came from one of my nightmares. That's why I had to quit the band. The more I poured my soul into the music, the less control I had over dreams."

I heard the pain he'd captured in the lyrics and music of Isis. Parker's vocals, but Josh's voice. Emotional infant that I am, it just about slayed me.

What had it done to the artist?

I heard the band playing a ballad now, something slow and sweet, without the anguish of Isis. I'd bet Josh didn't write it.

I cleared the emotion from my throat. "I'm surprised writing, creating, didn't help stop the nightmares, like cauterizing a wound."

He chuckled. "You don't mind going for the bloody images, do you? Well, I thought it would work that way too. Instead, my writing gave the nightmares strength. It seemed to breathe life into them, and in each one after, my death got more detailed."

I studied his profile, memorizing his expressions for when I returned to Egypt. As I scooped the cool sand and let it fall between my fingers, I knew that for right now, there was nowhere I'd rather be.

"I'm sorry, Josh. I don't remember my dreams, not usually."

"Lucky you. I'd give just about anything to forget."

My phone bleeped. An incoming text. I sent Josh a 'gotcha' look and pulled my phone from its strap.

*Where are you? We have news about Josh's biological father. B*

I looked at Josh, my stomach jumping to my throat. His father...his real father. How would he react to knowing he was a member of the Felidia as well as the carrier of the Blood of Ra? "Let me answer this really quick. It's Bastet. If you think I worry, you should see her in action."

*Talking with J now. Do you know who he is?*

*Call me when you are alone.*

Cloak and dagger business, isn't that what Lorelei called it?

"Did you tell on me?" Josh tossed sand over my toes. "That I made you go out tonight?"

"No. As you said, I am perfectly capable of guarding you. I'll tell her when we get back."

"Will you get in trouble?"

I thought about it, picking up another handful of sand and letting it fall. Life, as Josh had said, was short – for most people. "Probably." I shrugged. When we got back to the house, Josh's life would change, whether he wanted it or not. "Not a big deal."

Once he understood his path as Felidia, maybe the nightmares would stop. The oracle could at least help him forget, before Josh ended up insane. It happened sometimes, which is why the Felidia community tried so hard to keep its members together. If a Felidia didn't want to be a Felidia, then the demi-goddesses did a mind sweep and let them go into the world. But you couldn't mind sweep away the Blood of Ra.

Could you?

If he really didn't want to believe, would the demi-goddesses offer Josh the chance to forget?

My heart twisted with uncertainty.

"We can go," Josh said reluctantly.

"No. Take your time." I couldn't protect him from what was to come. My talents involved weaponry and hand-to-hand combat. I couldn't put a sleeper hold on the truth.

"I was kind of hoping to mend a few fences tonight."

"Mend fences?"

"Parker and I had a big argument the night I quit. He had a talent scout interested in us, but...I couldn't stay. He blames me for them not being signed. The scout wanted the writer of Isis." Josh leaned his forehead on his drawn up knees. "It would've killed me, in real life, if I kept writing."

I reached out and rubbed his back. Ignoring the warning voice in my head, which sounded a lot like Sekhmet, I let my fingertips trace each vertebra, each rib, each smooth line of muscle. "It will be all right," I lied.

It wouldn't be all right. Josh would find out that his mother lied, again, and that there was a reason he kept dreaming of death. He was reliving his past.

"Here." I pressed on the sensitive spot between his neck and shoulder and lightly pinched his skin. "Feel that? If you ever find yourself in danger, this close, reach out, here, and squeeze hard." I felt him shiver beneath my fingertips. My blood heated as I imagined my lips on the spot I'd touched. "Now you know my secret."

"Thank you." He turned, staring at me in the moonlight, his cheek resting against his knee. "You are the first person I've ever known who totally gets me."

Because your mom stole you away from the pride...but that betrayal was for later. In the now, I said, "I understand more than you know. You feel different; you *are* different. But you shouldn't be afraid. Embrace your strengths."

"Nice line of politically correct crap, Shani. I thought we were finally going to be friends."

I saw the plea in his eyes, and I couldn't turn away. He needed a friend just as much as I did, and for the next half hour, I'd shield him against the world. After that, there was no guarantee of what place I might play in his life.

My chest ached with sorrow and regret. I didn't want the regret.

I leaned over, touching my lips lightly to his. "Friends."

We held hands and watched the relentless waves batter the shore. The flexible sand gave without really losing ground. I'm sure Bastet would find a lesson in there, but as I reveled in the feel of Josh's fingers clasped in mine, I didn't care.

He finally broke the companionable silence. "Thank you."

Touched, I whispered, "For what?"

"I think...I think just for being you."

Tears threatened to fill my eyes, but I held them back by blinking up at the star-heavy sky. Nobody had ever said that to me – ever.

Doing the math, I predicted that I had a fifty percent chance of him hating my guts once he learned the truth. "Come on." I jumped up, spraying sand everywhere. "I hear voices, a group of people are coming."

"I don't hear anything."

"*You* don't have the best hearing on the guard, so I'm not surprised."

Josh stood, his shadow blocking the moon. I shivered with premonition. Too bad I couldn't fine-tune a bad feeling to get disaster details.

"You're just scared that you kissed me," he teased. His blue eyes glowed with male satisfaction. "You like me. Admit it."

"I can't like you. You're a stubborn-"

His mouth shut me up in a hurry.

It's hard to talk when your lips are being devoured by Red Bull-flavored lust. The texture of his mouth was as soft as warm velvet, the light then hard, pressure of his kiss made my sandals fall off my feet. His hand slid to my lower back, caressing my hip as he brought me close. I couldn't get close enough.

I was starving and he was grilled rabbit.

"Josh...uh, dude, why are you kissing your cousin?"

Cabo's voice watered down my desire in a single splash of reality.

"She's hot, I'll give you that," Parker drawled. "But unless you move to Arkansas, it's illegal."

Mortified, humiliated, and already missing the warmth of Josh's touch, I leaned over and grabbed my sandals by the straps. "Do you want to stay and chat?"

"No." He shook his head.

"Let's run!"

Grinning, Josh took off down the beach, but I leaped ahead, leading us home over bushes, fences, and even a rooftop.

We made it home in ten minutes, barely breathing heavy.

"Amazing. I wanna do it again. You sure your feet aren't shredded?" Josh narrowed his eyes, obviously concerned I might be hiding an injury.

"No." My skin is made of much sterner stuff than regular human skin. "Like you, I heal fast. Do you think your mom is still awake?"

"And waiting at the door with a glass of wine in hand."

It would be nice, knowing someone waited for me. "I had fun, Josh, thank you." Please don't bring up the kiss.

"Yeah."

I appreciated his limited English skills.

Suddenly awkward, I dangled my sandals by the straps. "I'm going to check on Lorelei and then go to bed. We have a lot of work to do in the morning." We were no closer to figuring out who had broken into the library, I still had to call Bastet and send the picture of Ninja to Sekhmet. Depending on what Lorelei suggested, I might head back out to search for Ninja at the Waverunner.

Josh looked over my shoulder and squinted into the dark on the other side of the gate. "Hey, isn't that Lorelei right there?"

# ⟨HAPTER TWENTY-SIX

## SEEING IS BELIEVING

"Lorelei?" I don't know how Josh managed to pick her out of the shadows but he was right. That was my mentor jogging toward us with a wave and a smile.

First of all, I was thrilled that she was feeling well enough to get some exercise.

But midnight?

She'd taken medicine guaranteed to knock her flat for hours.

*And I'd been warned to trust nobody.*

True, it had been from my mother, but still, the warning rang in my ears. I kept my smile plastered on my face, even as my stomach dropped to my toes.

Suspicion ran its course as we waited for Lorelei to come to the gate so Josh could lock it after her. Why tell him that she could leap over the thing when he'd already had such a bad night?

"Are you all right?" Josh asked me. "You sure got quiet."

"Tired. What a day." And now, I had to face Lorelei and get some answers. I'm sure there was a way to casually bring up my suspicions. I couldn't think of one that wouldn't destroy our friendship.

Where could she have gone? Why would she have left Josh's house without sending word?

Ninja.

Ninja had been waiting at the bar. For Lorelei? There had been one chair saved. Maybe my friend, my mentor, was the leak in the Bazmeht compound.

*No.*

My stomach churned, and I swallowed three times in a row to avoid throwing up.

I chewed my lip. What was her motivation?

She was a talented Council Leader, respected and, yes, adored. Feisty, fun, but deadly and honest. Reliable. Did she work for the Uraeli? Had she been the one to vandalize the library, then maybe had a migraine and forgotten she'd spilled her drink – with the telltale Flamingo Pink by Jet lipstick on the rim of the glass?

Maybe she needed money. Though I couldn't imagine what for. The Bazmeht gave us unlimited access to funds.

How could she work for the Uraeli when they'd killed her daughter?

I couldn't believe Lorelei capable of deception, and yet...I couldn't afford not to keep my eyes open to the possibility. My love for her had to take last place, or at least behind my client – Josh – and the Bazmeht.

Emotion couldn't be a factor in the equation. If Lorelei were guilty of betraying the Bazmeht, I would take her down.

"You didn't have to wait." She leaned over at the waist and sucked in air. A show, certainly, unless she'd been running for hours. She lifted her head and winked at Josh and I. "I'm glad you did."

"Your headache is better?"

"Much. I think by taking my medicine at the first sign, I managed to beat it into submission. I feel terrible that I left you both to work so hard today, but it looks like you took a break too? Nice dress, Shani." Lorelei elbowed me and continued, "I wanted to clear my head, to be fresh for the morning."

Sounded plausible. Ten minutes ago, I would have believed her, without question. But until she'd uttered that last sentence, she hadn't looked at me.

"I'm just glad you're feeling better. I know how miserable your migraines make you."

Lorelei tilted her head to peer at me. "Are you mad?"

So much for subtle. "No." I put my arm around her shoulders so she couldn't see my face. I'm sure I had tells too, and until I learned them, it was better to be safe than sorry. "Just tired. We've had a lot go on while you were down for the count."

I felt her relax against me. "Like what? It has to do with what you and Josh were doing in the library, behind locked doors, I would bet my sapphire ring on it."

Josh blushed, because he'd insisted she didn't know we were there.

"Lorelei," I cleared my throat, angry because I'd thought I'd hurt her feelings, when she'd betrayed my trust. "What do people do behind locked doors?"

"Shani!" Lorelei grabbed my hand and squeezed hard. "You'd better be kidding."

"I am." I laughed, as if she wasn't crushing the bones in my hand. Then I squeezed back and saw her wince. "Come to my room and let's catch up."

I saw a resigned expression cross her face before she agreed. "Let me shower and I'll meet you there." She released my hand and blew a kiss to Josh, who'd been quietly observing the exchange. "Night."

"See you in the morning," he said.

Josh locked the gate, and we walked into the dark house. His mother wasn't waiting up – at least not anywhere we could see – no Maria, either. We walked silently to the kitchen and sat in the gloom of the oven light.

"What's going on? Between you and Lorelei?"

Ruthless, I shoved emotion into the cave it belonged in. "Nothing. We'll work it out."

"You could really get in trouble if we hooked up, huh."

"Yes." I didn't offer further explanation, and we stayed quiet, facing each other at the small kitchen table. He took my hand, threading his fingers through mine.

"I want to be friends. I hoped we could be more."

"Impossible." I'd never forget a single word we'd said on the beach tonight. Or the way our lips melded with passion. But I had to let it go.

If Ninja worked with Lorelei then Josh was in serious danger. I had to get Lorelei to tell me the truth. She's a council leader, and I'm only a Level One Bazmeht with a lot to learn. She'd taught me all I knew, so I was at a disadvantage in more ways than one.

Squaring my shoulders, I tried to explain. "In order to do my job, I can't think of you as my friend. I have to think of you as my duty, my honorable job, or else I might not be able to perform to the best of my ability."

"I'm not in any danger, Shani." His tone was tightly controlled, angry, and I thought it best to keep it that way.

"I don't agree, Josh. And before you ask, I can't tell you anything more." I closed my eyes against the dangers he'd be facing soon enough. "Let me be the one to shoulder this burden, it is what I've been trained to do."

"You're a liar. You need protection more than I do – don't

think I haven't caught on to the fact that every time 'we' are in danger, the target is you."

I bowed my head and bit my lip before I blurted the truth like a novice guard. I'm not to give information. Need to know only.

"And last night, when Cadee brought you home? I noticed something weird about your skin. It moved, Shani. And when I helped cover your head with the blanket, you had cat ears. Yes, cat ears. I've tried to forget about that all day, but I can't, which is why I took you to hear Isis. You are the personification of every nightmare I've ever had. Every time I die, it has something to do with what *you* are. And guess what, sometimes in my dreams, I'm a lion. Mahes."

*Oh. Dear Goddess. What do I do?* I couldn't breathe past the shock. Mahes was a lion god whose priests served at a temple dedicated to fertility. *He was my ideal mate, and I couldn't have him.*

"I should hate you. Fear you. But I'm trying to be a friend. I'd like the same respect."

He left me at the table without saying goodbye. I listened to his footsteps until he reached his room, and then I stood, trying very hard to stay detached. His words hurt, but I couldn't let them make me bleed.

I broke into the library, more determined than ever to find answers. If Lorelei were behind the theft of the pages, then I'd need to find out what she'd done with them and get the information to Sekhmet. No emotion, no arguing, just the job.

I'd never felt more alone.

Zelda's neat piles of damaged texts offered no new clues. I noticed a super clean spot on the carpet, and saw the cup on the counter top where I'd set it earlier. Was it possible to take up close pictures and find fingerprints?

Thank Ra for smart phones. First, out of habit alone, I skimmed my messages, listing them in order of importance. Two from Bastet and one from Sekhmet – or Keket, who Sekhmet had do her texting. I'd read them later. Josh, in bed, could wait until morning to hear the identity of his father.

*Josh witnessed my change, and yet, he'd kissed me anyway. Mahes.*

Don't think about it. A text from Martina, wanting to know if I was ever coming home. I had my horoscope sent to me every day, and the weather channel sent me daily updates. I had the joke of the day and history tidbits in my inbox. I was never alone, not really.

*Emotions belonged in a nice cyber file to read when a girl was prepared.*

Staring at the pink mouth on the glass, I acknowledged that I had no idea if the pictures would help, but if I could clear Lorelei, it was worth the effort.

My vision is fabulous, even in the dark, but I don't have telescopic zoom. To the naked eye, there were no prints, and I'd been careful not touch anywhere but the bottom of the glass. Positioning the cup, lipstick side toward me, I zoomed to 200 percent with my iPhone and pushed the picture icon. It made a funny noise instead of a click. Had the immersion in sand ruined it?

I'd get it fixed, that's all. Taking off the back was easier than I thought it would be. Until I noticed the scratches – scratches I'd assumed had come from the beach but could have come from a tiny screwdriver prying off the back plastic case.

I lifted the battery of my phone and saw a Bazmeht tracking device.

*Betrayed.*

Lorelei had taken my phone after Cadee had found it.

"Shani?"

I dropped the phone on the countertop, next to the glass. Betrayal was bitter and it fueled my fury. "Lorelei." I turned, keeping my emotions in check, but barely.

"I waited in your room, but..."

Her words trailed and she put a hand to the towel wrapped around her supposedly wet from the shower hair. Not that I would ever take a word she said at face value again. For all I knew, she hid a bomb under that towel.

Lorelei flushed a soft pink as she noticed my beautiful orange phone in pieces. "I can explain."

"Don't bother."

Anger pinched her mouth. "Is that necessary?"

"You tracked me. Without my consent or knowledge. As if I was the one under guard, so let me ask you if my attitude is necessary?"

"Fine. Sekhmet wanted me to watch out for you. Is that so bad? Bazmeht is family and we take care of one another."

"This isn't taking care of me. It's spying." I lowered my voice as the realization dawned. "You were out jogging to see where I'd gone. When I went behind the sand dune, the GPS couldn't pick me up, so Bastet texted me." My belly ached. "None of you trust me!"

She glanced away. "I wasn't spying on you, for Goddess' sake. I was clearing my head."

I stepped away from her, my mind racing. "I'd prefer you spying on me. Because if you weren't following me, that means you had your own agenda. Does Sekhmet know that you're playing both sides of the game?"

"What are you talking about?"

"No need to be coy, Lorelei. Ninja was at the restaurant Josh and I went to tonight. In the bar, waiting for someone. Must've been you. Were you supposed to trick me into coming too? What then?"

"I would never betray the Bazmeht!" Lorelei roared, her pretty face contorted in anger. "Never."

"Well, here's a glass with your lipstick on it, found in this library where the texts with information on Mafdet were stolen or damaged." I kept my voice monotone. I had to be about the job, backing my instincts up with fact.

"Where did you get that?" Her face paled and her eyes glittered as she looked from the cup to me. "You believe I would do such a thing?"

Lorelei. My mentor, my friend. She held my gaze without blinking or widening her eyes. Her immeasurable power supported me, and she'd always stood by my side. She'd lied about following me, but she wasn't lying now.

I'd stake my life on it.

More importantly, I'd stake Josh's.

"Until this instant, I couldn't be sure."

Her hurt escaped in a tiny puff of breath.

I swallowed, unable to apologize for doing my job. "Which means someone set you up, and we need to know who before Josh is hurt."

"I don't understand." I watched as Lorelei morphed into efficient Bazmeht Bodyguard mode, overcoming her towel-hair and Victoria Secret PJs. Just as I, in my peacock blue disco dress and bare feet, would be ready for war. *We are Bazmeht.*

"Somebody knows everything that we know. We have to

assume, since Ninja is in town, that it's the Uraeli. They've wanted the Blood of Ra for a millennia or more. We try to make sure that they don't get it, and to my knowledge, we've succeeded. We've been peaceable enemies for five centuries, but I think the demi-goddesses are right and change is coming."

"I see." Lorelei's eyes narrowed as she noticed the stack of damaged books and scrolls. "Clues to the Myth of Mafdet were in those?"

"We don't know. I've sent the titles to Sekhmet and Control, and hopefully they'll find a separate copy of the text. Somewhere. But it would be easier to get back what was stolen."

"Who?"

I shrugged, my mind flitting on ideas before rejecting them. "Maria. Perhaps she's working for the Uraeli? We haven't seen her all day."

"Why?" Lorelei stood with her feet braced, listening respectfully to my thoughts. "She's a member of this family."

"She's the maid. She hates the cat sarcophagi. She *could* think that she is protecting Zelda and Josh by destroying the evidence of Mafdet."

Lorelei paced the room, her simmering anger evident in the short steps she took. "Possible. But why hasn't she done it before now?"

"Maybe she heard us talking, and she's figured out what Josh is. It changes things."

"But not for her. Her love for this family might cause her to act in a protective way, but this act of vandalism was very specific to the Myth. Who else would have a reason to want the myth deciphered?"

My hair kept falling in my face, and I couldn't think. I twisted it then anchored the thick mess with a pencil, jabbing too hard and piercing my scalp. "Ouch."

Lorelei arched a brow but kept pacing. "The Bazmeht are the only ones that know about the myth, to my knowledge."

"That can't be true. The Uraeli must know something of our entwined history."

"If there is a leak in our organization and Ninja knows about the myth and the new clues, then she should know that Josh carries the Blood of Ra in his veins. So why didn't she take him when you were at dinner tonight? No offense, Shani, but he is more valuable to them than you."

"None taken. I agree, even. My guess is she didn't know. Our decision to go out was very last minute."

"What about the French limo driver?"

"He works for the Uraeli." I chewed my lower lip in thought, then smacked my forehead. "As Josh would say, duh." I walked over to the glass. The glass with no fingerprints. "How does a person avoid fingerprints?"

"Gloves." Lorelei's dark brows raised.

"And who wears gloves? Really fabulous gloves?" I stretched my fingers like starfish and wiggled them. "Cadee found me and Josh last night, at dinner."

"She's been in this house." Lorelei took the towel from her head, her dark locks falling around her shoulders.

"She saw me change. It didn't freak her out – I think she had an idea of what we do."

"So she stole my lipstick and broke into the library?" Lorelei's tone questioned our logic.

"I know. Sounds strange, but maybe seeing my fur made her call Ninja, who told her to search. Goddess, I don't know, I'm babbling."

"Cadee." Lorelei paced, her hand on her hip. "It feels like we're on the right track. She'd leave a clue – a wrong clue – hoping to cause dissention between us. Maybe trouble all the way to the demi-goddesses."

"Mother Mafdet, she actually invited me and Josh in to meet her friends. Hello, Ninja."

"What's her motivation?" Lorelei loved to play Devils' advocate.

"Money. She has kids." I rubbed my arms against the sudden chill.

"Somehow she wormed her way into the Bazmeht system, and passed the background checks. I bet she doesn't have kids at all. If she's working for the Uraeli, then she's doing it for the cause. Their cause. To rule Egypt."

I sighed, staring at the glass. "Which means she'll fight to the death."

# CHAPTER TWENTY-SEVEN

## FLEXIBLE MORALITY

"I'm calling Bastet. Let's go to my room, we can put her on speakerphone, and maybe Sekhmet can be there too. It's time we all had the same information."

"Shani, I'm sorry about the tracking device." Lorelei reached out to touch my elbow.

"Let's not talk about it." I closed the library door behind me. "I'm furious, but that won't help me do my job right now, which is to protect Josh from the Uraeli."

Lorelei exhaled. "You are right. Let's get to work."

We sat cross-legged on my bed, Lorelei's phone between us. I didn't have the heart to put mine back together again. Not yet.

Bastet answered on the first ring. "Lorelei – have you found Shani yet? That girl has gone completely off radar."

"Hello Bastet. I found the tracking device under my battery." Hurt made my teeth ache. I kept my voice light. "Sneaky, sneaky."

"Every guard is getting one on their phone, it's a safety precaution. You just happened to be first." Sekhmet didn't bother with apologies.

"By not telling me, you let me know that you don't trust me..." I stared at the orange pieces.

"Bastet and I made the decision together for your own good. It is our prerogative. You'll need to get over it."

Right, as always. The hard to swallow truth stuck in my ego, though I'd sworn an oath to follow their orders to the death. The fact that I'd obviously not earned their trust or respect stung, but I would, absolutely, have to get over it.

Lorelei briefly covered my hand with hers. "Shani and I believe that Cadee is our vandal in the library."

"Ridiculous," Bastet scoffed. "She's working for us. She passed all the background checks."

"Ninja – the Uraeli warrior that killed me then escaped Bazmeht security – is in Miami. Sitting at the Waverunner, the same restaurant as me and Josh. We escaped detection by a whisker's breadth. Then, Cadee suddenly shows up, meeting 'friends'. I don't think she can be trusted."

"For what we pay her?" Sekhmet snorted. "We can trust her. We've asked her to gather information on the Uraeli activities in the area, and obviously she's doing her job."

"Did you know that she could read my mind?"

All three women gasped. "When?"

"Right after I almost drowned..." Last night? No, the night before. I rolled my shoulders to ease the tension.

"What happened?" Bastet wanted details so I gave them. She said, "It had to be because you were vulnerable. Then afterward?"

"I just didn't do it. It didn't seem right, so I built the wall back up."

"Smart. We need to consider this, Bastet. What if we're wrong?"

"Cadee is lovely, she sends me chocolate."

"Chocolate!" Sekhmet yelled. "The fate of the world cannot depend on your being tempted from reason by a box of Godiva."

"If it is Cadee," I interjected before they both started screaming, "then there is an easy answer."

"What?" the demi-goddesses demanded in unison.

"Give me and Lorelei her address, we'll break into her house and get the documents back."

"You are thinking more like a burglar than a bodyguard," Bastet clucked her tongue.

"It is an excellent idea. Hold on, I'm calling Dahlia in Control. And Shani, put your phone back together."

Finding guts I didn't know I had, I said, "I will. But the tracking device won't be in it." Lorelei's eyes grew round.

"Are you disobeying me, Shani Nebit?" Sekhmet's voice held undercurrents of repercussion.

My knee trembled. "Yes."

"You think you know better than I how to run a mission where so much is at stake? You think to bring your personal pride before the good of the Bazmeht?"

Goddess, when she put it like that, it seemed selfish and wrong. But... "Sekhmet, I respectfully request that I be treated the same as the other guards."

"Fortune smiles on you, else I would be there right now to box your ears."

"Sekhmet."

"You *will* put the tracking device back in your phone. It is thanks to your unique *inadequacies* that we are allowing cell phones in the field at all. You've done enough in the name of-"

"All the guards are getting assigned phones for field work, personal cell phones will still be off limits," Bastet clarified. "But for now, we would feel better if you would use yours until your *probation* is over and you can come home."

Lorelei bit her lip to keep from laughing out loud, but her shoulders shook.

Bastet's reminder coupled with Sekhmet's explanation made it easy to back down. "Forgive my impertinence. I will do it right now."

I did, under Lorelei's watchful gaze. "It's done," she said.

"Keep it that way," Sekhmet ordered.

"Have you found the maid yet?" Bastet cleared her throat. "Once we find Cadee innocent, we will need to have another place to look."

"Here's the address on file. Dahlia ran another background check and hacked into the files at the limo company. The addresses match, so you might be in luck. You'll need it to make me forget about your rebellion."

I scratched my throat. "Ready." I jotted the address into my iPhone and pulled up Mapquest. "We can be there in fifteen minutes, maybe less, depending how fast we get out of the house."

"Time is of the essence," Sekhmet said dryly.

"Oh…before we go, did you find out who Josh's biological father is?"

"Didn't I just tell you to hurry?"

She ended the phone call over Bastet's protests and Lorelei shook her head in amazement. "You have nerve, Shani. I haven't seen something like that since your mother insisted on having radios put in all of our rooms. Sharifa loved to dance."

My mother loved to dance?

"Anyway, let me grab my tennis shoes. Do I need to dress in black? What is the proper attire for breaking into a possibly innocent woman's home?"

"I don't know. Maybe we should toss Maria's room first. Just to be sure."

"You sound like a professional. This is going to be very

invigorating!"

Lorelei left and I slipped out of my dress into black leggings, and a long-sleeved black t-shirt that had a dark purple peace sign on the front. Close enough to all black.

I tiptoed past Maria's room and put my ear to the door. Silence – not even the sound of her breathing. Where had she gone? What if she'd really been the one to take the pages then hide before the storm came?

It didn't make sense. I reached for the knob anyway, concentrating on creating just the right amount of pressure to pop the lock.

The door didn't want to open. I felt a metaphysical force opposing my energy, and the knob turned hot beneath my hand. "Ow! Not fair."

"What's going on?" Lorelei whispered softly so there would be no chance of anyone overhearing.

"Something's not right. The doorknob is hot."

"She's a witch, remember? Spanish voo doo."

"Well, where is she?" Unease tickled my nape.

"Let's hurry. We can try again when we get back from Cadee's."

"I feel like – something's wrong." I stared hard at the housekeeper's door, as if seeing through solid objects would suddenly be my new super power. It wasn't. It gave me a headache. "We have to find her."

"When we get back, we'll search every inch of the house. I'll help."

Lorelei had covered her hair with a black sock and painted black stripes of kohl beneath her eyes. She wore a one-piece, black body stocking that could get us arrested for indecent exposure.

"We better not get caught." I led the way out the back kitchen door – no Maria, and the kitchen television wasn't on – and easily jumped the twelve-foot fence. We ran silently through the night, our thoughts separate, our footsteps in tandem.

"This is it." I stopped before a small bungalow styled house, single story. There wasn't any foliage around the perimeter, nothing we could hide behind as we tried to break in.

I dipped my head, concentrating on widening the canal to my inner ear. I heard the scratch of a palmetto bug's wings on the windowsill and the high-pitched hum of the alarm system.

"Nothing to it," I whispered to Lorelei. All Bazmeht can hear better than the average human, but my ability is truly a gift. Balancing on my toes, I motioned Lorelei to stay right at my heels as we ran for the back of the house. No trees but no streetlights either.

"I don't hear anything at all, other than the alarm system. No heart beats, no snoring, no pets."

"Why are you leading?" Lorelei put her hand on my arm.

"Because Josh is my client, you are here as back up."

"Oh. That's right."

I paused, my elbow poised to break the glass from the back door. "Just don't let me mess up to teach me a lesson, all right? I swear by the Goddess's Spear that I will learn just as well if you tell me before I screw up."

Lorelei laughed, the balance between us restored.

"We're lucky, this alarm is a keypad with a time delay. I'm going to rip it off the wall then unplug the phone line. I think it might be connected. I have four seconds. On three."

My adrenalin kept me crisp and focused; my training prepared me for this exact moment. "One, two – three." I jabbed with my elbow, reached in through the broken glass, flicked the lock back, and turned the knob. Went to the left, tore off the alarm panel, and unplugged the phone next to the refrigerator.

"Made a little noise," Lorelei observed. "But not bad. She'll know we were here."

"Look at the neighborhood. She'll know *someone* was here. Anybody could break in." I looked around the vacant room. "I thought she'd have better taste."

"True."

Lorelei went left, and I turned right, checking each room with a thoroughness aided by night vision.

We met in the tiny living room.

"Notice anything strange?" Lorelei's mouth was a hard line.

"Lots. Where to start? No sign of children. The rooms are bare. The furniture isn't worth donating to the poor. This is a front."

"There's one last room – the master bedroom, if 200 square feet can be called that."

We stayed shoulder to shoulder as we walked down the hall. "I sure miss my Glock right about now." I'd palmed my blade, and noticed that Lorelei did the same.

Lifting my nose, I sniffed then shook my head and grabbed Lorelei's shoulder before we went into the room. "That smell – sort of sweet – it was like Ninja's perfume."

"The Uraeli?"

"Yes."

"I don't smell anything."

All I had to do was reach and open the door. Just...

"Do it already!"

"Ah." I twisted the handle, expecting resistance, but the unlocked door swung inward. The bedroom was dark, except for the giant glass aquarium, back lit with a black light.

Instead of nice fishies swimming in salt water, this aquarium had a snake as thick as my wrist coiled within the center.

Lorelei stumbled against me, and I held her upright. The air reeked of rotten cantaloupe, and I checked the cage to see if the snake had a thing for molded vegetation.

Nothing. I waved my hand beneath my nose.

"What's wrong?" Lorelei asked, scanning the rest of the bedroom.

"How can you not smell that? It's awful!" I pinched the bridge and breathed in through my mouth.

Lorelei looked at me as if I was insane and moved toward the lid of the cage. The wire top didn't seem near sturdy enough to contain a huge, dangerous, poisonous, deadly and disgusting snake. "We have to kill it," she said matter-of-factly.

"Yes." According to the Bazmeht manual, we should have done it already.

The only good snake? A dead snake. Tefnut actually made a pair of boots from snakeskin, which we all agreed was pretty twisted.

The sleeping cobra made my belly churn with nausea. Memories of venom spewing through the air as Josh yanked Ninja from my dying body gave me strength. He'd saved me. Now it was my turn.

The queen-sized bed took an entire wall, next to the tiny closet. The doors wide open. A waiter's black and white uniform, the white shirt stained red, hung next to a limo driver's uniform. Not monstrous, like the French guy, but petite, like Cadee.

Leather gloves lay on the little side table next to the phone.

"This is definitely her place. She has a roommate, too. The Uraeli waiter. I'll search for the papers." I turned, but Lorelei smacked my arm.

"Not so fast," she said. "I already found them."

I knew what she was going to say, even as my eyes scanned the reptile cage. The enclosure had plenty of room for a few pieces of ancient paper stuffed in the corners. What better guard against a cat shifter than a five-foot venomous snake?

"I hate Cadee. I do. She's mean."

"Very mature, Shani. At least it's sleeping."

Yes, we had to be grateful for the small things. Still, I choked on a shriek when it opened its eyes. Dark, familiar eyes. As it lifted its head and stuck out its forked tongue, I swear I almost gagged on my own bile.

I knew this snake, had faced him in human form.

Memories of a dark time in my hidden psyche leaped to the front of my terrorized brain, urging me to flee or – even worse – fight.

My jawbones cracked as my face changed. Powerless, I fought for control as my body morphed into a feline warrior. Semi-anthropomorphically correct – a strong mix of a woman's super strength with the face and muscles of a cat. My carnassial teeth on either side of my upper premolars and my lower molars formed so that I could easily tear the snake's head from its body with a scissor-like bite.

*Serpent Slayer.*

Lorelei jumped back, her eyes dark in her pale face. "What are you doing? What's happening?"

"I'm not doing it on purpose. The smell of the snake is triggering a primal reaction, I can't stop the change." My mouth watered in anticipation of a good fight and the victory kill. *It was physically impossible for the waiter to full-body shift into a cobra.*

I scratched my feline ear. *Wasn't it?*

"What can I do to help?"

"You're asking me?" I relied on instinct alone to guide me through the next stages of battle. If my vision had been clear before, it crystallized now. My sense of smell told me there was a pair of Rottweiler's two houses down. My hearing, so acute it bordered on painful, yet...I am finally me.

𓂝𓆑𓏤𓈖𓆑𓂋 𓊪𓅱 𓈖𓆙𓄿 𓂧𓈖𓄿𓏤𓆓𓏤𓂻

My shoulders rolled, and the flexibility of my bones allowed me to twist and jump to the top of the bureau. Crouched on my haunches, I peered into the deadly eyes of the cobra.

Scared, it flared its hood and hissed.

Unimpressed, I hissed back.

With curved teeth bared, it darted forward, knocking the lid off the cage and lunging for my face. I sprang back, out of the way. The cobra fell to the floor with a loud *thump* and slithered beneath the bed.

Lorelei, smart and quick, jumped forward, grabbing the papers that belonged to the Felidia and the Bloodline of Re. They stank of snake.

She ran for the door, but the cobra must have decided Lorelei was the most immediate danger, and before I could hop down from my perch, the damn cobra had its fangs sunk into her calf.

I saw red. Blood red, passionate red, furious red. I granted no mercy. My duty is to destroy the enemy, and the cobra had no chance to survive as I took my fury and embraced it, shredding the snake to bits with my claws and teeth.

Could Lorelei survive the kiss of death?

# CHAPTER TWENTY-EIGHT

## DEATH'S DOOR

I called Josh. He said he'd 'borrow' his mom's car and meet me in front of Cadee's house. I didn't give a lot of details, and he didn't ask a lot of questions. I cried. Scared him, I think.

*Lorelei was going to die.*

The realization blossomed like a tumor, overwhelming all hope. All reason. Cat shifters don't survive snake bites, they just don't.

*Other than me.*

No cure, not since Mafdet, and she took the secret with her to the crypt. Lorelei didn't move, her body sprawled across the threshold. The carnage in the bedroom might scar Josh for life, and I don't know how to do a memory wipe.

Taking the comforter from the bed, I turned it inside out and laid Lorelei's body on it. I took the papers she'd been killed for and stuffed them inside my waistband. The lack of power hurt as if I was the one suffering from poison.

*No emotion.*

I pulled the edge of the blanket, with Lorelei on it, into the living room to wait for Josh. My heart ached as I held the agony at bay. Lorelei moaned. I kneeled and smoothed her hair from her sweating forehead.

Irrationally, Zelda's reading of the Myth of Mafdet echoed in my head. Tears dripped as hot as acid from my eyes as I accepted my mentor's death. But...maybe – *maybe* if I could survive a snake's venom like the Ancient Mother, then it might be possible for me to save Lorelei from it too.

Wouldn't that really piss my mother off?

Lorelei's face was pale. Not pale – waxen. Dark circles already formed beneath her eyes. Her breath came in fast pants and her ears changed form of their own accord. Fur sprouted like soft golden velvet across her forehead.

"You can't die." The order sounded like a plea for mercy.

I felt her pulse. Thready. What was I supposed to do? This wasn't covered anywhere in the damn handbook.

At last, I gave in to the overwhelming onslaught of feeling, praying with all of my soul for a miracle.

*Dear Mother Mafdet, Ancient Healer, guide me, save my friend, even in exchange for my own life. Lorelei is worthy, Mother, worthy of a miracle. Let my hands, my body, be the vehicle.*

I bowed, emptying my brain of all thought, opening the door for whatever, or whoever, might come in.

Mafdet's intrusion into my head wasn't gentle, but I welcomed her just the same.

*Cut the poison. Take the poison into your mouth. You offered to make the sacrifice, foolish child. I will take you up on it and you will owe me one more life. Do you accept?*

*I accept.*

*Then get to work before the poison reaches the tissue!*

I sliced the body stocking at the knee and saw the two puncture holes from the cobra bite, frothing with venomous pink foam.

The smell, so sickly sweet that I gagged, forever etched into my memory. I cut an X over the wound and leaned down, sucking the toxins into my body. I spit out the thick mess and did it again.

Lorelei convulsed, her body going into shock.

I sucked, spat. Prayed. I don't know how much time passed, but my tongue turned numb and my ears rang.

Josh came inside the house and still I sucked poison and spat it aside, unconcerned with what he thought of me or his heritage as I fought for Lorelei's life.

Finally, Lorelei's blood ran clear.

"It's done." Josh took his t-shirt off. "You might wanna, I dunno, wipe your mouth." He ran to the kitchen and brought me back a glass of water to gargle with.

Black spots did the mamba in front of me, and my mouth raged like fire.

"Thank you," I croaked hoarsely.

"I, uh, don't suppose you would be willing to go to the hospital?" He ran his hands over the light covering of fur on Lorelei's forehead.

*The game is over, Mahes. Now you know.*

"Yeah. Now I know."

I'd never been so dizzy. Or maybe I had. I'd just agreed to

give my life in exchange for Lorelei's. Another death. Theoretically, moving me to a Level Three Bazmeht by default, if the demi-goddesses could bring me back.

If my mother didn't gather more council members to vote me out.

"Get us home, Josh. There are jars, beneath the bed. Call Sekhmet. Call Bastet."

"You call them, Shani. You are staying awake. You get a nice dose of old fashioned castor oil, make you puke all that nasty poison up."

"What? I don't want to puke. I promised a life."

"You're not dying, so get used to hangin' your head in the toilet bowl."

The exact details of how we got into the car remain fuzzy, but the next thing I knew, Zelda helped me into the kitchen, dosing me with something very nasty tasting. Oily, slick, and bitter.

Mafdet's laughter reverberated in my skull between heaves.

*No good deed goes unpunished. I'll spare your life. I'm beginning to like you.*

*I am not in the market for new friends.* I rested my hot cheek against the porcelain. *I want to die.*

*Another time. You owe me.*

Morning came and went. I slept like I was already dead and not just balancing on the edge. Fragmented dreams filtered image flashes like a movie on fast forward. The red ball, the pink stone of the ruins in Bubastis. Muu, my mother, Bastet – always Bastet.

Josh put my phone to my ear so that Bastet and Sekhmet could each yell at me. They couldn't fly in and do it in person, thank the Goddess, because of the coming hurricane.

As if the weather was my fault.

We had the pages, and I didn't calm down until Josh promised to fax them to Sekhmet before the storm.

Zelda bathed my forehead with cool water and rinsed my mouth with aloe vera juice. Vaguely aware of my bodily changes, I realized there was no hiding my feline warrior self. My cat psyche and my human subconscious melded to make me, *me*. I had no choice but to trust the descendants of the Bloodline of Re.

"Do you want me to call your mother?" Zelda's concern shone from her oval eyes.

I almost said yes before I remembered that my mother hated me. "How is Lorelei?" I feared the worst. Just because I heard voices in my head, didn't make me a healer.

It made me certifiable.

"She's breathing steady. Her skin is back to, er, normal." I wondered at Zelda's calm. And hoped that if this rotten experience helped with anything, it would be her acceptance of Josh when Sekhmet and Bastet revealed the identity of Josh's true biological father.

"Thank you."

"It's truly been an honor. I've already decided to return to Egypt, at least part time. My brother will just have to get used to a little scandal in his life." She smiled, her eyes soft. "I'll return the treasures to Egyptian soil, where they belong. I've stumbled over my pride long enough."

\* \* \*

When I woke again, my room was dark. The sound of Josh's video game bleeped quietly from the corner.

My own guardian? The idea made me absurdly, ridiculously happy. I touched my ears, relieved to find they were back to normal human ears. No fur along my cheeks or nose, just skin.

No scales, despite the cellular changes I'd put my body through. Surely this proved my fitness to the council?

I could smell snakes. I would be able to detect the previously undetectable enemy. That had to be an ace in the hole, enough to grant me my place in the Bazmeht.

Wind raged outside my bedroom window, and I listened for Lorelei but she was too far away in her plaid room. I waited until I heard the death knell for Josh's character. "Hello."

"Hey!" He tossed the game on the foot of my bed and came to sit beside me. "You won't sleep through your first hurricane."

"Wouldn't want to miss that," I assured him. He stared at me, his perusal without judgment...just searching.

"I can't freaking believe that you're real."

A short laugh slipped from me before I realized I might need to treat the subject seriously. We'd probably be having this conversation again very soon. I reached out and touched his knee. "I'm real. As real as you."

"This explains everything. Well, not *everything*. But a lot."

"About?" I pushed at his chest so he'd stop staring at my face. "You are creeping me out. Enough already."

"The nightmares. Obviously, I took in more of Mom's stories than we thought."

His leg bounced nervously on the bed.

"What?"

"Well...now probably isn't the best time to ask, but, well, do you morph into Cat Woman like, all the time?"

"Cat Woman." I rolled my eyes. "For your information, Cat Woman never 'morphed' – Halle Barry just strutted around dressed in tight, black leather and flicked a whip."

"Hot." Josh sighed.

This time, I welcomed the laughter that escaped. "You are a pervert. I don't even own a whip."

"I checked for a tail..."

"You did not!" My cheeks flushed.

"True. Mom wouldn't let me."

"I am not telling you anything else." I glared at him, daring him to cross the line of decency.

Josh, ever the gentleman, said, "Fine. But I'll find out..." He leaned forward and dropped a kiss on my nose. "Eventually."

The wink he gave me was sexy. S E X Y. A promise that our future together was far from over.

My toes curled beneath the bedspread.

He got up, giving my leg a pat before walking toward the door. "I told Mom I'd call her as soon as you woke up. You might wanna brush your teeth or something."

I threw my pillow at him. With one hundred percent accuracy, I got him in the nose. The jerk took my pillow with him when he left.

Grinning, I got up and showered before anyone else could insult me. *That* is when I noticed my canopic jars at each corner of my bed. Stunned, I dropped to my knees, lifting the jar with the lynx head and bringing it to my cheek. The cool limestone jar filled with the soil of Egypt - only the demi-goddesses could have instructed Zelda and Josh to put it at my feet.

Talk about getting a speed course in history, not to mention, very secret ceremonial practices.

Bastet and Sekhmet must have been out of their minds with worry. I sent them each a text before brushing the gunk from my teeth and turning on the shower.

I opened the door from the bathroom after a steamy vanilla scented cleansing, ready to face the next step of my karmic journey. Zelda, Lorelei, and Josh sat on my bed, waiting like a jury of three.

"Thank the Goddess I dressed!" I'd picked a clean, white tee, black skinny jeans, and kept my feet bare. I'm not a big fan of shoes, unless they're fun. I've mostly hidden my taste for bling.

I gave Lorelei a hug and kiss, then took a position leaning against the wall. "You look like those three monkeys. Hear no evil, see no evil, speak no evil." I laughed but Josh sent me a look that reminded me I wasn't funny.

Lorelei held my empty canopic jar, the one to hold my ashes when I took my final rest. "Sekhmet and Bastet deciphered a clue. Cadee ripped off anything that said 'Mafdet' on it, mostly repetitions of what we already knew. But she got lucky and so did we."

My mentor's face, drawn from her recent bout with death, lacked her signature lipstick. She wore long pants, hiding a possible bandage. I hated to see her suffering.

"Just tell me. I can take it. I'm Bazmeht." I tossed the towel over the vanity chair and crossed my arms over my chest. I jerked my thumb toward Zelda and Josh. "Can they hear what Sekhmet found?"

"Yes. After what they've witnessed in the past twenty-four hours, Bastet has made them honorary, second tier Bazmeht employees."

Josh nodded, his heart-stopping grin nowhere in sight.

I missed it.

Rather than blurt out my suspicion of Josh's dad already being a bonafide Felidia member, I chewed my bottom lip. "Hit me."

"Sekhmet found the missing section of the Myth of Mafdet in a museum in Spain. Dated to 3200 B.C."

"I understand." I restrained from tapping my toe impatiently.

Lorelei leaned forward, holding my jar. "Inside one of these."

"What?" *Impossible.* "Predynastic jars held the organs for the afterlife – always."

"How'd an Egyptian canopic jar get to Spain?" Josh jumped up from the bed, knocking Zelda and Lorelei sideways. "I'll be right back." He ran past me, and I stared at Zelda and Lorelei as they righted themselves.

"He's excited about Egypt." Zelda shrugged proudly.

"A sign of maturity is containing one's excitement," Lorelei pointed out in a dry tone.

"The scroll said?" I itched to get to work, to find answers.

"It's a stanza, a four line piece of a bigger poem – at least, that's what Bastet thinks." Lorelei closed her eyes and recited from memory, "Nine jars must come together, weigh my soul against Ma'at's feather."

"Whose Ma'at again?" Josh slid into the room, his laptop in hand. At his mother's warning look, he chose to sit in the vanity chair instead of on the bed.

"Ma'at literally means truth. She's a judge in the Underground. It's thought that when you die, Thoth puts your heart on the scale of truth, balanced on the other side with Ma'at's feather. If you have led a truthful life, the scales balance and you go to Paradise or the Field of Rushes. If not," I shrugged. "Your heart is tossed to Ammut who devours it with her crocodile mouth in a single gulp."

"That is so cool." Josh shook his head in wonder.

I rubbed the bridge of my nose and prayed for patience. "Is that all Bastet has?"

"No. What we were able to get from Cadee's house actually gives half of the poem, supporting Bastet's theory that each canopic jar holds a four line stanza. We need to find all nine jars before we are can unlock Mafdet's crypt."

"Where is Mafdet's crypt?" Josh's fingers flew over the keyboard as he searched for Re only knows what.

"At the tip of our inverted pyramid." My fondest memories were of tending the flowers before the stone door. I loved knowing that I, who was without a mother most of the time, could talk to Mother Mafdet whenever I chose.

Lorelei cleared her throat. "Well. Symbolically, that is true." She bobbed her head and stared at the ceiling.

"What?" My sore insides clenched, anticipating another blow to the gut.

She exhaled heavily and rolled my empty jar between her palms. "*Symbolically*, Mafdet rests in the tip of the inverted pyramid."

"Where is she *really*?" My jaw cracked as I ground my teeth.

Had my entire life been a lie?

"It was the turn of the millennia before we realized she wasn't there."

Josh, obviously still working on being mature, snorted. "Freaking awesome. Like, as in, the *zero* hour? I can't believe this." He drummed his fingers against his knee, wearing that dopey grin I loved.

I sent him a glare. This was serious business and he had no right to be so cute. *"Where* is she?"

"We don't know. That's why solving this riddle is imperative."

"Don't want to sound like a moron, but don't you need to know where the crypt is before you can unlock it?"

I threw my hands in the air. "That is exactly the question I was going to ask."

"Cool. We can be morons together."

"Josh!" Zelda clucked her tongue.

Lorelei's gaze filled with worry and despair. "Change is coming, the oracle, Bastet and Sekhmet agree on that when they argue over everything else. We need the mother awake before the world is destroyed."

"Are we talking spiritually? Metaphorically? Or ka-boom, and there's a mushroom cloud?"

"This is no light matter, Joshua." Lorelei's pretty face hardened, and I couldn't swallow over the fear in my throat. "This isn't an exaggeration, it is a literal translation. The mother must be woken to stop the end of the world."

"That's ridiculous." He peered over his nose at Lorelei, who sent him a look in return – one that corrected my attitude many times over the years.

"The Mayan's predicted the end of times to happen in 2012," she said.

Josh cut her off. "But that's been de-bunked."

"There are other prophecies. Who are we to say which will come true? We cannot afford to take chances. We need to find the jars, which will lead us to the crypt and the key so the world is safe no matter what."

"Can we get to the rest of the poem, please?" No conjecture. I required facts. Clear, analytical facts.

"Hey. I typed in Spain and Egyptian artifacts and guess what popped up? Who knew there was a pyramid in freaking

Spain?"

Zelda made a dismissive noise. "Not now, Josh."

I took out my phone and pushed the record button. "I'm ready."

Lorelei met my gaze and began.

*"Nine jars must come together*
*Weigh my soul against Ma'at's feather*
*Pride is my sin*
*Let the punishment begin."*

"That's the part Sekhmet found in the jar from Spain." I worked the words over in my mind, committing them to memory as well as to audio.

"Yes." She reached behind her for the paper we'd rescued from the snake cage. "The rest goes like this – but we don't know where in the poem it is – the middle, the beginning, or the end." Her brow furrowed as she deciphered the words.

*"I am Mafdet, Goddess of the Underground*
*The key to the sacred crypt must be found*
*Re has promised that I may wake*
*And save the world before it breaks*

*Battles happen behind closed doors*
*Love will start another war*
*The enemy's face is a familiar one*
*Bring me, Mafdet, to Re, the Sun*

*Warrior of Justice, in Mafdet's name*
*Save the world from death's dark flame*
*Nine lives are passed to thee*
*To carry Me through eternity*

*My pride caused the fall - my punishment begins*
*Scatter the Council of Nine to the winds*
*East, West, North, and South*
*Over mountains, to the ocean's mouth*

*Felidia, hide me, keep me safe*
*I have dealt death to the Uraeli race*
*A debt they owe, and a debt they'll pay*
*Until the child of both is born to Re."*

𐤉𐤀𐤉𐤀𐤉𐤀𐤉 𐤀𐤉 𐤀𐤉𐤀 𐤀𐤉𐤀𐤉𐤀𐤉𐤀𐤉

"Is that it?" I turned off the recording and paced the room.

"What the hell does that mean?" Josh raised one brow. "I typed it as you said it so we can all have copies. But I gotta tell you, I don't care how often I read it, it still sucks. Mafdet might be a great Slayer of Serpents – kinda like Shani – but she's no poet."

"There was more to it," Lorelei shrugged. "But I think the snake ate it."

# CHAPTER TWENTY-NINE

## FERN

"You call this a little breeze?" The shrill force of one hundred and twenty mile an hour winds wreaked havoc on my eardrums. I couldn't see outside thanks to the protective hurricane shutters, but bursts of air managed to sneak through and ruffle the curtains.

I longed to go outside and watch Nature at her most furious.

Josh casually lifted one shoulder. "Good thing Mom fortified the house for a Cat 5, right, Mom?"

Zelda glanced up from studying the partial poem Josh printed out for each of us. She'd cut the paper into four line stanzas, rearranging them on the coffee table as if connecting the dots. "We should have bought the bigger generator. I'm concerned about Maria."

I also worried. Day two, and no phone call. Did Ninja have her, or was Maria working with the Uraeli's? "Has she ever left without word before?"

"Never. I checked her room. She's not there, and she didn't pack any of her things. The minute this storm is over, I'm driving to the police station. They refused to even consider her missing when I called earlier. I don't care whether you girls approve or not, Maria is my friend." Zelda sighed.

"I'll drive you, Mom. Maria is *family*. Anybody else hungry?" Josh leaned back, leaving the page detailing Egyptian-Spanish pyramids open on his laptop. "I'm starving."

"Me too." I rubbed my stomach, which growled obligingly.

"Surprise, surprise," Lorelei said from her perch on the barstool. "Thank the Goddess for a fast metabolism, Shani."

"I do!"

"Josh, I put together some snacks in the basket on the kitchen counter. Do you mind getting it?" The lights flickered eerily. "I can go with you," Zelda offered, rubbing her arms.

"Stay here, Mom," Josh teased. "I'm not afraid of the Boogieman. Should I grab some drinks, too?"

"I'll go with you."

"I got it." Josh shook his head, motioning for me to stay put. "It will take me two seconds." He held up a finger as I stepped toward him. "It's just the kitchen, Shani. This house is secured tighter than the U.S. Embassy." He winked at me. "Unless you want to hold my hand?"

I turned, hiding my amusement as he darted out the door. A crack of lightning lit the room. Chills prickled my neck and upper arms.

"Lorelei, haven't you found *anything* yet?" Impatient, I pushed aside the stack I'd already gone through. Nothing matched the poem.

"No. But we're halfway there."

"Little Miss Sunshine," I accused, picking up the next book. "At least we don't have to worry about Cadee or Ninja, thanks to the hurricane. The TV weatherman said the police can arrest anyone outside in a hurricane."

"They also can't send emergency vehicles out in the storm. If we needed help, we couldn't get it." Zelda studied another line of the poem.

"You have us, Zelda. We're much better than the local police." Her delicate snort showed her gratitude.

Lorelei scratched her ear, ignoring us both in favor of staying focused. "Once we find the book the poem came from, we'll need to locate the other eight jars. Do you realize how many canopic jars there are? Each cat sarcophagus has four and there are thousands of sarcophagi. A minimum of one hundred right here in this house." She blew out an overwhelmed breath.

"We only have to find seven," I corrected, as if this made everything easier. "Sekhmet already had one. It wasn't until she found the jar in Spain that she realized what she had." My phone *bleeped*, signaling a text. I checked it and groaned. "Mom." What could she want?

"What does she say?" Lorelei's look let me know I'd better read it and not delete it.

I sighed and clicked the envelope icon. I read aloud. "Hope you are safe from the storm. Glad you survived the battle with the cobra. Sharifa." I tossed the phone on top of the stack of books. "And you wonder why I don't call...can you imagine how awkward *that* conversation would be?" I shuddered.

Zelda stood, stretching her back. "Why am I not surprised

you don't get along with your mother?" She sat on the arm of the couch, facing me and Lorelei. "Your mother is probably a lovely, misunderstood woman."

"This is not the same as you and Josh," I defended myself.

"We are becoming friends." Zelda waved her hand in front of her face. "We just had to clear the air."

"You already *loved* each other." I rubbed my knuckle into my eye to stop the twitch my mother caused. "Mom and I don't. We never will."

Zelda gasped at my harsh pronouncement. "I'm going to my room to get a sweater."

I watched her leave, her head held high. "Oops."

"Behave yourself, Shani. You and your mother love each other, and maybe someday you can have a relationship with her that is less...combative?" Lorelei went back to reading, then stopped. Her eyes filled with tears and she tapped my arm. "Here we are talking about everything but the fact that you saved my life." She stared at me, her eyes clear. "I don't want you to think I'm ungrateful, but thank you seems so inadequate. Especially considering that you took snake venom from my leg into your body. We both should have died. And yet...Mafdet has blessed you."

I dipped my head, uncomfortable with the praise. "You would have done the same for me."

"No." She wiped her misty eyes. "It never would have occurred to me to do what you did, never in a million years." Lorelei hopped off her stool and gave me a hug. "I just want you to know that I will do everything in my power to convince the council you belong not only in the Bazmeht, but in the leadership training program. As a council head."

I drew back from her embrace, searching her eyes to see if she joked, or lost her mind. She appeared perfectly sane.

"Who are you kidding? I will count myself grateful if I'm allowed back into the pride, forget about leadership." I laughed dryly, terrified of the idea.

"The Oracle has always said that you will be an instrument of change. I think you may be the one that leads us into the next century."

Goddess help me, as much as I loved Lorelei, she needed a reality check. My belly in a knot, I shook her shoulder until she met my eyes. "I can't be a leader. Other than you, I don't even have friends among the Bazmeht."

"That makes you the perfect leader. No pre-formed alliances, and you only have the good of the Bazmeht in your heart." She smoothed my hair back from my face in a maternal gesture that warmed my chilled soul. "You are respected...or feared."

"If you are trying to build my self-confidence, that doesn't help." I pictured all the handmaidens quaking in their hammocks as Natalie scared them to death with tales of my snake battles.

Lorelei laughed. "She would never do that. Well, maybe."

I paused, realizing what just happened, and my shields went back up. "You read my mind."

"Oh..." Her eyes watered again. "You let me in."

Shoving lightly at her arm, I said, "Stop crying. Bastet said that I subconsciously have shields of steel and they're low when I'm vulnerable." I shook my head. "Cadee read my mind when I was practically dead, and Josh got me in the same state. You, Bastet, and Sekhmet are the only ones to get me when I'm just...me."

Lorelei gave me another hug. "That is the best gift. Thank you."

The lights flickered again and I searched the ceiling, uneasy. "Spooky. I'm glad Zelda has an automatic back-up generator. I wonder what's keeping them?"

A popping noise, louder than a shotgun at the shooting range, sounded just as the lights in the room went dark. The shutters made it pitch black.

Zelda screamed from the hallway and Josh shouted my name.

Lorelei and I exchanged a glance, automatically adjusting to night vision as we ran for the library door. The situation immediately turned ominous. Just the storm? I didn't think so.

Fear for Josh tapped through my veins with a sharpened chisel as I pulled on the doorknob.

It didn't budge.

Jiggling the handle and cursing didn't change the fact we'd been trapped inside the library. Josh, in danger, on the other side.

# CHAPTER THIRTY

## THE ENEMY HAS A FAMILIAR FACE

"Now!"

Lorelei and I used our *very* powerful legs and kicked the door down, not stopping as we jumped over the debris. Zelda stood on the other side, fear marking her face. "Why isn't the generator working?"

Danger pulsed in the air, electric. I took a second to form a plan. "Lorelei, you and Zelda go to your room and protect the sarcophagi. I'll get Josh and meet you there. Lock the door."

"Josh." Zelda's moan gripped my heart, but I gave her the mental *heave-ho* to the proverbial curb. A Bazmeht can't afford any distractions, and emotional tugs counted high on the list. She had my sympathy, but she couldn't have my attention.

Lorelei took Zelda by the forearm and urged her forward to the stairs. I raced for the kitchen, opening my ears and all of my senses to locate Josh.

Very faint, I picked up the shuffling noises of struggling bodies. The low grunts Josh made as he exerted himself led me toward the dining room, opposite the kitchen.

I jumped over the stairs leading down, landing with perfect balance on my toes. I faced the long hallway to the dining room. The thick, cherry door at the end stood between me and my duty, my friend, my honor.

I delicately sniffed the air, welcoming the too-sweet smells of Ninja and Cadee.

*The fight is on.*

Considering my options, I counted out possible strategies. Go around to the side door, hopefully sneak into the room without them noticing. Or, and I liked this a lot better, ruthlessly plow down the door in front of me and spring right into the center of the trap Ninja and Cadee planned for me.

Patience is not my virtue.

"Shani, don't come in!" Josh's warning spurred me on.

Rolling my shoulders, I leaned forward, put on the speed, and allowed my body full strength. Fast, strong as a semi-truck,

I broke through the door like a blade through paper. As I stumbled to regain my balance, Ninja hit me across the back with a dining room chair.

"Not fair," I mumbled as I fell to my knees. Wind roared through the dining room, and I noticed the shutters torn off, the window shattered, wide open. Rain pelted the carpet and ruined the silk curtains.

I caught my breath and searched the room. Josh, sitting on a chair, his hands tied in front of him. A growl emanated from my throat but I stayed still, narrowing my eyes at Cadee. She stood at his shoulder, a knife poised in her leather-gloved hands to keep him in place. She snarled at me, her eyes protected from the weather by night-vision goggles.

Ninja, not one to follow codes of combat, whacked me across the shoulders to get my attention. I twisted out of her reach and threw my arms around her shins so she landed hard on her side. The soaked carpet squished beneath our weight.

The loud night air shimmered with the occasional *zing* of lightning, leaving a trace of energy that stank of ozone. Sulfur.

I pushed off her, getting to my feet in a fluid move the envy of Bazmeht trainees. "Nice," Ninja said.

"What happened to the generator?"

"It broke." She grinned, her curved eyeteeth shining in the odd flashes of light. She mimed slicing something, so I assumed she'd helped the generator die. Turning, I picked up a broken chair back and slammed it on top of Ninja's head. She swayed in disbelief, then slumped.

Easy.

I turned to Josh and Cadee, noticing the thin line of blood welling at Josh's cheekbone. She'd marked him, and now I'd taste her blood.

"You shouldn't have touched a hair on his head," I told her in a voice rich with vengeance.

"You shouldn't have broken into my house." Cadee's mouth tightened with malice. "Then I wouldn't have had to cut your boyfriend." Josh kicked backward, and she tapped him on the head with the knife handle. "Move again, and I slice your throat, boy."

I clenched my hands into fists, controlling my deep anger. Cadee would pay, dearly, for each bruise. I sensed her hesitation, determined to use it to my advantage. She'd probably never murdered anyone before. Or perhaps she'd been ordered to keep Josh alive.

I wanted her away from him.

"Where's your boyfriend? Last time I saw him, he had a fork wound." I mimed stabbing into a shoulder. Cadee glared but didn't respond. I widened my mouth in a mockery of a grin. "Oh but wait, I saw him after that. Just the other night." I made a tearing motion with my mouth and spat.

"Murderin' bitch," she whispered, tightening her grip on the knife handle. She held the blade to Josh's throat.

"You don't want to do that." I slipped my switchblade into my palm, opening the blade with a click. Josh held his bound hands in front of him, as if I could cut him free from five feet away.

I'm not that good, I wanted to say. Pausing, I thought that I might be but now wasn't the time to test it.

"Come fight me Cadee, one on one. Or are you afraid? Tell me, human, why you side with the snakes? I did apologize, didn't I, for killing your lover?"

Cadee turned toward me, her mouth a slash of fury, her goggles glowing eerily in the dark. "You will."

I motioned her toward me. "Prove it."

She took a few steps, uncertain, but angry, then committed to lunging for me with her knife outstretched. Josh whipped his untied legs  to the side, tripping Cadee, who fell to her knees with a frustrated shriek.

I jumped between her and Josh, quickly slicing through the rope at his wrists just as she launched herself onto my back.

Spinning around in a circle, I flung her off in the opposite direction of Josh. "Get out of here," I called over my shoulder. "Run to the Scottish room."

I expected him to obey my command.

He didn't. He picked up a broken chair leg instead and stood, ready to fight. Cadee groaned, rising up to face us on wobbling legs, her knife across the floor.

"Don't be a hero. I can't do my job if I'm worrying about you." His grunt of defiance made me angry. And oddly proud.

"Isn't this sweet," Ninja said from behind me. "I still get to kill you both." I turned, angling Josh a bit toward the door. Ninja, on her feet, stretched sinuously before picking up Cadee's blade. When Cadee held it, I hadn't worried over the difference in blade size. Ninja was another story.

"The only dead body here today will be yours," I promised.

I couldn't leave Josh's side unprotected, which hampered my fighting strategy.

Me, Josh. Ninja, Cadee. The roaring wind, the crack of lightning, and the echoing thunder all served as a backdrop for our final battle. But so long as Josh stayed in the room with me, I was forced to play defense instead of offense.

Tension added a thick layer of suspense to the air as we stood off. The first to crack gave away the advantage.

As if he finally understood my dilemma, Josh took a back step toward the door leading to the hall.

Cadee jumped for him just as Ninja came for me. I heard the *thunk* of Josh's chair leg as it hit bone – presumably Cadee's – before I started defending myself against Ninja's lethal blows.

She's good.

So am I.

I leaped forward, punching her in the nose. I smiled at the satisfying crunch of cartilage, then ducked as she punched back.

I got her in the mouth with my knuckles. "You stole the pages from the library but we got them back."

Blood spurted between her fingers, and she looked even more ferocious than usual. "Who needs paper? You Bazmeht are using a system that is as archaic as the Goddess you swear fealty to." She sneered. "I wanted information, and I got it."

"You also lost a Uraeli."

She rubbed her bloody fingers together. "He'd become expendable."

Cadee growled low in her throat. "Linh? What are you talking about?"

Ninja had a name – Linh – and she said, "You turned him away from the cause, Cadee. He spoke of retiring in Ireland with you. Did you really think I wouldn't find out?"

So much for loyalty in the Uraeli ranks.

"I don't know what you are talking about." Cadee's pretty face hardened as she stared at Ninja.

"You are a traitor for hire," Ninja spat.

I dared a glance to the right just in time to see Josh grab Cadee by the shoulder. And squeeze.

She collapsed in a heap of unconscious fury.

"What is so important about an Egyptian legend?" I turned

Ninja's attention back to me before she decided Josh made an easy target. If he kept Cadee down, I'd concentrate on kicking Ninja's ass.

"Legend?" She laughed at me like I was the stupid one. "You still don't have a clue." She spit out a stream of pink just as lightning crackled behind her. "You deserve to die."

I gritted my teeth. "You tried that once." I am a Level One Bazmeht Bodyguard, trained to be a warrior. Ninja nothing but a shifty Uraeli soldier. I attacked with my hands outstretched and slammed her into the dining room table.

It broke down the center.

We scrambled to our feet, wiping blood from our eyes.

We circled each other until Ninja's back was to Cadee's prone body. The wind whipped the curtains around like silken sails, the sound slashing through the dining room. Ninja's spiked hair gleamed like black nails from her white scalp.

Josh stayed by Cadee, determined to keep her down. I wished he would go, leave the fighting to me, but wishing didn't make it so.

Impervious to the rain pounding through the window behind me, I shouted over the howling wind and crashing debris. "I will never let you take Josh."

Ninja swiped at her bloody lip, seemingly unconcerned as she stepped on Cadee's long, black hair. "What do I care about Josh? I can get him any time. I want to kill you." She sliced her finger across her throat. "Again."

"It's my turn." I stayed balanced. Defensive. Thunder boomed, shaking the room. I felt her hate and let it heat my own. "To kill you. Will you come back to life?"

Her mouth twisted in a cruel smile. I could tell we were both remembering the day my life's blood flowed at her hand.

My ears twitched with the desire to change, but I bit my lip and controlled the urge.

"Aren't you curious?"

"About the color of your blood, yes."

"About who the leak in the sacred Bazmeht food chain is..."

My belly tensed. *Not really.* What would I do if it were my mother? "I don't believe you."

"How else would I know what I do?" Her smug tone grated like salt in a wound.

I shook out my arms, keeping my body limber. Alert.

"Cadee's the leak."

"No."

Did it matter that much? I longed to subdue her, make her realized I had the upper hand. "You bore me. If you're afraid to fight, just say so. There's no shame in walking away." I concentrated on letting my fingers elongate so my claws could pop at a second's notice.

Her lips tightened.

Then she shrugged. Before I finished blinking, she leaped over Cadee to pin Josh to the ground. Her mouth opened, and she leaned toward his throat.

*Mother Mafdet!* She was supposed to come for me.

I sprang after her then yanked her spiky head back, shivering at her exposed, curved fangs. Twin spots of blood marred Josh's neck.

My client. *My heart.* She'd bitten him? The instant rage triggered each primal instinct, and my body, already pumped for change after the last few days, released the go ahead. Goodbye self-control, welcome vengeance.

Red fury colored my actions. "For every drop you took I will make you suffer that much longer." I breathed in deep, calling to the power inside me. My inner warrior. Ninja, the enemy. "I am Justice."

I tossed her far from Josh's side, her expression surprised and yet obviously pleased as she watched my body morph. Josh scrambled to his feet, scrubbing at his neck. Had this been the real trap? To prod me into change?

It was too late to control my wrath.

"So it's true." Ninja stood, staring at me with wide gray eyes.

My face transformed, my jaw shifted. I bared my teeth at her, the eyeteeth that could snap her spinal cord in two with one bite. "You should have kept your teeth to yourself."

Her nostrils flared. "You can't kill me. I haven't told you-"

With a primitive growl, I jumped over her head and swatted at her back with my deadly claws. A Bazmeht's claws are poison to a snake, and I was careful to just barely cut through the black leather of her tight fitting coat.

Ninja sucked in a pained breath.

"The first time we met, I was new."

She kicked out at me, and I ducked back.

"I couldn't leave my post. And yet you kept hammering at me with those," I reached forward and punched her in the jaw twice, "quick jabs."

Ninja put her hand to her face. I sensed her fear in the rotten smell of decaying fruit.

"Now? I am even stronger, thanks to your bite."

"You should be dead." She threw her knife at my head, narrowly skimming a lock of hair. "Come here, kitty, kitty."

Play time over.

I tackled her, my mouth foaming as I leaned in for her neck.

Lower and lower.

My tongue touched her cold, reptilian flesh.

"Stop!"

I blinked, holding Ninja hostage with my knee to her throat. Rage coursed through me, the need to finish the enemy intense. Irrational.

Lorelei beamed a flashlight in my face and I snapped my jaws closed, struggling to understand.

"Don't do it, don't do it...you are blessed by Mafdet. Filled with her warrior spirit. Your duty is to kill this Uraeli." Lorelei walked toward me, her palm out, entreating with soft, low spoken words. "But we need to know who is behind this, within the Bazmeht. She should die," Lorelei bopped Ninja on the forehead with the butt of the flashlight and Ninja immediately stopped struggling against my hold as she lost consciousness. "Goddess knows she should die. But I need you. Healthy, not fighting off snake venom. Josh, Zelda, we need you Shani. Let go, now. Let go!"

Lorelei's gift for spreading calm brought me back to myself. She talked in soothing tones, giving me time to master my body, my mind. My teeth and claws retracted and the insane hunger for Ninja's flesh receded into primal memory.

We'd fought before, Ninja and I.

We would fight again.

# CHAPTER THIRTY-ONE

## BRINGER OF PEACE

I got to my feet in the gale force wind, stumbling on shaky, adrenalin–spent legs. Josh took my arm, keeping me steady.

He didn't have any fear of me, of what I'd become - I sensed acceptance. "How are you?"

Lorelei stared at Josh's neck. "What's that?"

"She sucked on me like a damn vampire. Am I going to die? I'm way too young to go to the Big Surf in the Sky."

Sick, I looked at Lorelei.

"I don't know," she said, sounding exhausted. "I don't know."

Before anybody could stop me, I leaned in and closed my lips over the wound at his neck. Josh smelled of salt and sunshine, and I accepted my love for him. I bit down, gently probing for poisonous venom in his skin.

He pushed at me, but I held firm, gathering a mouthful and spitting it to the floor. No venom, just clean blood. "She toyed with me. She wanted me to change."

Josh glared at me and rubbed his neck. "What do you mean? Hurt like a son of a bitch, and I bet I'll have the biggest hickey in the history of the freaking world."

"I mean," I brushed his angry cheek with my fingertips, appreciating the feel of his healthy skin. "She didn't poison you. She bit you to make me lose control. It worked."

"What a bitch." He tugged at his hair. "I'm sorry, Shani."

"Don't be. I am your bodyguard. It is my duty to save your life. You're just going to have to accept that." It would take more than Bastet and Sekhmet could throw at me to keep me away from Josh for long. The fear I'd felt at losing him made my own death insignificant.

He kicked at the shredded doorframe. "I helped you. I did the sleeper thing."

"You showed him how to do that?" Lorelei shook her head.

I nodded, letting Josh brag a little. "He was *awesome.*"

"Worked like a charm. Took Cadee out, man. We should

probably tie them up, you know, until morning."

"Good idea." I breathed in slowly, deliberately staying calm. How much could my body take? Inventorying aches and pains, it scared me to admit I felt better than fine. Alive, aware. Invigorated.

Josh kneeled, tying Cadee's wrists and ankles tight with a piece of the silk curtain. Then he did the same to Ninja. I admired his eye for detail.

"We found Maria," Lorelei said, shouting a little over the wind.

"Is she all right?"

"She is just fine," Lorelei answered with an edge.

"Where was she?"

"Guarding the cat sarcophagi. My job, as she pointed out already. *Bruja.*"

Josh laughed. "I told you. She's family."

"Thank the Goddess you found her," I said. "What should we do with Cadee and Ninja?"

Lorelei eyed the limp, tied bodies with distaste. "The kitchen?" She walked toward Cadee.

"We can lock Cadee in the pantry," Josh decided. "She's a human," he paused as if not believing those words came from his mouth. "Like me. A pantry will hold her. Ninja, the snake chick, should stay with us."

"Logical. We'll question her when she comes to." I bent down to sling Ninja's dead weight over my shoulder. Josh took her from me, daring me to protest. I didn't. I had an idea we'd both be learning the meaning of compromise.

Lorelei dragged Cadee into the kitchen, where we quickly locked her in the pantry, shoving a chair beneath the door handle for good measure. Stomach rumbling, I grabbed the basket of food still sitting on the counter.

"Is Maria hurt? Do we need a first aid kit?" Josh paused with his hand on the cupboard door beneath the sink.

"No. She's hungry mostly, with a knot on her head." Lorelei speed-walked down the hall toward the tower. "She was going back to the kitchen after cleaning my room, which is why she had the glass with my lipstick, when she heard someone in the library."

I listened for any changes to Josh's deep breaths as he followed. I would take Ninja at the first sign of him tiring. *He is all right.* "Maria was there."

"Cleaning," Josh countered. "And it was Lorelei's glass."

"Circumstance. Maria found Cadee tearing pages out of Zelda's books and told her to leave. When Cadee didn't, she and Maria tussled, which is why the library was such a disaster. Maria knocked her head on the table and when she woke up, Cadee was gone. She felt like she'd only been out a minute or so, and she'd heard enough about the Myth of Mafdet to worry that the hidden museum collection might be in danger. Bleeding, she made her way to the room – I was sitting with you, Shani - to see that the 'dead kitties' were safe. She forgot the door automatically locks from the inside."

"She's been there for two days? Why didn't we hear her?" I tapped my heart.

"Zelda wasn't lying when she said that she fortified that room to withstand a nuclear blast. Steel. And I didn't think to look there because I was under the impression I had the only key."

"That poor woman."

"Can we walk faster? I swear she's getting heavier by the footstep." Josh switched Ninja from one shoulder to the next. "Is she awake?"

I saw Ninja's finger twitch and gave the Uraeli a pinch.

Ninja relaxed. "Not anymore."

"Cool." Josh eyed the stairs to the tower and the third floor.

"Want me to help?" The offer was sincere, and matched his snarl. Ego.

We walked up, Lorelei unlocking the upper door. Maria, propped up with plaid blankets and pillows from Lorelei's room, smiled in greeting. Candles rested on every available non-flammable space, giving the steel room a cozy glow.

Josh dropped Ninja to the ground where he could watch her and leaned over to give Maria a kiss on the forehead. "I was worried about you."

"I'm fine, *hijo.*" She opened the hamper, unpacking cheese, crackers, water, and grapes. After spreading cheese on a piece of flatbread, she handed it to Josh, who settled in next to her.

"*Gracias,*" he said with a crunch.

"I told you we needed the bigger generator." Zelda smoothed the blanket over Maria's feet.

"It wouldn't have helped," I said, leaning over for a slice of cheddar. "Ninja and Cadee destroyed it, and the dining room...it's flooded."

"My silk curtains? My antique chairs?" Zelda covered her mouth with her hand.

"Time to remodel, Mom. Insurance will cover it."

Zelda sighed. "This turned out to be the safest room in the house after all."

The cat coffins were a priceless collection...I tapped my lip.

"What are you thinking?" Josh nudged me with his foot. "I see smoke."

He'd seen me change, and he'd seen me fight. He'd proved he could handle the truth. "Felidia have been using canopic jars ceremonially since the beginning of time. Because of what we are, we never had our organs removed at death." I was so honest he paled. "Regular cats, when mummified, would have their organs put in the jars. We are looking for Felidia sarcophagi only."

"Is there a sign on the box?" Josh glanced at Ninja, I did too. She remained still as death.

But I knew I wasn't that lucky.

"There would be. Every Felidia is going to have Mafdet somewhere on the outside of the sarcophagi." Lorelei rubbed her hands excitedly.

"She is our Mother," I agreed. "It would be a way to give honor to her name."

"Nine jars, to be brought together." Lorelei hopped to her feet, barely avoiding kicking Ninja in the head.

She walked through some of the rows of coffins, pointing with an apple slice. "Nine jars. Nine council heads. 'Scatter the pride to the winds'. What if we are looking for the original nine council leaders – their coffins? Their jars?"

An image of Mafdet jumping up and down around a ceremonial bonfire, shaking her spear in triumph came to mind as clearly as if she were in front of me. "Yes. That's it."

Shaking with excitement, I reached for my phone to text Bastet. It was gone.

"My phone!" I darted for the door.

Josh grabbed my foot. "You can't go back down there."

"I have to find my phone." My breathing came fast as I fought panic.

"Are you kidding?" Josh grabbed a candle and peered at my

face. "You kick ass but cry like a girl if you lose your phone." He shook his head and smiled at me like I was a mystery that he didn't want to understand.

"I'm not crying."

He shrugged. "I'm coming with you."

"Fine."

"Shani?" Lorelei took a step toward us.

"We'll be back – just watch Ninja. Do you have your phone, Lorelei? Call Sekhmet, tell her we need the names of the original Council of Nine. It should be in the archives. Then we need to find out where they all went. I'm guessing it will be documented somewhere."

"Good idea." Lorelei whipped out her phone. Pressed some buttons. Cursed. "No service. What is the matter with everybody? Josh, you said this was just going to be a little wind!"

"Do I look like a weatherman?"

"Joshua!" Zelda reprimanded.

"I have the book," Maria interjected.

"What book?" I kneeled beside her.

"The book Cadee tore the most pages from. Here." She handed it to me, content to chew her cheese and crackers.

I accepted the book and it was like being hit by a volt of energy. My hair stood on end and Josh fell backward.

"I don't even want to know what that was." He crawled back to my side. "Can we get your phone later?"

I stared at all the expectant faces around me and reluctantly nodded. Panic ebbed, lingering at the edges of my psyche.

Josh put his hand on the nape of my neck and kneaded at the tension. "Good for you, Shani. We're all here, anyway. Who do you need to text?"

He was right. I opened the book, easily deciphering the ancient hieroglyphics. This book, though old, was a copy of an older book, which was more than likely a copy. Mafdet wasn't to blame for the bad verse.

"Do you need the candle?" Josh started to reach for one.

I shook my head. "Night vision. Ready? Uh, here... 'Uraeli have a wrong to right, but Felidia must forgive a slight. Return my spear, let my mane unfurl and I will run to save the world'."

"It's *very* difficult to take this seriously."

"Shh." I elbowed Josh and went on to the next verse.

"'Felidia guard the secret space and hide the mother from the Uraeli race'." I looked at Lorelei. "Somebody within our group knows where that crypt is."

She shrugged and met my eyes. Truthfully. "I don't know, Shani."

"'Until the time is right to blend, Uraeli and Felidia must be friends'." I put the book down. "That can't be right."

"We'll send it to Dahlia, Control might be able to get a clearer meaning." Lorelei crossed her arms over her chest. "Well. That doesn't help us right now. We might as well start looking."

Searching all of the sarcophagi would take days. "I was really hoping you wouldn't say that."

"Show me the symbol to look for. I'll help."

Josh wasn't the only one who wanted to help. Zelda and Maria each wanted a copy of the Symbol for Mafdet – a spear, with a knife attached, and a cat on the pole.

There is something appealing about being on a quest with friends. I shared my love of history as I read some of the hieroglyphics aloud.

I learned that laughter eases apprehension, and that it's easy to forget reality after a near death experience.

Josh and I flirted, but I made him work for his stolen kiss when we both bent to check the bottom row of cat sarcophagi.

His lips fit perfectly against mine. "You aren't afraid of me?" I whispered the question, able to bear the answer better in the dark...the next best thing to texting for emotional barriers.

Josh kissed me again. "No. I'm fascinated. One hundred percent, totally committed to Egyptian history."

I dipped my head to hide a smile. "You'll excel at school. You'll be teacher's pet."

"About that. In between life changing experiences, I've been doing some serious thinking."

"All right." I braced myself for his news, like he'd decided to take Ms. Paris back or he preferred a friend who didn't morph into super cat.

"I'm special."

I laughed and Lorelei looked my way. I waved and got back to searching cat coffins for the Mafdet symbol.

"I need protection. Preferably twenty-four hour protection."

I wiggled my ear. "Sounds like you need a bodyguard. Don't

you already have one?"

"Yeah. But see, I happen to know she plans on going in search of the jar things to save the world – whatever – and I..."

What would he say? Got any hot Bazmeht friends you can send my way? I held my breath.

"I made the mistake of totally falling for my bodyguard."

My stomach leaped in a figure eight. "You did? Even if she is never going to be, by any stretch of the imagination, normal?"

"She is perfect."

I would have kissed him right then and there, but I heard a noise by the only door in or out of the room.

My happy bubble exploded like a hand grenade, and I pushed away from Josh before I did something even more stupid than forget Ninja was tied up.

Or at least she had been.

"Lorelei – the door!"

She must have heard the panic in my voice because she vaulted over the row of shelves to get to where we'd left Ninja. She cursed in three languages and I ran to join her.

"What happened?" Josh asked.

"She's gone," Lorelei said.

"It's my fault. She must have morphed. Do they full body morph? I assumed they were like us and only did it part way, as Re intended." I rubbed the spot behind my ear.

"It's not just your fault. I didn't think of it either, and I have a lot more experience. I should have." Lorelei bent and picked up the strips of curtain.

"How would we tie a snake?" Level Two Bazmeht Bodyguard seemed an unreachable dream. Mistake after mistake.

"We should've used a giant burlap bag," Josh said.

I inhaled, smelling fruit. Realization dawned. "The Uraeli smell like cantaloupe! Wait here." I raced down the stairs, my senses open wide as I tracked the sickly sweet scent of Ninja. It was strongest by the library, and I wondered if she'd managed to change back to human form quickly.

There was so much I didn't know, perhaps none of the Bazmeht knew or remembered. Josh and Lorelei, ignoring my directive, followed me into the kitchen.

"We are too late," Lorelei said, her voice sad.

The pantry door, torn off and tossed to the side, served as Cadee's death bed. Ninja had exacted her revenge by plunging my switchblade into Cadee's heart.

Rain washed in through the open back door, flooding the kitchen. I turned to Josh, who couldn't stop staring at Cadee.

I'd grown up with death, he had not.

"I am sorry. I lost focus." Flirting with Josh distracted me from Ninja. Now Cadee lay murdered, and Ninja escaped – again. I'd put the Bazmeht at risk for a kiss and a few silly heart palpitations. *Mother Mafdet*, forgive me. Emotions equaled foolish flights of fancy for girls, not Guardians of the Underground. How many people would die for me to remember that?

*Not Josh.*

"We all did." Lorelei put a comforting hand on Josh's shoulder and pulled him back.

"The leak must've been Cadee," I said in a hard voice, determined to make things right.

"She paid." Josh met my eyes and held out his hand.

I looked away, putting emotion aside to do my job. "Lorelei, will you arrange the shipment of Cadee's body to Bazmeht headquarters? Maybe there's something Control can get from it. I'm going to the library for my phone." To see if Ninja really had stopped there and maybe left a clue.

"Shani?" Josh jogged behind me. "Can we talk instead of run?"

"No time." I steeled my heart against his imploring voice. "What happened upstairs, well, it can't happen again." I turned to face him, my expression stern and bad-ass. "I am your bodyguard, and that is all I can ever be. You and I together would be *disastrous*." My heart of concrete shattered like fragile glass as I deliberately broke any hope of us being together. "My allegiance has been and always will be with the Bazmeht. I am a bodyguard, and you are my *client*."

Josh left, but I didn't cry until I was safe within the confines of the library.

I found my phone and sat on the couch, my tears creating prisms in the candlelight. I scanned the room. The books. The shelves.

My vision caught on the lone cat canopic jar.

Alone.

I texted Sekhmet. *Bring me home.*

# CHAPTER THIRTY-TWO

## KARMA

"Shani, put your back into it, girl." Sekhmet bellowed the order, more to impress the Bazmeht in training than to intimidate me. Boos and cheers came from the benches around the courtyard.

I put my back into it. Pulling granite bricks with a rope across the training field was an honor, I reminded myself as sweat poured into my eyes.

The punishment for disobedience went back to the predynastic age when bored Power Hungry rulers routinely tortured their loyal servants just for kicks.

"Do you want to go around again? We aren't torturing you. This is what happens when you choose to kiss a boy and let a dangerous prisoner escape."

Sekhmet refused to listen to reason.

Bastet sent me a tiny wave of encouragement and I plowed on like a mule in the fields.

*If it weren't for me, you wouldn't know that snakes smell like rotten fruit.*

*If it wasn't for you, we would have that Ninja in our grasp, and we'd know who the Bazmeht informant is!*

*Ninja's name is Linh, and Cadee was the leak. How was I supposed to know that everybody would rather watch me kiss Josh than take care of the prisoner? Or that Ninja would morph completely into a snake and slither her sorry way to freedom? You never told me they could do that!*

*Whose prisoner was it?*

I stuck out my lip, stubborn as the mule I was portraying. *Mine.*

*Good girl. Pride is the greatest sin a Bazmeht can commit. Well…along with dallying with a member of the Blood of Ra – and a Felidia to boot.*

*I don't want to talk about it.*

I lifted my shields, allowing Sekhmet to vent her fury

vocally again, which gave the audience something to jeer about. My friends to enemy ratio was heavily mixed. Dendera, holding Muu, gave me a thumbs down.

I made the last turn of the circuit and kneeled, exhausted and sweaty, before the demi-goddesses. "Forgive my transgressions. My heart is full of sorrow for the disappointment I've caused." *But kissing Josh had been worth every sweaty step.*

Bastet tapped my shoulder with her golden Sistrum, the rattle used to call down the favor of the gods. She shook it over my head and prayed that the gods decided justice had been met.

Sekhmet banged her staff on the wooden deck. "Shani Nebit, the gods have forgiven you." She batted the staff on my left shoulder, then my right. It took all of my strength not to cry out in pain at her enthusiasm. "Re has forgiven you!"

The Council of Nine, my mother included, stood. All wore ceremonial white. I'd started out in white, but it was now a dirt-encrusted rag.

*My lot in life is to be humbled.*

"It is time." Bastet rattled the Sistrum. Sekhmet kissed the Ankh of Life.

"If any object to Shani Nebit being reinstated to Bazmeht, speak now, or forever hold your peace." Sekhmet's scowl let the council know what she'd think of any who would speak against me.

For the first time in my life, nobody did.

"Welcome Shani! You are finally a Level Two Bazmeht Bodyguard. Welcome home."

So I cried. Just a little. It turned to mud on my cheeks, I could tell as the salty tears dried.

I didn't get to bask in my glory long before Bastet pulled me to her side. "Shani. I know that you've made great sacrifices on behalf of the Bazmeht. You requested a week to just 'veg' – whatever that means."

I bowed my head, knowing I wasn't going to get my week of rest and disco dancing.

"But you see, your mother needs you."

"She's got Natalie!" I looked over to where my mother, Natalie, and Keket all huddled together around the sherbet fountain.

"You'll have to pack for the Mayan jungle."

"Huh?" My mother dressed in khaki pants and hiking boots. I wouldn't be able to show off my new pedicure.

"She needs you, Shani. We're sending Natalie to Germany."

"No."

"You are Bazmeht. You don't get to say no." Bastet clucked her tongue at me.

"But–"

"Now. Go pack. You will leave before dusk falls."

"Bastet, what kind of emergency in the Mayan jungle could require me missing my own Leveling Feast? Honeyed almonds, hummus, roasted duck–" My stomach rumbled and tears, tears that threatened more often thanks to finding unrequited love, filled my eyes.

"Grow a backbone," Bastet chided. "I'll get you a plate to go."

"You don't understand."

"This 'meddling aunt' understands a broken heart perfectly well. The best thing to do is throw yourself into a new project. Saving the world is a worthy adventure," she teased.

"I could never really tell you no." I kissed her cheek. "But you realize that if you send my mom and I into the jungle together, only one of us might come out."

\* \* \*

I wasn't sure what to say to my mother as Lorelei drove us to the airport. It helped a little that she didn't know what to say to me. Home for less than twenty-four hours, I'd given Muu permanently to Dendera, taken my evil glares from Keket, and said good-bye to the empty room that didn't feel like it belonged to me anymore.

My heart beat in Miami.

My new hiking boots pointed toward Mexico.

Lorelei pulled to a stop in front of the airport. Our private plane piled on the miles, thanks to the quest for the canopic jars. I wondered if my mom thought she'd found one. So far, the Bazmeht had three out of the nine needed to locate the key.

The pressure to find the sacred crypt fell on my shoulders, because Mother Mafdet seemed to favor me. I knew Death, which held no fear. Revenge left a bitter aftertaste that only vengeance could assuage. Ninja. My nemesis. I spared a glance toward my mother. What role did she play?

No matter the circumstances, I would be fine. After all, I'm a Level Two Bazmeht, and highly trained to kick ass.

I sighed. There'd been a time when that was all I'd wanted.

Lorelei patted my arm. "Good luck, Shani. Sharifa. I'll be in touch as soon as we find out where the next Council member went. Tracing someone's actions from four thousand years ago isn't easy."

"Thanks Lorelei." I held up my regulation Bazmeht cell phone. Serviceable gray. "You can find me, down to the last jungle leaf."

I got out of the car, holding the door for my mom.

She held my gaze, the Cairo sun shining on her red hair and turning it to gold, which matched her golden eyes. Her skin, flawless porcelain. Cold and aloof. How could she be my mother?

I turned, pulling my one suitcase behind me like a ferret on a leash.

We entered the cool, air-conditioned airport, and my stomach was a riot of nerves. Our pilot, a Felidia woman named Rashi, greeted us as we took our seats.

Apprehension sat next to me. Even buckled in. It occurred to me that I didn't know if my mom preferred the window seat or the aisle.

She took the seat behind me, the window.

We wouldn't have to talk. I buried my hurt that she avoided me even now. The months ahead stretched dimly.

I heard Zelda's voice, and I shook my head, sure I was hallucinating, probably from lack of roasted duck.

She greeted Rashi as if they were old friends. My mother groaned.

Pulse quickening, I wondered why Zelda was on the plane. I thought of Josh, hoping she'd drop bits of information into the conversation. How he liked school, or if and his girlfriend were back together. Was he writing again? If he still hated me.

It amazed me how much I missed him. Sekhmet, cruelly but intentionally, forced me to stay and finish my forty days in Miami. The worst time in my life.

Josh and I tried to ignore each other but it was impossible. So I'd retreated behind my Guard persona, and he took ridiculous chances just to see me lose my cool.

He'd dated a string of blond, curvy girls who all made it clear they were *very* available. He'd trampled what was left of my heart. I'd lasted until day forty, and then I'd flown back to Egypt.

Zelda waved at me, then made room for Josh.

I was certain that my wishing him near had finally made it so.

His blond hair, streaked with dark brown, made him look like a dangerous angel. I closed my eyes. Had Bastet known he was coming? *How mean.*

My mother tapped my shoulder. "I didn't know. I'd been warned that Zelda might come, but Josh – this is a surprise to me too."

"The best way to study Egypt is in the Mayan jungle – right? Shani! Darling, tell Josh he's being stubborn."

Zelda dressed head to toe in white with navy accents. Her hair was sprayed and coiffed as if she was going to dinner at the Breakers instead of touring through the rainforest.

"Cairo. The pyramids," I managed to say. "I have no idea what we will find in the Mayan jungle." I couldn't be Josh's bodyguard again. I'd barely survived last time.

Josh glared at me, then his mom, before slinging his duffle bag into the storage above the seat.

"I'm Zelda," Zelda told my mother.

"How do you do," my mother answered in clipped tones. "I've heard so much about you."

Laughing, Zelda pulled a travel pillow from a silk case. "Most of it is true," she shrugged. "My brother insisted I prove my intentions toward the family are pure, so here we are."

Josh dropped into his seat, the one directly in front of mine. I unstuck my tongue from the roof of my mouth.

"Hello," I said softly.

He closed his eyes. "Don't even try to talk to me."

*Mafdet's mercy.* An ache lodged in my throat.

The love of my young life hated me still.

I felt the engine of the plane rev, and my pulse slowed in time. Breathing past Zelda's overpowering Chanel perfume, I inhaled Josh's unique scent of sunshine. I opened my mind, absorbing everything one sensory image at a time. Closing my eyes, I knew my mother tapped her armrest impatiently, even as Zelda fussed with the seatbelt over her lap. I attributed Josh's tension to sharing a plane with me.

He didn't understand that I wasn't the master of my own

destiny. I'm part of a team, and the other guards count on me to pull my weight. Maybe spending some time together in the jungle would help us at least be friends again.

*Being Bazmeht is worth any sacrifice.*

I pretended to sleep so that I wouldn't cry.

# About the Author

Award winning author Traci Hall is multi-published in paranormal fiction for adults and teens. She specializes in family oriented stories with happy endings. Traci lives in Florida with her own slightly dysfunctional but adored family, including two dogs and a cat.

## Find Traci online at:

www.tracihall.com
http://twitter.com/tracihallauthor
http://www.facebook.com/traciella
www.babesinbookland.wordpress.com